SKEL
IN THE CLOSET

A DRAGON BUSINESS ADVENTURE

NEW YORK TIMES BESTSELLING AUTHOR

KEVIN J. ANDERSON

Caezik SF & Fantasy
in partnership with
WordFire Press

ISBN: 978-1-64710-120-6

Caezik/WordFire May 2024.
1 2 3 4 5 6 7 8 9 10

An imprint of Arc Manor LLC

www.CaezikSF.com

www.WordFire.com

PROLOGUE

I n my drafty throne hall, the sound of a minstrel's lute brings back
fond memories.

Traveling minstrels are the most efficient and cost-effective way of
transmitting news in a medieval society. They go from tavern to
tavern, singing songs of great heroes and legendary deeds. What better
way to spread stories?

Over the years, I've commissioned many songs about my own
exploits—King Cullin the Brave, King Cullin the Dragon Slayer.
Some of them are actually true, although edited for content or revised
to make them appropriate for family audiences.

Thanks to famed minstrels like Nightingale Bob, my daring
exploits with Sir Dalbry, former Princess Affonyl, and rough-and-
tumble Reeger are popular among the great unwashed (which is a very
large audience, since few people bathe). Yes, a singing minstrel with a
harmonious lute always makes me smile.

Unless it is my son Maurice making the attempt.

The prince just doesn't have it in him. I wince at the dissonant
twang of a string that brings to mind a whisker being pulled from a
wet cat.

"No, no, my prince!" groans his exasperated tutor, Nightingale
Bob. "The second course, not the first one! Those are simply not the right
notes." Bob moves Maurice's fingers to the proper placement and
adjusts the quill plectrum in the lad's right hand.

1

Frustrated, Maurice glares at his lute. At fourteen, he has been pampered with princely indulgences, but knows very few practical skills. His pale brown hair is washed, primped, and curled in a way that will one day make maidens long to run their fingers through his locks. The young prince has studied the ballads, read courtly tales of adventure and romance, but he's only just begun to take an interest in music.

When Maurice pleaded to take lute lessons, his mother encouraged him ... as she encourages every other momentary passion he finds. I am, however, familiar with my son's fleeting interests and his lack of talent, so I declined to buy him the expensive professional-model lute he drooled over in the music store. I told him to be content with a practice lute from the secondhand shop.

Good thing.

Seated on a stone step in front of my throne, Maurice scowls at the strings. He has a narrow face and features made for showing angst. He paws at the strings in his struggle to find a tune.

Nightingale Bob's face pales with dismay. Maurice tries to make up for the jangle with increased exuberance, until he is not so much strumming the lute as flaying it.

At least it's better than the time he insisted on learning to play the accordion.

Nightingale Bob, a highly paid and expert minstrel, changes the boy's finger positions again. At least Maurice isn't inclined to give up. That makes me proud.

"It never hurts to prepare for alternative employment, son," I say from my seat on the throne, "in case your situation dramatically changes."

He blinks up at me. "How would it dramatically change? I'm the royal prince."

"What if, say, orcs were to invade the kingdom, and you were forced to flee into exile? Skill with the lute would prepare you to work as an itinerant minstrel—a very respectable profession," I say.

My son responds with a serious nod. "Yes, the oldest profession."

He's a good kid, but he's very naïve for fourteen.

After more atonal minutes, Nightingale Bob has cringed enough for the day. He stands with strained patience. "Keep working on it, my prince. Practice your chords." The minstrel slings his professional lute over his shoulder and bows to me. "*Sire, I have done all I can. If he devotes his life to practice, practice, practice, he will become a princely minstrel someday.*"

"*Thank you for your effort, Nightingale Bob. I always enjoy your music.*" I cock an eyebrow. "*Maybe you could write a few songs about the prince's golden singing voice?*"

The professional minstrel is uneasy, and his voice quavers. "*But we haven't even begun singing lessons, Sire!*"

I rest an elbow on the arm of the throne. "*Perhaps it's best not to overextend ourselves, but a catchy ditty about the boy's prowess would be much appreciated.*"

Nightingale Bob lowers his voice, all business now. "*Same rate as for songs about your own exploits, Sire?*"

We negotiate a discounted price, because Prince Maurice doesn't have the legendary status I do, but I sweeten the deal by commissioning an additional work-for-hire ballad about some other adventure of mine. I give him carte blanche to follow his muse.

Before he goes, the minstrel looks up at the battered, ugly dragon head hanging on the wall behind my throne. "*Aye, that was a tremendous beast, Sire.*"

"*And certainly a tremendous story,*" I say with a sigh. "*Those were the days.*"

The stuffed reptilian beast was recently refurbished by the kingdom's best taxidermist. I consider it true art, even if the critics don't appreciate preserved monsters as a decorative style. Based on past experience, I hold a low opinion of art critics.

Maurice regards the dragon head on the wall without interest while fiddling with the strings of his practice lute. He's seen the trophy all his life and heard all my stories about the dragon business. Noticing his interest (or lack thereof), I lean forward on the throne. "*Son, if you want to be a true minstrel, you need to know plenty of tales for the finest inns and taverns.*"

"*I plan to play only love songs,*" says Maurice.

The minstrel takes advantage of the distraction and scurries away.

"*Love songs!*" I sneer. "*You think the bawdy tavern clientele at the Scabby Wench want to hear love songs?*"

The boy pouts. "But they're sweet. Someday I'll use romantic ballads to woo my lady fair."

"I'm a king, and you're a prince—we can arrange a lady fair whenever you want one." I lean forward with great intent. "Did I ever tell you about the time I traveled with a two-headed dragon?"

Maurice sniffs. "There's no such thing as a two-headed dragon."

I shrug. "Not so long ago, you insisted there was no such thing as dragons at all. Now you're an expert about how many heads they can have?" I raise a finger. "But there is such a thing as stories—*you can't argue with that."*

The prince shifts his lute aside. "What does a story have to do with dragons?"

"Everything. Not all stories have dragons, but the good ones do. Now, let me tell you. Back in my younger days, I wandered the land in search of fame and glory."

"I thought you always traveled with Sir Dalbry and Reeger," the prince says.

"This is just a solo adventure, when I was on a break."

"A side story?" Maurice frowns. "Because it doesn't fit well with the continuity?"

"It's a fine tale regardless. I was seeking treasure and adventure, sowing my wild oats ..."

"You wanted to be a farmer?"

As I said, he's very naïve, even for fourteen.

"Far to the north, a king's devastated outer wastelands were being ravaged by a horde of lava monsters from a nearby erupting volcano, and he feared they would invade the rest of his lush and fertile kingdom. So I answered a classified ad to go confront the fiery beasts."

The prince narrows his eyes. "But there are no volcanos in the kingdom, according to my geology tutor."

"As I said, it was in the volcanic regions to the north, with mudpots and fumaroles," I say, then quickly continue. "But if the monsters advanced, they could cause a great deal of damage to noble estates, the green orchards and farmlands, and some of the kingdom's best golf resorts. Something had to be done! But, considering the strength of the fiery horde, I knew I couldn't face them alone."

Maurice grins. "Is that where you brought in Dalbry and Reeger?"

I feel a little embarrassed. "No, I told you this is a standalone adventure. *Actually, I joined up with a down-and-out two-headed dragon who was looking for some contract work. The poor dragon had two dry throats and a fondness for ale, so they'd spent their entire treasure hoard draining the kegs at the local brewery. I offered to pay them as extra muscle when I fought the lava beasts."*

"Them?" The prince is full of questions. "You said it was one dragon."

"Yes, but two heads, so the dragon used they/them pronouns. The heads were named Ee and Orr, but better names might have been Manic and Depressive."

"A dragon with personality, then?"

"A split personality, but their moods balanced each other out. Ee and Orr debated, but both agreed they were thirsty, so off we went, with the promise of refreshing ale afterward.

"The monsters and the erupting volcano had devastated the terrain, but so far they'd made no move to cross the nearby river. When I saw the size of the fiery, lumbering army and felt the scalding temperature in the air, I realized I didn't want to be cooked like an egg in my armor! Even with the two-headed dragon as backup, I doubted we could vanquish the entire horde. That's when I remembered pertinent advice from my old friend Sir Dalbry—that evacuation is often the best plan. I considered running off to a nearby tavern with an outdoor biergarten that could accommodate a large two-headed dragon with a powerful thirst."

Maurice's surprise is clear. "You were just going to leave a job unfinished? *The Knight's Manual strongly advises against that."*

"Indeed, and I was very chivalrous." Also, *I needed the money the king was offering, and I had to pay Ee and Orr.*

"So, I devised a super-weapon, something that would strike fear in the lava beasts."

The young man's eyes are sparkling. "A super-weapon? Like a giant catapult? Or an enormous ballista?"

I lean closer to whisper, "A horse trough!"

He seems disappointed, but he's listening.

"We approached so that I could shout a request to negotiate, and that's when I learned that lava beasts have temperaments equivalent to

their temperature. They hurled flaming blobs of fire at us. Fortunately for us, their aim was terrible.

"It was time to deploy the super-weapon."

"The horse trough?" Maurice is clearly skeptical.

"The horse trough!" I say. "The dragon carried it in their claws, filled it from the nearby river, and flew overhead, pouring the entire load of water onto one of the shambling magma demons. In a gush of steam and conflicting temperatures, the lava beast hardened instantly, while waving a blocky fist at us—then it shattered into lumps of rough lava rock!

"Ee was gloomy and depressed, Orr crowed with triumph and swooped away as other lava monsters hurled vengeful fireballs into the air. When the two-headed dragon returned with a second load of water, I shouted again to the leader of the flaming beasts.

"Now that we'd opened a dialogue, I could express my employer king's concerns about the devastation to his lush and fertile lands. I was pleased to learn that the lava beasts loathed anything moist and green, and they particularly hated streams of running water. They had no intention of moving, whatsoever.

"So, as the two-headed dragon flapped in place overhead with the threatening trough of river water, I brokered a peace settlement. It's always best to negotiate from a position of strength. The flaming monsters promised to remain in their devastated lands and avoid the rest of the kingdom. It was a win-win situation—and I certainly won, because afterward the king was delighted with our hard-fought outcome. (I didn't tell him the monsters considered the rest of his kingdom to be an unpleasant eyesore.)

"So, fully funded again, Ee, Orr, and I did indeed go to a tavern with a large outdoor biergarten and celebrated until most of the reward was spent."

Maurice is not convinced, but I give him a meaningful nod. "I keep that lump of lava rock on display in the dining hall as proof. You've seen it."

"That only proves you once found a lump of lava rock."

"Indeed!" I am glad to see his gullibility has its limits. "There are other stories, son—adventures, derring do, treasure and treachery! I

even know some stories that don't have dragons. How about one with ghosts, for instance?"

The prince's expression twists as if he's just sniffed strong artisanal cheese. "There's no such thing as ghosts."

I sigh. Do we have to do this again? "Ghosts are what you make of them. Better yet, ghosts are what you make other people believe! Sit back, son. Let me tell you about the time I haunted a castle and overthrew an evil orc army."

I chuckle to myself as I get warmed up.

CHAPTER
ONE

R iding at the head of the group, Sir Dalbry cut a dashing figure in his suit of armor and scaly cape, which he claimed was from the hide of a dragon. The old knight sat tall in the saddle as they all rode into Queen Amnethia's capital city.

From behind, Cullin couldn't see much more than the horse's ass in front of him—not referring to the seasoned knight, but the actual rear end of Dalbry's mount, Drizzle. The horse had seen better days, as had the old knight. The gelding was gray with black speckles, but Dalbry insisted that his steed was purest white beneath the stains, because a brave knight deserved a white steed. The name Drizzle had been from the dregs of names, after other horses had used all the more dramatic weather-based monikers, such as Stormy, Lightning, and Thunder.

Behind the brave knight, young Cullin rode a pony named Pony, followed by an old mule (which had thus far eluded being named) bearing Reeger, who scratched his armpit and adjusted his burlap jerkin. For the past hour, Reeger had complained about saddle sores, but at least that was a much-improved conversation from previous descriptions of his hemorrhoids.

Reeger shifted the long wrapped parcel tied to the mule's saddle. "Rust! We haven't been able to sell our story in the last three king-doms. What makes you think Queen Amnethia will buy it?"

Dalbry didn't turn around, partly because his plate armor

provided little swivel ability. "Obviously, we will have to be more convincing."

Reeger spat a wad of phlegm to the side. The mule grimaced with distaste. "I always do my best."

He unwrapped the flap of the package to expose the basis for their current con—a bleached whale rib that had washed up on the distant coast. Cullin and Reeger had cleaned the long bone, sharpened the point, then glued scavenged sharks' teeth along the edge. The unnatural and terrifying "kraken tusk" inspired gullible onlookers to imagine the nightmarish sea creature.

"I've heard that Queen Amnethia has problems with her short-term memory," said Dalbry. "That might make her more amenable to hiring our services."

"So long as she doesn't forget to rustin' pay us," Reeger grumbled.

"All in good time." The knight reached into a small leather sack at his side and drew out a dried apricot. Dalbry's magic sack of apricots never grew empty, because he remembered to buy more dried fruit whenever his supply ran low.

"I've been working on my mournful expression," Cullin said. "It's sure to make the queen more sympathetic."

"I've seen the lad practice," Reeger said. "Even been coaching him. He's got the disgusted grimace down pat, too."

Cullin offered one of the well-practiced grimaces, and Reeger nodded in approval.

He wished that pretty Affonyl could be riding with them, but the former princess had gone ahead to secure a vendor stall in the royal flea market, and she was busy making a few honest coins. Extravagant cons might earn extravagant payoffs, but consistent money kept a quail or two on the cookfire.

Cullin had once practiced his mournful expression for Affonyl, who wasn't impressed. She said he was much better at the "love-struck mooncalf" expression, but he didn't know what she meant.

Approaching the outskirts of the city, the three riders took on their roles. The queendom was landlocked and far inland, with crops and grazing meadows, forested hills, and mountains in the distance. The ocean was a distant rumor, and that allowed Dalbry, Reeger, and

Cullin to embellish their seafaring stories, and few would contradict them.

The castle stood on a rise, an architectural hodgepodge of thin towers and blocky battlements, defensive parapets and airy balconies. Renovations had changed the style over the centuries to fit the sensibilities of successive administrations. Judging from the colorful displays along the main road up to the castle, Amnethia's preference tended toward petunias. Her predecessors might have left a permanent legacy by building new wings or parapets, but this queen wanted to be remembered for her flowerbeds.

As pedestrians, farmers' carts, and noble carriages filled the town streets during the afternoon rush hour, Reeger wrapped up the kraken tusk again. Sir Dalbry raised a gauntleted hand and gestured up the steep road. "Ride ahead to the castle, Cullin. Announce our presence and tell the queen she should prepare to be amazed."

Amnethia's throne room was heady with the scent of potted petunias, bouquets of spiky gladiolas, and cheery, fresh-cut daisies. Though he had practiced his lines, Cullin was so nervous he forgot to wipe his feet on the castle's doormat, and he tracked mud across the tile floor. An annoyed court sweeper followed him with a straw broom, erasing all marks of his passage.

The queen sat on a gilded, girly-looking throne next to a smaller chair for her consort, Lord Dither. (The lord insisted his name was pronounced with a long "I" sound, but nobody in court referred to him as such.)

Amnethia was a thin, middle-aged woman with an aquiline nose. Her pale hair was done up in so many hoops, loops, and braids that if she were to walk in a forest with low branches, she would surely end up snagged and suspended from a tree.

Lord Dither sat with slumped shoulders and heavy-lidded eyes. A shadow hung above him as if his life had become an unbearable weight. Amnethia and her consort were not married, and parts of the queendom were scandalized about the two of them living in sin. It was rumored, however, that Dither had certain masculine problems, so there wasn't a great deal of "sin" taking place.

Between the queen's ornate throne and Dither's junior throne, a table held a teapot and two china cups. The two sipped their tea as Cullin proclaimed the imminent arrival of the famed Sir Dalbry, of whom the minstrels sang. When Amnethia and Dither gave him a blank look, Cullin hummed part of Nightingale Bob's most famous tune and sang the familiar refrain, "Brave Sir Dalbry ... standing in the hallway."

Amnethia was sure she must have heard the song, but had forgotten it. She was easily convinced that Dalbry must be well known. "I am always pleased to receive guests, especially famous ones."

As soon as Cullin finished the preparatory work, Dalbry and Reeger arrived. As the knight entered through the great doorway, Cullin called out his name in a voice that should have been impressive, but since the young man was still at the tail end of puberty, his voice cracked with an embarrassing high lilt.

Dalbry strode across the freshly swept floor in his gleaming armor, dragon-skin cape, and clean boots. Reeger slouched along behind him, carrying the long canvas-wrapped tusk in his arms.

Reeger preferred to do the unpleasant, but necessary, work behind the scenes, because his skulking abilities were legendary. Other times, though, his unkempt and unsettling presence added veracity to the setup. In best-case scenarios, people paid handsomely just for Reeger to go away.

Despite his armor and his creaking joints, Sir Dalbry bowed before the throne with surprising grace. "Queen Amnethia, I have traveled to your far queendom all the way from the rugged seacoast to bring you a relic of incomparable value."

The queen was delighted. "Oh, I can't wait to see what it is!"

Lord Dither's half-lidded eyes widened just a bit.

Reeger lurched forward with the burden in his arms, and Dalbry flipped open the wrappings to reveal the whale rib studded with glued shark teeth. "Surely you have heard of the kraken, Majesty— the monster that all sailors fear!"

The queen glanced at Dither, who nodded, then she turned back to the knight. "Why, yes, we have heard of it, but I'm afraid there are no krakens around here. We are far from the sea."

Wearing a serious expression, Dalbry stepped closer to the throne and lowered his voice. "When the fierce kraken sets upon a sailing ship, few men survive. But I did! I fought the monster and slew it out in the ocean."

"That must have been quite the challenge," said Dither.

"A challenge indeed. I was traveling aboard the ship with my companion Reeger, here." He gestured to the unkempt man at his side. "We sailed to the New Lands to seek our fortune, but a terrific storm whipped up from out of nowhere. Our sails were torn to shreds. The captain lashed himself to the wheel in the pouring rain, and our poor vessel rocked from side to side. Many crewmen were thrown overboard."

Amnethia took a sip of tea to calm herself from the exciting story.

Dalbry lowered his voice. "Tentacles thrashed in the water as those poor lost souls were seized and drawn into the monster's fanged mouth!"

Lord Dither gasped. Cullin added his own gasp for good measure. Reeger grunted.

Dalbry continued, "Hungry for our ship and crew, the kraken smashed the hull, used tentacles to tear down the masts. Reeger and I tried to save the doomed crew, but there was nothing we could do. Our ship was wrecked, the captain killed, all the sailors devoured." He drew the long sword from its scabbard at his side. "But as a brave knight, I have slain dragons and fought ogres. You may have heard the songs about me?"

"Yes, yes! We remember clearly," said Amnethia. "Something about a hallway."

Dalbry nodded, satisfied. "I clung to a bit of debris and drew my sword to face the kraken. I fought the monster in its own element, stabbed it with my blade, pierced out its eye, and drove the sword between its gills!"

Reeger pulled away the rest of the wrappings to reveal the full kraken tusk.

The old knight shook his head in dismay. "My poor companion, though, was struck in the side of the head with a yardarm, and he's not been right since. I keep him with me because I feel sorry for the poor lack-witted man."

Reeger flashed him a sarcastic glare, but Dalbry didn't notice.

"Before the slimy carcass could sink beneath the waves, I hacked off one of its tusks as a trophy. For days, Reeger and I drifted among the debris of the ship until at last we washed up against the shore."

"It sounds like quite an adventure," said Amnethia.

The knight gave her a respectful bow. "I've carried the tusk ever since. This far inland, you've probably never seen any real kraken artifact, but I show you now."

Reeger brought the ominous-looking object closer so Amnethia and Dither could get a better look.

"Alas, it has been my burden for far too long," said Sir Dalbry. "This magical tusk has protected me on my travels, lo, these many years, but I would like to offer it to you as a protective talisman ... for a reasonable price."

"Or a large price," Reeger mumbled, and the knight gave him a quick glare.

"As I said, my companion is not right in the head." Dalbry continued in a warm, lecturing tone. "Everyone knows that a kraken tusk imparts an aura of protection. With such a talisman hanging in your castle, Majesty, your queendom would surely be free of threats, with no chance of war or pestilence."

"Or famine," Cullin piped up, helping to sell the story.

"But why would you part with such a relic?" Amnethia asked.

Dalbry cast his eyes down. "As a brave knight and dragon slayer, I have many travel expenses, and we would appreciate any fair sum for it. But the true answer is that as an adventurer, I cannot rest on my laurels. I have slain many dragons, but I don't carry their heads with me—only this cape." He swished his scaled dragon skin. "I'd happily sell you this kraken tusk, because it would give me the incentive to go hunt another kraken."

"The sea is lousy with them" Reeger said.

Dalbry continued, "The tusk would be better off with you, Majesty."

Cullin pointed to the wall. "It would look nice hanging right over your mantel there."

"You'd go all the way to the ocean to fight another aquatic monster?" Dither asked. "Seems like a long way."

Dalbry bowed. "As a knight, it would be my duty."

"Why, there's no need for that, good sir," Amnethia said with a smile. "We have our own giant lake monster right here in my queendom."

Dalbry was at a loss for words, and Cullin flashed him a quick glance.

Amnethia continued, "Yes, the awful creature has devoured many hapless fishermen and sunbathers. On the morrow, I'm sending a group of intrepid hunters to kill the lake monster. You can join them and do your duty."

CHAPTER
TWO

W hile Dalbry's kraken tusk intrigued the queen, she was more motivated to dispatch her own lake monster. She invited the brave knight, Cullin, and Reeger to join her and Lord Dither on their joyous expedition to slay the ferocious beast that terrorized her favorite resort lake.

Amnethia beamed at Sir Dalbry. "Having you with us will ensure that my mercenary fisher-hunters do the job properly. You'll let them take first crack at it, won't you?"

"They have already been paid a retainer," Dither said in a sour voice.

"By all means, Majesty." The old knight was all too willing to let others do the monster slaying. "I shall observe their technique with interest."

Amnethia stood before the fireplace mantel, smiling. "Your kraken tusk would look very nice mounted here—perhaps next to a monster fish head."

Cullin was anxious to meet with Affonyl in the town market so he could tell her where their plans stood, but the queen insisted they stay in castle guestrooms. She gave Sir Dalbry his own quarters, while Cullin and Reeger shared a smaller room with bunkbeds. The young man was not happy with the sleeping arrangements, knowing that Reeger farted and snored throughout the night. On most nights, when their group camped under the trees with plenty of ventilation and other forest noises, that wasn't such a problem, but that night in the stuffy enclosed chamber, Cullin was so miserable that he actually looked forward to hunting a monster at dawn.

After a breakfast of the queen's favorite waffles, the grand fishing expedition prepared to set out, including liveried heralds with long horns to announce the queen's presence, in case the lake monster wasn't paying attention. "Killing a terrifying beast is no small task," Amnethia said, "and must be done with appropriate pomp and circumstance."

As an honored guest and dragon slayer, Sir Dalbry rode with the queen and her consort in the main carriage, while Cullin and Reeger sat in an open cart filled with mercenary fisher-hunters, who intended to make names for themselves.

Queen Amnethia's carriage headed away from the castle, followed by her liveried honor guard and the heralds, who tooted their long horns as they warmed up for the true fanfare. Last came the big wagon with Cullin, Reeger, and the fisher-hunters.

Drawn by a pair of plow horses, the cart of mercenaries bounced along. The rough men told tall tales and fish stories, exaggerating past successes and building up their confidence. When Cullin asked them to introduce themselves, Reeger just rolled his eyes. "Waste of time, lad, if they're all going to get eaten."

"What if we need to sing songs of their heroic deeds?" Cullin responded in a low voice.

"Rust, then we can just make up names!"

But the fisher-hunters were brash and proud, eager to tell their stories. "I am Heller," said a man with shaggy hair and a cockeyed stare. In a contest for most unpleasant facial features, he could have given Reeger a run for his money. "Or you can call me Mike, if you buy me an ale."

"Heller it is, then," Cullin said.

A lean man with shaved head and bushy goatee scoffed. "I prefer wine, no matter who's buying. My name is Dug."

The other two fisher-hunters were a burly older man with a gladiator look about him named Paxinos, or Ted for short, and a weathered, bearded Viking type who pounded his chest. "And I am Vilgerdarson! Cecil Vilgerdarson!"

Both men said they would be content with any sort of alcoholic beverage.

During the ride, the mercenaries tried to outdo their rivals with displays of testosterone. "I once caught a cutthroat trout five handspans long. Biggest trout I ever saw!" said Heller. "I had to wrestle him out of the brook and throw him on the shore, where I dispatched him with my gutting knife."

"I once caught a tuna as big as my outstretched arms." Vilgerdarson demonstrated by stretching out his arms, which were indeed very long. "I speared it at an isolated lake to the north." He thumped his spear on the bed of the rattling wagon. "Took me half a day to drag it onto shore, so I could kill it and have a feast."

"Tuna aren't freshwater fish," said Paxinos.

"You'd never find a giant like that in an isolated lake," added Dug.

Vilgerdarson reddened. "The tuna came there to spawn! I harvested half a barrel of tuna roe after I gutted the monster and filleted all the meat."

"Come on, Cecil, how did a fish that big get to an isolated lake?" asked Dug.

The Viking showed another wave of scorn. "It was a spotted northern tuna, fool! With big fanlike fins. Spotted northern tuna can *fly* to their spawning grounds!" He thumped his spear on the wagon bed again.

The old gladiator lowered his voice. "Now, the hardest ones to catch are minnows. That's a real challenge for any fisherman! Minnows wriggle and dart away so fast! That is how a true fisherhunter proves his prowess." Paxinos leaned against the wall of the cart with a grunt. "I have caught many a minnow in my day."

Listening to their ridiculous stories, Cullin noted which parts he found difficult to believe, so that he could offer tale-spinning advice to Sir Dalbry.

The procession left the city behind and traveled through the forest, into the hills, and finally reached a large mountain lake. Docks extended from the shore near a striped royal pavilion. Farther along the lake stood the queen's summer fishing cabin, as well as stables and a boathouse. Empty picnic tables sat in front of souvenir stands

SKELETON IN THE CLOSET

(now closed, because the lake monster had driven off the tourist trade). In front of a food tent was a faded sign with peeling paint that announced, "Fish Fry every Friday night."

As the party pulled up to the empty lake village, the eager heralds finally got to blow their horns. Lord Dither climbed out of the ornate carriage and extended his hand for the queen. She stepped out as if expecting a great reception at the lake, but she heard only wind whispering through the pines. Sir Dalbry emerged last, adjusting the shiny pieces of his armor.

The four fisher-hunters sprang out of their open wagon, ready for fish conquests. While the wily mercenaries planned how to outwit the lake monster, Reeger and Cullin joined Sir Dalbry at the colorful pavilion, where the queen and her consort would have a good view of the slaughter.

Since they were not on the list for the pavilion, unfortunately, Reeger and Cullin had to sit at one of the empty picnic tables.

The docks near the fish-fry tent held three rowboats. After bailing greenish rain water from two of them, the fisher-hunters placed their weapons aboard—Dug and Heller in one, Vilgerdarson and Paxinos in the other.

Dug, the bald man with the goatee, carried his hooked spear like a harpoon. Heller, who had taken such pride in catching a large cutthroat trout, carried a bow and a quiver of arrows. In the second boat, Paxinos, the gladiator who claimed great prowess in catching minnows, carried an old sword. Next to him, the Viking kept glancing warily at the skies, as if worried about flying tuna.

Queen Amnethia stood at the pavilion and called Sir Dalbry forward as an example for the others. "This brave knight slew a kraken in the deep ocean and brought its tusk to me. Now he and his companions will watch you men slay the terrible lake monster. Show them how it's done!"

The four mercenaries bowed to the queen, and when she snapped her fingers, her royal footman rushed back to the carriage. He came back with two enamel pots, which he formally presented to each pair of mercenaries.

Amnethia said, "This is a final gift to you, my brave fisher-hunters. These pots are from the chambers of my Royal Fertilizer, the man responsible for fertilizing the flowers in my copious royal flowerbeds."

The footman removed the lids to reveal that each vessel was filled with squirming pink earthworms.

"These sacred chamber pots contain special worms. Use them to attract the lake beast." The loops and hoops of her hair jiggled as she gave them a formal nod.

Carrying a chamber pot aboard each rowboat, the fisher-hunters set off across the placid lake. One man rowed and the other crouched at the bow, peering ahead in search of monsters.

In the first boat Heller pulled out a small drum and began pounding with his palm. Dug removed the lid from the chamber pot, dumped the squirming worms into the water, then stood holding his harpoon ready. Setting down his drum, Heller nocked an arrow and drew back the string, waiting.

In the second boat, Vilgerdarson pulled out a net and held it, alert, while Paxinos emptied the second chamber pot. The old gladiator smacked the lake's surface with the flat of his sword, which made the boat rock back and forth.

Lounging at the picnic table, Reeger grinned, showing his brown teeth. "This should be rustin' good."

They sat and waited. And waited.

In the open pavilion, Dither mused, "Fishing consists of interminable periods of nothing happening. Some men find it relaxing."

"Sounds like golf," said Sir Dalbry.

Before they could further discuss the tedious sports of fishing or golf, a giant monster lunged out of the water, its jagged fin like a huge sawblade—an enormous striped pike, half again as large as either boat. With a hinged jaw full of needle-sharp teeth, it chomped down on the first boat, splintering the wood.

Heller and Dug scrambled to defend themselves. Dug stabbed at the air with his harpoon, but the enormous pike bit his arm clean off. The bald fisher-hunter howled while his stump gushed blood. Heller launched several arrows.

The pike came up again, capsizing the rowboat and spilling the two men into the lake. With swift efficiency, the hungry fish gulped them both down and sank beneath the surface. The placid blue lake now turned red.

Vilgerdarson waved his net in the air, as if to catch the pike if it should happen to take flight, and old Paxinos stabbed at the water with his sword. Both men showed such unbalanced exuberance that they capsized their own boat, without any assistance from the monster.

While the two fisher-hunters flailed, the pike circled back around and devoured them both. For good measure, it smashed the second rowboat into splinters.

From the picnic table, Cullin and Reeger stared in horrified awe. "Crotchrust! That thing's as big as a dragon."

"We're going to need a bigger boat," Cullin said.

In the striped pavilion, Queen Amnethia fanned herself in alarm, while Dither pushed out his lower lip in a pout. "Now we have to procure more royal rowboats, dear. That'll strain the treasury."

Amnethia sighed. "And our tax income has been low this year, due to the loss of tourism."

She folded her fan together, handed it to her royal footman, then faced Sir Dalbry. "It appears I will hire your services after all, brave knight. You don't need to go to the deep blue sea to find a worthy aquatic scourge. I will buy your kraken tusk as a decoration for my mantel, but we must negotiate an all-inclusive price for slaying our lake monster as well."

CHAPTER

THREE

After their disastrous fishing expedition, Cullin needed to tell Affonyl what had happened. He couldn't wait to see the look on her face. Though he hadn't been in any actual danger himself, he was sure the former princess would be impressed.

Because she had studied natural science, alchemy, and astrology, Affonyl had proved to everyone that a brainy girl was well worth having around. Using that knowledge, she had played a con of her own to escape a repressive princessy life with her father, King Norrimund the Corpulent. She had managed to deceive not only the king, but also the evil Duke Kerrl and numerous would-be dragon slayers. Afterward as part of their gang, the former princess had shown herself to be a skilled, useful, and feminine part of any con. Affonyl usually knew what to do.

And regarding the man-eating fish, Cullin certainly needed some advice.

He found the young woman in the village market where she had set up a small table and an easel. A handwritten sign said "Caricatures, 5 copper coins. Amuse your friends! See yourself as others see you!" Then in smaller print, "Suitable for framing." She also had a clay pot next to a card, "Tips Accepted."

Affonyl's blond hair had once been long, as was customary for a princess ready for an unwilling and unpleasant betrothal. As part of her disguise, she had hacked it short, but by now it had grown out in a ragamuffin style. She wore a colorful peasant dress, so she fit in with the locals in the village market.

The willowy girl was busy sketching a whimsical figure of the town baker, who sat wearing a forced smile. Seeing Cullin arrive, she beamed, but kept drawing the baker's caricature, and he anxiously waited for her to finish.

The plump baker had flour on his nose and apron. Affonyl's caricature made his eyes round, sparkling with homey mirth. His big smile, plump cheeks, and extra chin were a testament to the tastiness of his bakery's products. In bold letters under his face she wrote, "Hamilton's Bakery. I enjoy loafing around!"

She tore the paper off her easel and handed it to the satisfied man. He held it in flour-dusted hands. "I'll put this in the bakery window. Maybe I'll even have it painted on a placard."

She grew more businesslike. "I offer a limited commercial license. Copyright remains with me, but you may use the artwork for promotional purposes."

"Thank you, thank you!" He plunked five copper coins into her hand, paused, then dropped another into her tip jar. "Come by Hamilton's Bakery for a treat. I have a special new pastry named after myself: Kris's Kringle."

"Kris with a K?" she asked. "Nobody in the Middle Ages spells Kris with a K."

"Part of my branding," the baker said. "Kris's Kringle. You should try one."

When the happy man strolled off, she finally turned to Cullin. "Squirrel! I've been waiting for you."

Though he was glad to see her reaction, Cullin said, "You're still calling me Squirrel? After all the time we've known each other, shouldn't I have graduated into a larger rodent by now?"

She tapped a finger to her lower lip. "Hmmm, would you prefer jackrabbit? Hedgehog? Muskrat? Or maybe a nice marsupial—a wallaby, perhaps?"

Cullin sighed. "Squirrel is fine." At least it was a term of endearment.

She had him take a seat on the stool next to her easel. "Have you been keeping Queen Amnethia busy? Did Dalbry sell that kraken tusk yet?"

"The queen is making an all-inclusive deal," Cullin said.

As she listened, Affonyl sketched on her big pad, and his voice grew more urgent as he grew caught up in his tale. "There's a monster fish in the lake and the queen hired us to kill it! Well, she hired Dalbry, but you know he doesn't do anything alone."

The former princess gave him a curious frown. "I suggest baking the large fish with lemon and dill."

"I saw it eat four fisher-hunters with my own eyes! It rose up out of the lake, smashed two rowboats, then snapped up those men like bugs on the water. Now Queen Amnethia wants *us* to reel it in!"

Affonyl gave him a skeptical smile. "Squirrel, if you make up *convincing* stories, they'll pay off better."

When they all got back together, he would have to bring in supporting testimony from Dalbry and Reeger. In the meantime, he changed the subject. "So, how was your day?"

She wiped a smudge of charcoal dust from her fingers. "Oh, it's busy here in the flea market! I really have a knack for art, you know."

Cullin nodded. "I saw the avant-garde embroidery work you did in your father's castle."

In her stifled life as a princess, Affonyl had been trained in all sorts of princessy things, but she had resisted the indoctrination by using guerilla needlework. She eschewed traditional patterns and created chaotic tangled designs, which soon caught on as "modern embroidery." Across the land, the knotted examples of her lack of stitchery expertise were celebrated as an innovative style.

King Norrimund had insisted over and over, "A princess is a princess. Don't go thinking of yourself as a person." But Affonyl knew she *was* a person. Cullin certainly thought of her as a person, and a very pretty one at that, although he was more experienced in dragon slaying than in flirting.

After Affonyl fled her father's kingdom and renounced all claim to daintiness and princessy pastimes, she joined Cullin, Dalbry, and Reeger in conducting innovative scams. She also loved selling her original artwork at village festivals, town markets, even once at a futuristic event called a Renaissance Faire. Because she was technically an outlaw, she didn't dare sign her works, taking only cryptic credit as "the artist formerly known as Princess."

Now while Cullin fidgeted on the stool, she focused on her easel, sketching quickly. "I'm so much happier now, Squirrel. Footloose and fancy free! And I made thirty coppers today."

Cullin grinned back at her. "That's great news, because Reeger and Dalbry want to meet at the tavern. We need to plan how to kill the giant fish, and thirty coppers will buy ale and maybe a few meat pies."

"Good thing one of us has a stable job." Affonyl picked up her tip jar, jangled the few coins and patted the pouch at her waist. "I'll help you come up with the proper way to slay the beast, so you don't embarrass yourselves." She finished her sketch with a flourish and turned the easel so he could see it. "It's my masterpiece, don't you think?"

The wonderful caricature portrayed Cullin as downright adorable, winsome, with a big Adam's apple, a mop of unruly hair, and pond-sized eyes. His heart fluttered to think that this was how she viewed him. "Can I keep it? Suitable for framing!"

"Of course." She tore it off the pad. "But it'll be hard to carry around in a big frame."

He carefully folded the paper and tucked it inside his tunic, close to his heart. "I like it a lot."

"You'd better." She folded her easel and packed up her charcoal sticks and lead stylus. "Let's go to the tavern, so I can learn more about this fishy business."

CHAPTER

FOUR

The capital city had a plethora of inns and taverns that catered to the seedier sort of customers. In such places, everybody knew your name, and everybody knew what to expect: splintered tables, smoky atmosphere, loud conversations, bad manners. An occasional minstrel with a poorly tuned lute might sing bawdy songs, while wenches served foaming tankards of ale and brushed off rude amorous advances.

Those seeking a higher class place had to look in the city directory for "bistros" or "wine bars."

The Mountain Oyster was not a place like that. Reeger had chosen it out of all the possibilities because it met his needs and expectations, which were admittedly low. Dalbry had suggested an establishment called The Three Legged Pony, that was cleaner and served a renowned chicken pot pie, but Reeger was quite fond of the fried oyster specialties served here, even if they tasted different from any oysters he had ever had on the coast. Heather, the tavern mistress, coyly refused to answer any questions, claiming that her Mountain Oysters were a secret recipe.

As tavern owner and lead wench, Heather Jones had originally established the place for weary and hungry travelers, offering reasonably priced food and lodgings. As a play on her name, she had named the place Ho-Jos, but decided she didn't like to be called Ho, and thus settled on the Mountain Oyster.

When Cullin entered the tavern with Affonyl, he saw that Reeger and Dalbry had claimed a small table in the shadowy corner. They already had tankards of ale in front of them, although Affonyl was the one with copper coins to pay. They were all accustomed to being penniless, and they knew alternative ways to settle their bills (including sneaking away). They preferred, however, to concoct a satisfying tall tale that was well worth the price of a beverage or two.

Affonyl sat on the wooden bench opposite Dalbry, and Cullin took his place beside her. He flagged down the tavern wench to bring two more tankards of ale.

"Already ordered a basket of them oysters," Reeger said. "We can have a feast."

Dalbry brushed a spot of mud off his shining armor. "We'll need our strength for the mission we're about to embark on."

Reeger made a raspberry sound. "A fool's errand, if you ask me—and I'm no fool."

"Some would beg to differ," Affonyl quipped, then leaned closer to her companions. "I hear you got hooked into a giant fish story."

"Wasn't no rustin' story," Reeger said. "We all watched that monster eat four men and two boats."

"Not to mention two chamber pots of worms," said the old knight.

"I told you, it's true," Cullin insisted to her. "And now Dalbry here is on the hook for slaying that monster pike."

Their voices were loud enough that other customers cocked their ears.

Dalbry tried to be more discreet. "Now we must decide the best manner to kill the beast. Surely it can't be much more difficult than slaying a dragon, except that it's in a lake."

"Maybe we can shove our kraken tusk down its throat," Cullin suggested. "Then we'd at least get rid of the thing." Like most of his suggestions, it was quietly ignored.

Heather bustled back with two more tankards of ale and a basket of the fried mountain oysters Reeger enjoyed so much. He nudged Cullin. "Eat your fill, lad. Happy Hour special."

Affonyl and Dalbry each daintily took one of the fried oysters, though the former princess had never been a fan of them. Cullin chewed on the rubbery breaded squishiness. He was not fond of the flavor, although a healthy dollop of barbecue sauce helped.

Reeger ate with great gusto, and his words were even more garbled with his mouth full. "While I'm a fan of valorous deeds, this might be one of those times when running away is the better part of valor."

"Without our kraken tusk?" Dalbry said, alarmed.

"Without our pay?" Cullin asked, concerned with financial matters.

"At least we'd have our rustin' limbs intact and not bitten off by a pike!" Reeger said.

"That is indeed an important consideration," admitted Dalbry.

"There's still one rowboat left at the lake," Cullin said, as if that were a relevant part of the discussion.

Affonyl managed to finish her mountain oyster, decided against taking another one, and cleansed her palate with ale. "You watched the monster eat four experienced fisher-hunters. If you just take a rowboat out on the lake, even with your sword, you're bound to fail. We should think outside the box."

"I'd like to see that pike chomp through Dalbry's armor!" Reeger said.

"I would not," Dalbry added.

A man interrupted their discussion from a nearby table. "Hey! Are you Sir Dalbry the dragon slayer?" It was the cheerful baker Affonyl had caricatured.

The knight lifted his chin. "I am indeed, although in this particular instance I am Sir Dalbry the kraken slayer. We come from the coast with many tales, and I recently presented the queen with the tusk of a horrific sea monster, whereupon she engaged my services to slay the horrific lake monster."

"And what do you know about fish?" asked a fisherman. He tapped the side of his head. "*I* know the mind of a fish!"

"Then go kill the giant pike and take the reward for yourself," Reeger suggested with a snort.

The fisherman backed away, slurping his ale. "Well, I don't know the mind of a *big* fish."

"We've experienced countless adventures fighting sea serpents and sirens and great storms," Cullin said. "We could share those stories, for a modest price." Maybe that would pay for their drinks and at least the first basket of mountain oysters. Better to save Affonyl's copper coins for a rainy day—and rain was quite common in these lands.

As curious patrons pulled their chairs closer, Sir Dalbry retold the story of the great kraken battle, with embellishments from Cullin and Reeger. Oddly, the townspeople seemed skeptical, even insulting, and Cullin was concerned that they wouldn't pay for the drinks after all. Apparently, the people here had often been tricked by itinerant scam artists claiming to be dragon slayers.

Hearing of the copycat scams darkened Reeger and Dalbry's mood. The knight grumbled under his breath. "That was our intellectual property!"

"Damn right," Reeger said, "and it was our idea, too."

Cullin whispered, "Maybe we should go somewhere else to discuss our plans?"

"I hear the Three-Legged Pony is nice," Dalbry said. "I would enjoy a good chicken pot pie."

"That's a bistro, not a tavern," Reeger snapped.

Affonyl spoke up, distracting the patrons. "I was a mermaid, you know—a real mermaid."

The audience fell into quiet, confused muttering. "A mermaid? Where's your fish tail?"

As a group, the patrons bent over to look at her long peasant dress, wondering how it could cover a scaly lower body and wide tail fin.

"We saw you walk into the Mountain Oyster!"

"I'm not a mermaid *anymore*!" She crossed her arms over her chest. "Clearly, you aren't familiar with mermaid legends. I emerged from the sea and gave up my mermaid form for true love." She fluttered her eyelashes at Cullin, and a sudden heat rose in his cheeks. "Now I walk the land."

The mutters changed to snickers of disbelief. "You gave it all up for that scrap of a lad?" said the man who understood the minds of fishes. "He's nothing more than a twisted rag of a boy!"

"I'm a squire," Cullin said defensively.

"True love is true love." Affonyl blinked her wide, earnest eyes and leaned close to stroke his arm, which brought even more heat to his cheeks.

He reminded himself it was just a story she was telling, but often there was truth in stories. He took a long gulp from his tankard.

"If she's a mermaid, why isn't she topless?" said a portly man lounging against the fieldstone fireplace. "I know my stories. Mermaids never wear a dress or a blouse. Take it off! How else are you going to prove you're a mermaid unless you show us your breasts?"

Affonyl stiffened, the anger visibly building up inside her. "What will that tell you? All women have breasts."

The portly man said, "I've studied quite a number of breasts in my day. I'd know the difference."

Understanding the obligations of chivalry from reading the Knight's Manual, Cullin stood to defend Affonyl's honor, though he realized he wouldn't do well in a tavern brawl against so many men.

Affonyl kept her icy calm. "I can prove it another way." She raised her voice and called for the tavern wench. "Bring me a pot of pure water!"

"Pure water?" Heather said, aghast. "Nobody drinks water here. All we have is ale."

"The ale might as well be water...." said Reeger, eliciting a round of chuckles from the other customers.

"I have dishwater from the rain barrel in the back," the tavern wench suggested.

Affonyl sighed. "That'll have to do."

The former princess had a satchel of necessary items, which she had carried ever since escaping her father's castle. She replenished the contents whenever they found a tinker, a witch, or an apothecary. Cullin was always amazed by what she had.

Now she pulled out a triangular fish scale that fit neatly in her palm. Clasping it between thumb and forefinger, she showed the tavern patrons. "A mermaid scale," she said in a whisper.

Cullin remembered that Affonyl had acquired a handful of scales from a dead marlin in the fishmarket. She had obviously been planning this trick for some time.

"This is a talisman from when I had my mermaid tail—a reminder of what I once was, everything I gave up." She glanced at Cullin. "It longs to return to the water. I'll show you proof." She looked boldly around. "Then you'll owe me and my friends a round of drinks."

"And another basket of oysters," Reeger interjected.

The fish scale had been coated with a chemical film that shone with rainbow hues in the inn's smoky light. The tavern fell silent.

"Watch what happens when it gets a taste of the water again."

She dropped the scale into the pot of dishwater. Nothing happened for a moment, then tiny bubbles began to appear, a fizz like fermenting cider. Suddenly it roiled, burbled, and frothed. Energetic foam splashed over the rim.

The tavern patrons gasped and drew away.

Cullin was impressed as always. In addition to her artistic talent, Affonyl knew much about alchemy and natural science from her years studying under Wizard Edgar. The bubbling froth reached a crescendo.

The people gaped at Affonyl, and she said in a wistful voice, "I do miss my ocean life, but I've made my choice, and I'm determined to be happy." She picked up one of the last fried tidbits in the basket. "Although our sea oysters taste much better than these mountain ones."

Reeger called out to the tavern mistress. "You heard what she said! Another round of ale for us—and more of these oysters."

Sufficiently impressed, Heather put another order in to the kitchen.

Affonyl turned a hard glare on the intimidated customers. "Now, some privacy for me and my friends! You don't want me to invoke the mermaid's curse."

Indeed, the bar patrons did not. They warily left Affonyl and the others alone.

The former princess finally got back to the matter of slaying the giant fish. "As I was saying, you don't need a boat and a sword."

"Then how do we kill the lake monster?" Cullin asked.

Affonyl glanced at the skittish patrons. "Superstition and natural science are a potent mix. We need chemistry, not bravery."

CHAPTER
FIVE

C ullin agreed as soon as Affonyl suggested her idea, but Reeger and Dalbry required more convincing.

The former princess showed them the mathematics to prove her scheme would work (though neither of the men could follow the differential equations or alchemical symbols). They finally relented when she reminded them of her explosive success during their previous dragon-slaying adventure.

Once the plans were made, she and her companions simply had to put them in motion.

Sir Dalbry entered the throne room and presented himself to the queen with a deep bow. He noted that she had already mounted the tooth-studded whale bone above her mantel.

"Majesty, I'm a daring dragon slayer and intrepid kraken killer—I do not intend to be outsmarted by a fish. My courage is greater, as is my brain capacity. My companions and I will face the monster late tonight, when its energy will be at low tide."

"An excellent plan, Sir Dalbry," said the queen, "although a mountain lake experiences no tides."

Dalbry swished his scaled cape over his shoulder. "If I do not return victorious on the morrow, then I have been devoured by the great pike, and you'll need to find another fish slayer."

Meanwhile, Affonyl took Cullin with her to acquire the necessary ingredients from apothecaries and herbalists, while Reeger went searching through the castle for a triple-pronged siege hook. "Any fisherman knows if you want to catch a big fish, you need a big hook!"

The group regrouped at nightfall to set off for the distant mountain lake. Cullin and his companions intended to do their fish business well after midnight, when no one else would see, in case something went terribly wrong. In the worst-case scenario, they could all run away, and Sir Dalbry would keep his legendary reputation intact, though he would be presumed eaten.

They retrieved Pony, Drizzle, and the surly old mule from the royal stables.

Reeger brought a small rickety cart to carry a maggot-infested sheep carcass he had purchased for a surprisingly good bargain. While the others held their noses, Reeger chortled, "Rust, we've got to have bait, don't we?" The smell of the rotting sheep carcass lingered around them in the cool night air as they rode out of town.

Riding Pony, Cullin looked down at the squirming maggots in the decaying mutton. "Well, we know the giant pike likes worms." Sitting behind him in the saddle, Affonyl wrinkled her nose.

In the darkest hour of night, they arrived at the uninhabited lakeshore town, with the queen's pavilion, the abandoned souvenir stands, and one remaining rowboat. Cullin tied Drizzle and Pony to a tree, but Reeger led the mule and the cart right up to the dock. Bending over the cart, he pulled out a braided rope with the grappling hook tied to one end. He tossed the rope's other end to Cullin. "Tie this around a sturdy tree on the shore. Make sure the knot is tight."

The young man trotted off and did as he was told. During their time traveling the coast, a veteran sailor had taught the young man myriad knots. Cullin had mastered none of them, although he was good at tangling up the strands, and the old seaman had called that good enough.

Now, he tied the rope around a thick oak on the edge of the water, then double- and triple-knotted it to make sure. As soon as he was finished, Reeger called him to the dock. "Now the real fun starts, lad. Help me with this!"

The cockeyed man had worked the sharp prongs of the hook into the rotting carcass, anchoring it firmly through the spine and rib cage. "Carry this out to the end of the dock and throw it into the water. Just be gentle, or some limbs or organs might fall out."

When Cullin looked at the noisome carcass, his stomach twisted into knots far tighter than anything he had worked into a rope. "Are you sure this is a job for me? Couldn't you ...?"

"Rust, I can't have all the fun for myself! You're my apprentice, and I'm teaching you tricks of the trade. Plenty of folk would pay a princely sum to learn Reeger's secrets. Well ... not that many people. Come on, give me a hand."

The mule snorted, impatient to be relieved of its odoriferous burden.

Cullin grimaced as he dug for a handhold among the mangy patches of wool. His fingers popped through the hide, and the insides had a consistency more like pudding than meat. But he found a bone and a joint, which gave him a good grip. He tugged, and Reeger took hold of the other end. The sheep sagged as fluids dripped out.

"Move quick," Reeger said. "Don't want to waste any of this."

They scuttled down the dock with the carcass. The boards creaked, and small ripples of water touched the pilings, but otherwise the lake was silent. With the three-pronged hook firmly embedded in the carcass, the long rope trailed behind them. Cullin let out a loud grunt of disgust as a loop of sheep intestine dropped down, nearly tripping him.

"Just a few more steps—one, two ... three!" Together, they swung the sheep back and heaved it out into the water as far as they could, which was not actually far, but far enough. Buoyed by bubbles of decomposition gas, the sheep floated like the bobber on the line of an amateur fisherman.

Reeger cupped his slime-covered hands around his mouth and shouted, "Here fishy, fishy, fishy!" He offered a cockeyed grin to Cullin. "How can it resist?"

In full armor, Dalbry strode onto the dock and walked out to the end over the water, drew his sword, and stood waiting.

As Affonyl finished her own preparations at one of the picnic tables, she called to the knight, "With our revised plan, Dalbry, you won't need to actually face the monster."

"It is the best way to promulgate the mystique of knighthood," he said, remaining in place with his sword drawn.

Cullin looked in disgust at the goop covering his favorite tunic, but he wasn't inclined to wash himself off in the lake. He hurried over to Affonyl and asked if he could help her.

She wrinkled her nose and turned away. "You could help by standing at a fair distance."

Disappointed, Cullin moved downwind.

On the picnic table, the former princess fiddled with a small cask like the ones Queen Amnethia used for peppermint schnapps. She pulled out a flint and steel from her sack of necessary items and affixed a string through a hole in the top of the cask.

They all stared at the lake and the floating lump of maggot-infested mutton. "Here fishy, fishy, fishy," Reeger called again.

"Maybe the monster's asleep," Cullin said.

A striped torpedo-shape lunged up from beneath the dark waters with a huge splash. The jaws opened wide and chomped on the woolly carrion, dragging the whole sheep down. Water splashed into the air. The rope unreeled, then went as taut as a bowstring.

"The hook is set!" Reeger crowed.

The giant pike thrashed in the water, fighting against the line. It arced up in the air, its mouth gaping to show the grappling hook caught in its jaw. The monster let out a gurgling roar, which Cullin found alarming.

With her background in natural science, however, Affonyl said, "A fish shouldn't even have lungs or a larynx to make a sound like that."

From out on the dock, Dalbry explained, "Monsters are designed to make scary noises."

Reaching the end of the rope again, the pike swung back toward the dock. Its dorsal fin sliced the water as it hurtled toward the waiting knight.

"Dalbry, get out of the way!" Cullin yelled.

The former princess kept trying to strike a spark from her flint and steel.

The knight lunged to one side, landing in the shallow water just as the lake monster crashed into the dock. Dalbry scrambled in his clanking armor toward the shore. "That's enough to establish my brave mystique."

The pike raced back out into the water, and once more abruptly reached the end of the rope. The sturdy oak anchoring the other end groaned, and the shore mud shifted. Under the powerful strain from the fish monster, the entire tree came out of the mud, roots and all, and toppled into the water.

Affonyl finally managed to strike a spark to the fuse in her small schnapps cask. Cullin had helped fill the tiny barrel with her special chemical recipe, and he certainly hoped it would work. He ran to the end of the damaged dock and hurled it into the lake.

The cask splashed into the water near the thrashing pike, landing upright so that the fuse was not extinguished (which was good, because Cullin would not have wanted to swim out and light it again).

The monster fish, its mouth still full of the hooked and rotting sheep, lunged up in anger—and swallowed the cask.

Just before it exploded.

The loud sound was muffled because the explosive keg was down in the pike's gullet, but the result was spectacular. Flames and smoke shot out of its yawning gills, and the sleek body split open as if filleted by a thunderbolt.

Cullin and Affonyl ducked away as lake water rained around them, followed by hunks of raw fish. The ripples settled quickly, and the dead lake monster floated like a large capsized canoe.

Cullin and the former princess whooped and hugged each other, until she again smelled the rotting sheep on his jerkin, so they separated and shook hands instead.

Reeger danced around. "How's that for rustin' indigestion?"

"The foul beast is slain." Sir Dalbry strode toward the lone rowboat still tied to the damaged dock. "Now we must obtain proof to present to Queen Amnethia."

Then, as a surprise secondary reward, hundreds of normal-sized fish floated to the surface of the lake—bass, bluegills, trout, even smaller pike stunned by the explosion.

Reeger put his hands on his hips. "That's a year's worth of Friday-night fish fries."

Affonyl grabbed several shopping baskets from one of the empty tourist shops so they could collect all the fish. Cullin volunteered to accompany Dalbry in the rowboat; now that the lake monster was dead, he wanted to wash himself off.

The two rowed out to the huge carcass, and the knight leaned over the side, using his sword to hack off the pike's head, after which his duty was done. The large and unwieldly trophy filled the rowboat.

So, after the scaly head was dropped on the shore, Cullin and Affonyl rowed out again and gathered up baskets of fish. The young man took the opportunity to dive in and rinse himself off, although now that everything smelled so strongly of fish, the rotting sheep odor on him was less noticeable.

Reeger brushed out the maggots and clumps of wool from the cart bed. "I knew this would come in handy. What a haul!"

The mule let out a disappointed bray at having yet another burden, just when it thought it had the night off.

CHAPTER
SIX

The grand celebration whenever they returned from a successful monster slaying (whether or not the monster was real) aways provided great fodder for minstrels to write songs about ... but their timing in defeating the giant pike was unfortunate. They had blasted the fish in the middle of the night, and it would be awkward to return with their trophy (not to mention a wagon filled with fish) before dawn, because everyone would be too sleepy to do much celebrating or rewarding.

So, Dalbry and Reeger napped inside the fish-fry tent, and Cullin built a campfire to roast a nice perch he had found floating on the lake, which he shared with Affonyl. Then, well-rested and washed up at the lake, they headed back to the capital city at sunrise. Dalbry proudly sat astride Drizzle, Cullin and Affonyl rode Pony, while Reeger drove the mule and its cart back to town.

Businesses were just waking up—candlemakers, potters, grocers, cider sellers, and bistros offering coffee and brunch specials. When the townspeople noticed them, and turned up their noses at the strong reek of fish, Cullin began shouting, "Brave Sir Dalbry, slayer of the lake monster! All hail Sir Dalbry!" He paused, hoping for townsfolk to take up the cheer.

Affonyl added her voice. "We bring the head of the terrible scourge! Killed by brave Sir Dalbry!"

Reeger yanked away the canvas to reveal the giant fish head gaping up at them.

Eventually, onlookers were impressed enough to take up the cheer. Some even danced through the streets singing a perky tune. "Ding dong, the fish is dead!" The ever-growing crowd followed them up the flower-lined path to Queen Amnethia's castle, where the sweet smell of petunias offered a pleasant counterpoint to the unpleasant odors that had accompanied them throughout the night.

Cullin and Reeger dragged the huge pike head with them, while Sir Dalbry strode into the throne room bearing the heavy burden of his own greatness. Affonyl carried a basket of fish as further evidence.

Queen Amnethia and Lord Dither were delighted and impressed, although less so when Cullin and Reeger dropped the slimy, glassy-eyed head onto the tile floor. Nevertheless, the cheering, singing townspeople made the queen forget her dismay.

Dalbry gestured toward the mantel. "The mounted fish head will make a fine accompaniment to my kraken tusk, Highness. A package deal."

The queen pretended to have forgotten about the combined fee, then distracted them by announcing a celebratory feast.

That night in the grand hall, Cullin and his friends enjoyed a big fish dinner of the gigantic pike, as well as a little fish dinner of all the bass, perch, and bluegills that had also floated to the surface of the lake. The large group of royal guests dined on enormous portions of roast fish, fish fillets, and, to Cullin's delight, breaded fish sticks.

When the dinner conversation fell into a lull, Affonyl flashed a smile to catch the audience's attention. "I'm very well acquainted with fish. You see, I used to be a mermaid, but I gave up my tail to join Sir Dalbry's band of adventurers." Other voices came to a halt as everyone listened.

"Oh, how interesting," said the queen. Some of the banquet guests gave Affonyl skeptical looks.

Cullin blurted out, "She even has the mermaid scales to prove it!"

Taking her cue, the young woman removed another chemically treated fish scale from her bag of necessary items. She used one of the finger basins of water to perform her astonishing trick with the foaming, bubbling scale, and Queen Amnethia applauded with giggling exuberance.

After the long banquet was over and they were stuffed with fish, the queen once more offered them guest rooms in the castle—Sir Dalbry in his fine chamber, while Affonyl had to join Cullin and Reeger in the bunk-bed room. Cullin offered to sleep on the floor.

The next morning, the three mounts set off with their saddlebags full of gold from Amnethia's reward and the purchase price of the kraken tusk. Reeger donated the smelly old cart to a needy orphanage, and the group was once again free to seek adventures.

While the current scarcity of dragons might have been grounds for celebration among the nobility, peasants, and other potential victims, it did affect the job security of the band of supposed dragon slayers.

Cullin was not eager to face another ferocious scaly beast, even though the dragon business was a lucrative scam. Over the last year, they had occasionally ventured into the ogre business and the kraken business, with the possibility of including other mythical beasts. They would just have to be creative.

Cullin inhaled the fresh air. "Let's see where circumstances take us."

Reeger grunted. "Back to the seacoast so we can gather more mermaid scales and another kraken tusk."

The old knight rummaged in the small leather sack at his side and gave a disappointed grunt. "First we must stop in the farmer's market so I can refill my magic sack with dried apricots."

Maurice is surprised that my tale is finished so soon. He stands up from the stone step and rubs his buttocks. The pampered boy has delicate gluteals, which he used to rub and perfume daily, but I put a stop to that. "You're done already?"

I feel proud. "Ah, you were so captivated by the tale that you want it to go on and on."

"No, it wasn't the tale you promised," Maurice says. "You said it had orcs and ghosts. If you tell your audience that and then give them a

Big Fish story, they'll be dissatisfied. They'll write terrible one-star reviews."

"Nobody reads those reviews," I say, a little too defensively. *"But I'm not finished yet. That was merely an introductory adventure, a hook to remind readers of beloved characters and provide setup for the main tale."*

"You mean like a prologue?" Maurice says. *"Most people skip prologues."*

"That is why I didn't call it a prologue." No matter what he says, I am satisfied with my literary device. *"And now that we're rolling, we can get on with the central storyline, which is filled with excitement, peril, monsters ... and evil!"*

"Does it have dragons in it?" Maurice asks.

"This one has orcs, and ghosts! In fact, it has orcs that go bump in the night." I chuckle at my cleverness, but it sails right past Maurice. I grow serious again. *"Have a listen. I'm sure you'll enjoy it."*

CHAPTER
SEVEN

Well-rewarded after slaying the ferocious lake monster, the band rode out from Queen Amnethia's kingdom. They were in a sunny mood, talking and laughing, and even the mule seemed pleased not to carry any burdens other than Reeger.

"We shall head to the coast. And the coast is ..." Dalbry gestured uncertainly off into the distance. "That way, I think."

Reeger halted the mule next to a fat birch tree and dismounted. "Better consult a map." From his stained jerkin, he drew out a battered piece of parchment showing the boundaries of known kingdoms, queendoms, principalities, and budding democracies. The terrain details were sparse, as if someone had drawn it from memory with their eyes closed, but waypoints and geocaching spots were marked, along with points of interest and environment-friendly horse-refueling stations.

He stuck the map on a twig against the wide birch trunk. "Let's choose our route in a scientific fashion." He kicked a mark on the ground several steps away and pulled the dagger from its sheath at his hip. Squinting one eye for aim, and squinting with the other eye for a better aim, he hurled the dagger, which nicked the left edge of the crude map. "Looks like we head west."

"Now, we should all get a say," Dalbry objected. From his seat in Drizzle's saddle, he threw his own knife at the map, cutting a gash on the right side.

Not having a vote, Drizzle, Pony, and the mule munched on grasses and weeds beside the trail.

"My turn." Cullin jumped down from Pony and pulled his knife. He shifted from side to side, studying the map, envisioning where he wanted to go. Remembering all he had been taught about knife work and self defense, he inhaled a deep breath, exhaled slowly to concentrate, and let his sharp blade fly.

He missed the trunk entirely.

Impatiently waiting for her turn to cast a vote, Affonyl passed her throwing dagger from one hand to the other. "We should determine this by rational means, not some willy-nilly pin-the-tail-on-the-cartography." She flung the dagger with a brisk flick of her wrist, and the point skewered both the map and the birch bark. "There. You know how good I am at science."

Cullin ran up and put his finger on the knife hole in the map. Affonyl's scientific route-finding directed them to a busy trading port on the coast. The handwritten label identified the land as belonging to KING JOHN.

"Mount up," Dalbry said, though he had never dismounted. "We're off to the land of King John."

At nightfall several days later, they had given up on finding a star-rated inn or even a low budget hor-tel (a lodge that catered to travelers on horseback). They came upon a campfire and three gangly teenage minstrels—two beanpole boys and one beanpole girl.

Cullin heard the sounds of ragged music before they saw the meager camp. The beanpole young woman plucked the strings of a harp. One of the young men strummed a battered old lute, while the other tooted noise from a harmonica.

Surprised by the unexpected visitors, the itinerant minstrels stopped their attempts at music and scrambled to their feet. A few sparrows and a squirrel were roasting over the fire.

"Fine people, may we join your camp for fellowship and good cheer?" Dalbry asked. The minstrels looked at one another, uncertain, until the knight added, "We could share food—I have a magic sack of dried apricots."

They settled in together with the uneasy comfort of travelers, and the musicians introduced themselves as not only minstrels (which was obvious), but *mercenary minstrels*. "We work in the gig economy," said the young woman harpist, whose name was Debbie. She claimed to be well educated, with a Musical Doctorate, though she looked barely seventeen.

"Songsters for hire. For a price, we'll write you a tune and spread your brave legend to anyone who will listen," said the lute player, Hinkley.

Reeger let out a rude grunt. "Anyone who listens? That limits the audience."

"I myself have had numerous songs written about me," said Dalbry. "I am well aware of the power of propaganda."

"He's Sir Dalbry, the brave dragon slayer!" Cullin interjected.

"And a kraken slayer," Affonyl added. "And Big Fish slayer."

"Sir Dalbry, hmmm ..." said Stephane, the young man with the harmonica. "Isn't he still in the hallway?"

"It was a forced rhyme," Dalbry admitted, "but it was the best that Nightingale Bob could come up with."

"Nightingale Bob is a classic," said Hinkley, setting his lute aside. "But we cater to a younger audience, the more medieval-savvy generation."

Debbie absently plucked her harp strings in a very doctoral way. "We've written tunes for Sir Quinton the salamander slayer and Sir Rolf the wyvern slayer."

The harmonica player nodded. "Don't forget Sir Tom the firedrake slayer or Boris the basilisk slayer."

Debbie frowned as she hit a sour twang on her harp string. "Boris didn't turn out so well, and he never did pay us the completion fee."

Cullin looked at his friends, who all seemed uncomfortable with the news. Reeger grumbled loudest. "Rust—wyvern slayer? Firedrake slayer? Salamander slayer?" He hawked a wad of phlegm and spat it into the campfire, where it sizzled in the embers. "Next you'll be singing songs about earthworm squishers or toad fighters. What you have here is Sir Dalbry, a real knight, a hero! Why, he's the OG dragon slayer."

In the awkward conversational pause, the mercenary minstrels shared around their tidbits of squirrel and each took a sparrow. The old knight offered apricots.

Debbie tried to revitalize the conversation. "Nightingale Bob songs play well in classic inns and taverns, but our work is better suited to alternative clubs and avant-garde taverns."

"And bistros," said the lute player.

"A more culturally literate audience," said Stephane, with a toot on his harmonica.

Once the rising moon shone sufficient illumination for traveling onward through the forest, neither Cullin nor his companions felt compelled to spend more time with the humorless gig minstrels. Dalbry climbed back into Drizzle's saddle. "Well, we'd best be off."

Relieved, Cullin headed for Pony. "We're in a hurry to our next big adventure. We're off to the land of King John."

Gathering information that might prove useful, Affonyl turned to the minstrels. "Have you been there? Can you share any details about King John?"

"Oh, King John!" said Debbie. "He truly appreciates fine art. His masterpiece collection is known throughout the land. He has an exquisite eye."

"And ear," said Hinkley. "At his court he had us play our entire repertoire. A copper coin for each song."

"The rest of the court didn't appreciate it as much, because they couldn't hum along or dance to the beat," admitted the harmonica player with a roll of his eyes. "But we don't write our songs for the likes of *them*. Our work is for a far more discerning ear."

"When you reach the king's court," the harpist said, "ask if he'll show you the treasure of his castle. Few commoners get to see it."

Stephane added, "And even fewer understand it. Modern art and music are an acquired taste."

"Good to know," Affonyl said. Cullin could tell by the glint in her eyes that an idea was already forming in her mind.

"Any other pertinent facts we should know about King John himself?" Reeger asked.

Affonyl added, "Details that us commoners might want to know?"

"King John is quite tall, with very long arms and very long legs," said Hinkley. "That is why he's appropriately known as King Longjohn."

Sir Dalbry thanked them and waited while Cullin, Affonyl, and Reeger mounted up. "We shall remember that."

After a few more days of traveling, the pleasant morning birdsong changed into the raucous screams of circling seagulls.

When Cullin rode Pony to the top of a grassy hill, he could smell the salt tang in the air. The countryside was dotted with peasant villages, fertile farm fields and orchards. Far ahead he could see the rippling blue ocean, the white sails of trading ships on the water, and the busy port town. An impressive castle stood on a high promontory above the city.

Along the coast, the low hills were studded with rock pinnacles, narrow slabs that protruded from the ground like snaggly teeth. Quarry workers and excavation engineers worked at the smaller pillars, digging them up for unknown landscaping purposes.

"The kingdom seems to be thriving," Cullin said.

Reeger cocked an eyebrow. "You know what that means—King Longjohn is rich! And if he's rich, he can afford some much-needed dragon slaying."

Dalbry clucked his tongue. "I fear those scalawag wyvern hunters and salamander slayers have already saturated the market. They're putting the dragon business out of business."

"We'll come up with something else, then. We have brains and imagination," Affonyl said with a twinkle in her eye. "Well, some of us do."

As they followed the rutted dirt road through the rolling hills, they came upon bustling traffic, peasants with possessions piled on their backs making their way en masse, old men and women dressed in tatters, farming families with children, dogs on leashes and goats on leashes. Some walked with wooden staffs that could serve double duty as fishing poles (and Cullin considered warning them about the dangers of overly large fish).

"Excuse, me," Sir Dalbry called. "Might you be fleeing from a terrible dragon?"

"No dragons here," said a middle-aged farmer who prodded a stubborn goat. When the goat paused to defecate, the farmer moved his boot out of the way just in time.

"Then where are you all going?" Cullin asked.

The farmer's wife said, "From Point A to Point B."

"We're being relocated." The man seemed anxious to be on their way. "Left our old hovels for a new subdivision, but before we could move in, the whole development was unexpectedly condemned and all construction stopped. So, now we're heading back to the familiar tatters of our lives."

"We were supposed to have a new home," whimpered a little girl who walked beside a little lamb. "But now we have to go back to the old hovel."

"We'll redecorate, honey," said her mother. "King Longjohn will take care of us."

The girl sniffled and clung to her lamb.

More wagons rattled past as peasant families continued to move along. The people seemed resigned, as if they had done a lot of work for nothing.

"What was wrong with the new subdivision?" Affonyl asked. "Why did construction stop?"

"King Longjohn cleared some new arable land for the planned development." The weary farmer leaned forward as if sharing a secret. "And discovered an old, cursed orc graveyard!"

"An orc graveyard?" Cullin asked.

"Bones and everything! Armor, skulls, swords, and spears."

"Sounds like good pickings," said Reeger, who had substantial experience with graveyards.

"Ruined the property value," said another peasant as he wheeled a squeaky cart forward. "Nobody wants to build a new subdivision on a cursed graveyard."

"How do you know it's cursed?" Affonyl asked. "Instead of just a regular graveyard?"

"The orcs buried there didn't look too happy about it." The

peasant pushed his cart. "Have a look for yourselves. It's just over the hill there."

Cullin and his friends decided to do exactly that.

On the other side of the hill, the forest and meadows had been cleared, trees chopped down, holes dug. A faded sign pointed the way, announcing without enthusiasm, "Coming Soon—Serfdom Sunrise Acres. Peasant hovels for all income ranges."

Wooden stakes tied with ribbons marked out plats. New roads were laid out, and excavation had begun. But there would be no town square in the peasant subdivision, no new cottages, no black-smith's shop, not even the proposed strip mall.

When digging crews cleared sections of the open ground, they had found a mass grave filled with haphazardly buried monstrous skeletons. Upon discovering the buried orcs, the construction crew apparently dropped their spades and pickaxes and fled. The tools were still strewn about.

Reeger bounded forward with his rolling gait, followed by Cullin and Affonyl. "Look at the bones!"

Cullin pulled out an orc helmet, brushed off lumps of dirt. The metal was corroded, the brass studs tarnished and pitted. The big sword was heavy and dull—not a practical weapon.

The former princess bent down to study the rib bones, the grotesque skulls, the clawed hands and fingers, the thick cranial bones. "From this, I can extrapolate that orcs are ugly."

"Even I know that much science!" Reeger said. He picked up an orc femur and thumped it against his palm. "We can excavate these treasures. Sell 'em in a secondhand shop."

Affonyl hammered a large orc skull on a rock until it split open. "Very thick bone. Minimal cranial capacity."

"Exactly what I thought," Cullin said, trying to impress her. "But what does it mean?"

"Very tiny brains."

"Not much we can do with these at the moment." Dalbry turned Drizzle around while the others mounted up again. "Let's ask more questions in the port town. We have to prepare ourselves before we meet King Longjohn."

CHAPTER
EIGHT

A s they entered the busy city, they saw more evidence of the kingdom's economic prosperity. Longjohn's merchant ships traveled to and from the unspoiled New Lands, and the trade in exotic items kept the merchants wealthy, generated substantial taxes, and maintained a high standard of living.

A large harborside market held vendor stalls offering fabrics, trinkets, preserved meats, woody vegetables, dried fruits, and shrunken heads. They sampled many of the unusual food items, although Dalbry preferred apricots from his magic sack, which he replenished from a vendor, just to make sure the magic didn't run out.

Cullin and Affonyl strolled together through the market. He toyed with dangling gold necklaces, poked at a bit of amethyst, and considered buying a gift for her, since he had enough coins to purchase whatever he liked.

But Affonyl was interested in a showcase exhibit from a recently returned naturalist ship. On a table, glass jars held strange biological specimens preserved in some kind of potent alcohol. She scrutinized a spotted newt that drifted in murky fluid.

Seeing her interest, the vendor tapped the side of the jar with a thin stick. "Those critters were all gathered by our scientific ship, ma'am. Not good to eat right from the jar, but fun to look at, if you hold them up to the light." He jiggled the jar to make the preserved newt dance.

Tempted, Affonyl poked around in her bag of necessary things, but decided that the specimen jar was too large to carry around. "Maybe I'll get something from the next ship," she apologized and followed Cullin to the next stall.

The naturalist called after her. "I hear they're bringing in a giant fish said to be extinct for millions of years! Found off the coast of Madagascar!"

Cullin groaned. "We've had enough giant fish stories for now.

Affonyl rolled her eyes and muttered, "Like we're supposed to believe any country has a silly name like *Madagascar.*"

Nearby, Reeger befriended a salty old sailor named Honsl who was missing several teeth, and propped a pegleg on a crate in front of him. He wore an eyepatch and kept his one eye open for potential easy marks. Reeger was not an easy mark, but he was good at extracting information.

The old sailor adjusted his patch as Cullin and Affonyl rejoined Reeger. "You three look like discerning people. For a copper coin, I'll tell you how I lost this leg." He rapped his knuckles on the pegleg. "It was a kraken, I tell you! It wrecked my ship, killed my crew, and only I—"

Reeger held up a dirty hand to stop him. "Rust, we've already got a kraken story."

Taken aback, grizzled old Honsl regarded them with greater respect. "I see you're all professionals, too."

Reeger leaned closer so that his bad breath could compete with the old sailor's. "We will give you a copper coin, though, if you can provide information about King Longjohn, the primary imports and exports of the land, the economic status of the port city, and the latest gossip, so we can better plan our visit."

Honsl's one eye glinted. "So instead of a tall tale, you're wanting a social studies report?"

Now Affonyl was interested. "Exactly."

Reeger nudged Cullin. "Lad, give him a copper coin."

The young man did so, and the sailor rattled off the average temperatures and seasonal differences, prevailing winds, gross domestic product, population diversity, mean age, and mean income.

While chatting, Honsl took out a rusty nub of a knife and a small piece of driftwood. He flicked with the blade, whittling away curls of wood, tiny shavings, and fashioned the lump into a dolphin, or maybe a shark. Cullin couldn't quite tell the difference. The old sailor inspected the completed carving, turning it between his calloused fingers.

Affonyl was delighted, and Cullin thought he would offer it as a gift, but instead the old man tossed it over his shoulder into the harbor, then picked up another piece of wood and whittled again.

The grizzled sailor gave more background on the merchant ships, how King Longjohn had established trading outposts in the New Lands, founded several plantations which were worked by some of his footloose peasants who wanted to colonize.

"His most popular crop is peanuts—ground-gold, he calls them. Quite a delicacy. Longjohn's merchant ships bring in barrels and barrels of 'em. Roasted peanuts, salted peanuts, boiled peanuts. Even a spreadable butter made out of peanuts."

"We'll have to try some," Cullin said.

"Longjohn has expanded the market by selling to discriminating nobles up and down the coast. Because peanuts are a delicacy, he can charge high prices."

Old Honsl whistled through the gap in his teeth. "With all his peanut plantations, though, he'll oversaturate the market, mark my words. Prices will collapse, and then any commoner will be able to eat peanuts." His wider grin showed even more missing teeth. "That's fine, because I'm fond of peanut butter myself, even if it does stick to the top of my mouth."

Affonyl surveyed the stark cliffs, the quaint harbor town, the sailing ships on the water, the castle on the headlands above. "Very picturesque. Might be a good subject for a painting."

Cullin looked at the castle, and his musings took him in a different direction. "We hear there's a priceless treasure up there."

"Ah, Longjohn is famous for his treasure," Honsl said with a whistle. "Doesn't know how to keep his mouth shut, brags about his exquisite collection. He's been acquiring it for years."

Reeger cocked his eyebrow, intensely interested. "His treasure?"

The old sailor let out a snort. "His art collection! Thanks to prospering trade in imported items, the kingdom had vast amounts of gold and jewels, but to protect against changing economic times, Longjohn decided to diversify his portfolio and invest in fine art.

"The king styles himself as a connoisseur of sculptures, any shape or form, most of them better off in a modern-art museum—and I don't mean that as a compliment. For all his talk, Longjohn doesn't really have any flair for artwork. He just acquires whatever the critics adore, including woven bird's-nest tapestry hangings and primal mud paintings. Never seen the collection myself, though. You think the king would invite someone like me to tour his treasure gallery?" Honsl coughed, then spat down on the dock.

Reeger did the same, as if in a show of solidarity.

The old man lowered his voice. "You ask me, Longjohn is over-compensating."

"Overcompensating for what?" Cullin looked up at the castle high on the headlands. "Does he have a very small—"

"For his father, King Ferdinand—better known as King Grog," the salty sailor said. "Notice those sea caves at the base of the cliff right up against the tide line? Used by smugglers before the port town was built. Longjohn's father had a thriving business in smuggling moonshyne. That's why he was called King Grog."

Reeger said, "I heard of King Grog back in the day. I thought it was a nickname to imply he was drowsy all the time, but moonshyne makes more sense."

With deft flicks of his calloused fingers, Honsl whittled away at the lump of wood, but the end splintered into roots. "Grog's son John let the moonshyne business go to hell. Now, he just collects expensive artwork. Waste of taxpayer money ..."

Using his imagination, he transformed the splinters into the tentacles of an octopus. He admired the new carving, then tossed that one into the harbor as well.

Glad for all the background information, they thanked Honsl and went to join Dalbry. Flush with Amnethia's cash, they stopped at a fancy outdoor bistro, where they ate cod cheeks with white wine and drank fresh coffee imported from the New Lands. Affonyl taught Cullin how to sip his wine, but Reeger took one taste and ordered a tankard of craft ale instead.

"It does us no good to rest on our laurels," Dalbry said.

"Or Queen Amnethia's petunias," Cullin added.

"Shall we determine what sort of monster to slay in this kingdom? What seems most profitable?" The knight looked around at his comrades. "The land is certainly prosperous, and Longjohn can afford to pay us a substantial reward."

"We need to come up with a big enough scheme," Affonyl said.

Reeger nodded toward the harbor. "There's always the ocean. Plenty of giant fish."

"I've had enough of fish for the time being," said Dalbry.

Cullin agreed. "I'd rather do something completely new."

The former princess finished her salad and cut into the buttery cod cheeks. "Squirrel's right—it's time to step up our game, expand the dragon business, since we've seen so many cheap imitations cashing in on our work. We should consider something more ... artistic."

Two seagulls wheeled overhead, shrieking. Everyone covered their plates until it was safe.

Reeger was dubious. "You want us to become art thieves? Rust, I'm not running off with a bronze statue on the back of the mule!"

"Not art thieves—art *fabricators*," Affonyl said with exaggerated patience. "I'm a skilled artist in my own right. My innovative embroidery patterns took the land by storm, and my caricature designs are quite a hit with flea-market audiences."

Dalbry drank his coffee. "But King Longjohn has a mature appreciation for fine art. His tastes are quite refined. How can you create art that he will like?"

"Art is in the eye of the beholder—or the art critic." She sized up the old knight, imagining him in a different role. "You can be quite erudite, Dalbry—this would be a perfect match for you."

Cullin understood where she was going. "You want to fool King Longjohn? Sell him a fake art treasure?"

"Fake?" Affonyl smiled. "Who is to say how valuable an artist's work is?"

"The audience of course." Dalbry's voice trailed off as the wheels turned in his head. "And the critics..."

"Sounds like we need to create some rustin' artwork," said Reeger.

Pausing at a pivotal point in the story, I stretch my arms with an exaggerated yawn. One of these days I should have a recliner throne installed. I've gained a little weight since my days of roaming the countryside, having adventures, battling enemies (imaginary or otherwise). It comes with age and maturity, not to mention a comfortable lifestyle.

Recently, the queen used part of the treasury to install a personal gym down in the dungeons, and she and her ladies-in-waiting go down in colorful leotards and engage in group dance exercise routines. I think that's silly. If one wants a little aerobic activity, we already have the jousting field, the archery court, and the practice sword-fighting rolls.

Concerned about my diet, the queen insists that I eat fresh vegetables with each roasted haunch I gnaw. She also makes sure that Maurice keeps himself healthy, and it's all I can do to keep him focused on more important things.

"There still haven't been any orcs," the prince complains. "Except for the bones. I hope there's more than that."

"We're only two chapters into the main story, son! Be patient. A good storyteller builds dramatic tension, unfurls the plot threads. You'll learn to appreciate the art of it."

Maurice still seems skeptical.

I am about to explain further when a bell rings out in the courtyard. Glancing through the leaded-glass windows at the far end of the throne room, I can see it's late afternoon, though the skies are gray and cloudy. By the growling in my stomach, I can tell that it's almost dinnertime.

When the bell rings again, I gesture for Maurice to follow as I hurry outside. In the main courtyard, I can already smell the delicious smoke, the roasting barbecue, the sizzle of sausages on the fire.

Reeger and his wife Wendria have arrived from the Scabby Wench Tavern. On Fridays they bring a wagon into the courtyard with supplies and a keg of ale for a community cookout. The tailgate party has become a tradition.

"Reeger!" I shout, unable to keep the good humor out of my voice. In the castle firepit, he is happily roasting sputtering sausages on pointed sticks. "Throw on a bratwurst for me—no, make it two!"

Reeger's smile shows he is not at all ashamed of his bad teeth.

"King Cullin, Sire—two bratwurst it is. I see you've brought the young prince for a hearty meal instead of that sissy castle fare." He narrows his uneven eyes. "Got a special on blood sausages today, lad!" He catches himself for his casual tone. "I mean, your Princeliness, Sire."

Maurice looks trapped. "Do you have any ... turkey sausages?"

"I can call one a turkey sausage, if that would do," Reeger says. "Don't know what's really in 'em anyway."

Maurice acquiesces with good grace. He has been raised to fulfill the diplomatic duties of a prince.

Reeger is older, seedier, and stockier than he was when we went adventuring, but he's still Reeger. His lifelong dream was to own his own tavern, something like the Mountain Oyster, and we amassed enough of a fortune along the way so I could become a king and Reeger could have his inn.

He set up what he called "the finest tavern with the raunchiest name." He is proud of the Scabby Wench and its unpleasant wooden sign hanging outside; he says it attracts just the sort of clientele he wants. The name also discourages any rowdy, lusty, drunken patrons from demanding sexual services from Wendria.

I wonder if that has ever been a problem.

By the keg on the cart, Wendria twists in the stopcock and starts dispensing mugs of ale in disposable red tankards. The castle staff members begin to gather, now that it is happy hour.

Reeger hands me two crackling bratwurst mashed into cut-open stale bread rolls. Maurice takes his "turkey sausage" without the bun. Wendria pours me and Maurice each a portable tankard of ale and offers us a curtsy. The prince responds with an extravagant bow, which I think embarrasses her.

She's a perfect match for Reeger, scoring equally low on the attractiveness scale. She's a siege machine of a woman, her dark hair spiky and thick, tied with a red ribbon because she says her husband likes it. They arm-wrestle as often as they kiss (and frankly I prefer to see them arm-wrestle). He adores her, though, and she has been known to knock stupid ideas out of his head, although not all of them. She runs the tavern business, and together they've made the Scabby Wench into quite a success.

Reeger is happy with the increasing crowd of customers, and Wendria keeps pouring ale. He comes back with a sausage of his own, wiping a dollop of kraut and mustard from his thick lip. "Now, lad— umm, I mean Prince—what sort of ridiculous tales has the king been filling your head with? True ones?"

"I doubt it," says Maurice, "and he's taking a very long time to get to the meat of the story."

"All stories are true, in a manner of speaking," I say. "That's what fiction is all about."

My son raises his eyebrows. "You called it fiction. That means it's not true."

"True in a human sense, son. A mythological sense. Legends! And some legends are true."

"Whatever," the boy mumbles. "You promised me a story about orcs and ghosts, but I think it's a bait and switch."

"Nothing wrong with a good bait and switch," Reeger says. "Used it myself many a time for fun and profit. But if King Cullin is telling you the story I think he's telling you, you're in for a wild ride. A tremendous adventure." He glances down at Maurice's food. "How's the turkey sausage?"

The clouds overhead are thick and dark, and before the prince can answer him, thunder rumbles out. A few patters of rain fall in the courtyard.

Grabbing their meals, the castle staff members duck back under the overhangs, while others rush toward the cart so Wendria can fill the portable tankards to go. The rain quickly turns into a heavy downpour, and even though I'm getting drenched in the courtyard, I wolf down my second bratwurst. It wouldn't do to be caught inside the castle by a queen who doesn't approve of junk food.

Reeger and Wendria work together like a panicked pair of rabbits. She caps the keg and covers it with a tarpaulin. Reeger gathers his roasting sticks, puts the few unclaimed sausages in a sack, and scrapes together the condiments. He shelters everything with the bulk of his body as he rushes to get out of the rain.

Maurice and I call goodbye to Reeger and Wendria, who are eager to get back to the warm stuffiness of the Scabby Wench. I shout after them, "See you next Friday!"

Reeger raises a hand in a backward wave as he trots along behind Wendria's retreating cart. Thunder crashes overhead, and lightning skitters among the clouds. "We could retire to your private chambers, son," I say. "I'll continue the tale there."

"Or start it," Maurice says. "At least I can fix the strings of my lute while I'm listening."

I'm pleased that my boy has gotten so good at multitasking.

CHAPTER
NINE

D ue to the coastal weather patterns, as the peglegged Honsl had described in his social studies report, gloomy fogbanks often rolled in. Mist swirled up from the cold sea and blanketed King Longjohn's castle in chilly murk. The rock pinnacles that studded the hills looked mysterious and ominous.

Because this was an unusual scam for them (Affonyl preferred the adjectives "innovative" and "imaginative"), their group took the time to plan carefully. With discretionary funds from the Big-Fish reward, they bought the supplies they needed, new garments to fit their new roles.

Cullin left his fish-stained blue tunic with a laundry service and acquired a white lace-up shirt with tight cuffs and billowy sleeves, along with professional dark hose. He carried a leatherbound book with blank pages and a stylus so he could take notes. He called it Ye Olde Journal. All together, he cut the perfect image of a medieval executive assistant.

Dalbry underwent the biggest transformation. The veteran knight stashed his armor, sword, and shield in a rented storage unit, exchanging them for foppish clothes—green shirt, black doublet, and lacy collar and cuffs. He brushed out his flattened and unruly hair, which he disparagingly called "helmet hair," and even added a pretentious curl.

SKELETON IN THE CLOSET

Looking at him, Reeger couldn't stop guffawing. "What's next, my Lord? A bit of perfume in the armpits or the crotch?"

"Body odor would be unseemly for a man in my position," Dalbry said. He stroked the front of his doublet and sniffed the air. Cullin could see he was getting into character as a famed and respected art critic.

Affonyl coached the knight, since she was familiar with erudite art-world jargon, although he had difficulty getting into the proper mindset. "I've spent my life building my legend as a brave knight and dragon slayer. Think of all the songs Nightingale Bob has sung about me."

"We could always pay him to write a bawdy tune about Dalbry the art critic," Reeger teased.

"I prefer dragon slaying," Dalbry muttered. "But we shall see if this gambit proves successful. Cullin and I will do our best."

"It sounds like fun," the young man broke in, "and less dangerous than battling monster fish or giant dragons."

"Fewer explosives required," Affonyl said.

Reeger didn't seem happy about it. "Whenever you need me, I'm ready to do my part wading through swamps or digging in graveyards."

"Or latrines," Cullin pointed out.

The lumpy man scratched the stubble on his cheeks. "You never know what you might find when you dig in the right place."

Meanwhile, Affonyl set up her stall in the village market and began producing unsigned caricature portraits that astonished and amused the townspeople. She also dropped hints and spread rumors about a legendary artist who created grand-scale works of art, Affonyl NoLastName, which sounded mysterious and avant-garde.

After saddling up their well-rested mounts, Cullin and Dalbry made their way up to the castle in the thick coastal fog. It was a good day to meet with the king, because the art-loving monarch would not have outside recreational plans in the gloomy weather.

After tying up Drizzle and Pony in the courtyard, since they wouldn't be staying long enough to warrant livery in the royal stables, the two entered through the castle's main doorway. The young man tried to put himself into an artsy frame of mind, as executive assistant to the respectable critic.

59

An officious man-at-arms made them sign in on a clipboard, using a goose quill and an inkpot. When Dalbry revealed his profession, the guard said that the king would be eager to welcome them.

Longjohn's father Ferdinand, the renowned smuggler king, had been content with traditional dank stone walls with torches flickering in wrought-iron sconces. King Longjohn, though, had added a flair to the interior decorating, installing thick red carpet runners along the flagstone floors. Rather than faded tapestries and coats of arms on the walls, he had mounted dreamcatchers made of colorful thick yarn, macrame flowerpot hangers with dangling spider plants, or wooden planks on which flowers had been painted, then coated with thick varnish as decoupage.

The guard escorted them into a large throne room which doubled as a formal dining hall, so Longjohn could conduct the kingdom's business in a relaxed social environment. The guard handed the clipboard to a sleepy crier, who glanced at the name, cleared his throat, and yelled, "Sire, we present Dalbry, art critic and artists' representative, and Cullin, his executive assistant."

Dalbry still held himself like a knight, then he remembered to take on a more haughty air. Cullin walked dutifully beside him.

King Longjohn perked up on his raised throne, regarding them with great interest. "Critic? Artists' representative?" He noticed Cullin. "You must be extremely important if you have your own executive assistant.

"I am most critical, Sire," said Dalbry with the hint of a proud sneer in his voice. "Just as every knight needs a faithful squire, so an acerbic art critic needs an executive assistant." Taking his cue, Cullin pulled out Ye Olde Journal and started writing details.

The king was tall, long, and gangly, like a man who had been stretched on a torturer's rack for several hours longer than was good for him. His throne was at once too wide for his skinny hips and too short for his long legs, which stuck out well beyond the end of the seat. His arms were too long to rest comfortably on the sides of the ornate chair.

With an artistic and critical sniff, Dalbry bowed before Longjohn and somehow managed to keep his chin and nose lifted officiously in the air at the same time. "Majesty, your taste in artwork is world-renowned, as is your desire to acquire true cultural wonders for your private collection."

The king beamed. He had high cheekbones and a narrow chin, a neatly trimmed brown beard along the line of his jaw, and a shaved upper lip, because mustaches had fallen out of fashion in creative circles. "If you are indeed someone who appreciates the incomprehensibilities of true genius, I would be delighted to show you some of my favorite pieces!" He shifted one long leg over the other.

Dalbry allowed himself to sound skeptical. "I have a very discerning eye, Sire." Cullin dutifully wrote that down in Ye Olde Journal.

"Oh, I follow all the latest up-and-coming artists," Longjohn said. "Even the most obscurely famous ones."

"Ah ..." Dalbry said, drawing out the suspense, "then you must be familiar with the reclusive landscape artist Affonyl NoLastName?"

"Affonyl NoLastName?" The gangly king perked up. "Doesn't sound familiar to me. Landscape artist, you say?"

The old knight seemed to swell into his role. "She creates innovative works using the power of nature, primal materials. Each piece becomes a monument to her artistic vision. I am proud and humbled that Affonyl allows me to represent her interests, because she won't sully her hands with the commercial aspects. She's entirely consumed by her art."

As his excitement increased, Longjohn unfolded himself and rose from his throne. "Affonyl NoLastName? Yes, I believe I have heard of her. She exhibited some of her works in the neighboring kingdoms I believe."

"Yes," Dalbry said. "Affonyl does not seek fame, and she takes commissions only when the inspiration strikes her."

"I must have one! How can we inspire her?"

"With a signed contract," Dalbry said. "Negotiated through me. If I deem your kingdom to be a worthy location for one of her landscape masterpieces, I will speak with my client. The creations of Affonyl NoLastName are not for just anyone."

"A great landscape artist could find no better showcase than here in my castle!" Longjohn stepped away from the throne. "Come, follow me for a brief tour. You'll see that her work will be in fine company."

With significant strides, the king led his two visitors through a maze of unnecessarily winding hallways and then outside into an expansive private statue garden. Screaming seagulls wheeled above, unseen in the fog.

Graveled paths looped among neat hedges, which showcased an odd assortment of stone and bronze figures: a granite sphere engraved with a smiley face, a deep-thinking troll bent over with his chin on his fist, a twisted tumbleweed of rods and lumps that looked like an accident from a foundry, a huge stone moth with the head of a goat.

Longjohn led them along the paths, naming the obscure artists, listing the incomprehensible titles of the sculptures. Cullin felt confused and unsettled, but Dalbry pretended to be impressed. "Quite an eclectic collection." Staying in character, he pondered the stone moth with the goat's head. "I see the metaphor here. The essence of the human spirit, how we all wish to take flight, but we have wings of stone, and our minds are filled with a stubborn animal nature."

Longjohn let out a squeal of delight. "Exactly! I'm glad you see it, too."

"Oh," Cullin said, "now I see it."

The old knight continued to extol esoteric and ludicrous theories about what the artists must have intended. Cullin just tried to imagine what sort of hallucinogenic mushrooms the sculptors had eaten.

As Longjohn and Dalbry moved ahead to admire the unsettling statues, the young man heard splashing and scrubbing from behind one of the decorative hedges. Not interested in the critical commentary, Cullin went to investigate.

He poked his head around a shrub to see a young girl dressed in the uniform of a scullery maid. She had a wooden bucket filled with soapy water and a boar's-bristle brush. The scrawny girl in patched skirts was maybe eleven years old, clearly a tomboy. Her dark hair stuck out like the bristles on her brush.

She hummed to herself as she dunked the brush in the gray water and scrubbed a chuckling rotund bunny with a battle axe in one paw. The scullery maid scoured bird droppings from between the rabbit's ears.

Seagulls circled, and a fresh dollop of gray-white excrement splattered where the maid had just scrubbed. The girl lashed out with a sharp curse. "Get out of here or I'll tear your beak off and shove it up between your tail feathers!"

Cullin looked at the similarly stained statues nearby. "At least you have job security."

Startled, the girl spun about, holding the brush as if it were a sword. He raised his hands to show he was no threat. "I'm just here with my master admiring the statues."

"Admiring them?" she said in a sarcastic tone. "Not many people do."

"There's no accounting for taste. I hear they've gotten good reviews."

The waifish maid's eyes lit up. "Oh, you must be the executive assistant to that art critic."

"Word travels fast," Cullin said.

"I'm a scullery maid—I have to know what's going on in the castle." She scoured away the fresh glop on the bunny statue. "You're right. The work never ends ... every day with a bucket and brush scrubbing these statues. I think the damn seagulls enjoy the target practice."

Sensing that she might provide useful information, depending on how their plan proceeded, Cullin introduced himself. The girl responded with, "My given name is Sue-Pam, but that's too many syllables. We just shorten it to Spam."

"Nice to meet you, Spam." He nodded toward the dirty bucket. "That looks like hard work. Aren't there child labor laws in this kingdom?"

Spam sounded indignant. "Of course there are—but I'm almost eleven."

Cullin was relieved.

Two more bombardier seagulls scored direct hits on nearby statues. Seeing that Spam would be busy for some time, he took his leave and hurried to catch up with Dalbry.

CHAPTER

TEN

"A ssuming we can agree upon an exorbitant price," Dalbry said after much consideration, "I must make sure there is adequate placement for a significant new work of landscape art. Affonyl's singular creations are massive, both in physical size and in cultural import."

Longjohn felt he had found a true kindred spirit in Dalbry. Cullin made more notations in Ye Olde Journal as they walked the perimeter of the castle grounds.

The knight-turned-critic assessed terraces and garden spaces, shaking his head each time. "Not adequate for the majesty of her creation."

During their scheming in the bistro, the scope of Affonyl's vision grew to the point where Dalbry, Reeger, and even Cullin thought it was getting out of hand. But the former princess was insistent, claiming she understood how kings and art snobs thought. She quoted the well-known Gnostic scholar, "Go big, or go home."

The work of Affonyl NoLastName must be no mere caricature drawing, no framed canvas, nor piece of lawn statuary. Her landscape art would be big, bold, and audacious to the point where no one would dare suggest that it wasn't impressive—and it would be worth every gold coin to King Longjohn.

Since a shipment of peanuts had just arrived from his plantations in the New Lands, Longjohn's treasury would soon be filled. Once he liquidated the peanuts, or at least whipped them into butter, he would have all the funds he needed to commission a priceless artistic masterpiece.

Cullin and Dalbry both liked the sound of that.

Now, however, the lanky king began to look worried. "Just how, uh, large is the work going to be?"

"Sizeable enough for her to convey the scope and grandeur of the natural world," Dalbry said. "If she takes on a commission for such a discriminating and influential patron, we must have the proper space aligned with the earth's magnetic fields."

"And a nice feeling of feng shui," Cullin added.

"Then it must be her biggest piece yet." The king's eyes lit up. "Oh, I have just the right place for it."

With great strides, he led them to a side courtyard adorned with rosebushes and little fountains, a place reserved for open-air concerts and recitals. A bandstand was set up near a double door cut through the stone perimeter wall, so that bands could load and unload their instruments. On the grassy lawn, folding chairs could be set out for appreciative audiences to enjoy the concerts.

The king indicated all the open grass in front of the bandstand. "Would this be big enough to show Affonyl's new work? Right now, the space isn't efficiently used." He paced across the grass. "Recently, we had three young minstrels who specialize in alternative ballads and new musical techniques."

"I believe I've heard of them," Dalbry said.

"A harpist, a lute player, and a harmonica player?" Cullin asked.

"Yes, those are the ones! But they didn't draw much of a crowd."

Dalbry paced the perimeter of the courtyard, and Cullin followed him, writing down imaginary measurements. At last the fog had partially lifted and thin sunlight filtered into the courtyard.

The supposed art critic pondered. "This area could provide an expansive yet intimate venue. I will try to convince Affonyl. We shall see what sort of mood she's in."

Longjohn seemed nervous, desperate. "Wait, I haven't shown you the best part yet! My private collection—the real treasure. Affonyl must know that I am absolutely sincere in my love for the arts."

"Sincerity is the sincerest form of flattery," said Cullin, though he felt he might be misquoting.

Longjohn hurried them along. "Come, I'll give you a private showing." Once back inside, the lanky ruler led them down a side corridor, up a flight of stairs, then down two more. The entire castle was a labyrinth.

Then, he pushed aside a hidden stone doorway, pivoting it through a thick wall to reveal a secret passage. "The original architects were very security minded. My artwork is so valuable, it's good that very few people can find it." He chuckled as he took a torch from a sconce on the wall. "I myself get disoriented half the time."

Cullin was uneasy about getting lost in the shadowy passages, but the king led them onward, down and down, until they were deep within the bluff. Barely able to contain his anticipation, Longjohn began dropping hints about the wondrous marvels and the marvelous wonders they were about to observe.

With a flourish and a sigh of triumph (after several false starts down blind passages) King Longjohn presented his great gallery—a cave gallery grotto hacked out of the living rock and illuminated by numerous candles and torches. To Cullin, it looked like a dumping ground of objects that had been appraised at very high artistic value.

There were statues and paintings, colorful tapestries and faded ones, marble busts of handsome but forgotten historical figures, gilded urns with chipped enamel, framed paintings of well-dressed but not portrait-worthy noblemen.

"Beautiful," Dalbry lied, "and certainly valuable ... if you could find an art auction house that would take the whole collection."

"I would never part with it!" said Longjohn in dismay.

Cullin tried to keep an open mind, or at least get his mind around the fact that someone would admire all this. He admitted to himself that he didn't really understand art. In his opinion, the best art he had ever seen was the delightful caricature Affonyl had drawn of him in the town market.

In an erudite voice, Dalbry said, "Now that I have seen your collection, Majesty, I will convey its grandeur to Affonyl. I'll put in a good word for you, since we have agreed on a reasonable first offer for a new piece."

"Plus expenses," Cullin interjected, because that was his job as executive assistant.

"Yes, plus expenses," Dalbry repeated. "Cullin, make a note of it in your journal."

King Longjohn was giddy with the prospect of a new treasure to add to his castle. As Cullin stared at the exhibits, one of the paintings finally did catch his eye—an amusing depiction of cute dogs dressed in common medieval costumes playing cards around a table in a tavern.

He rather liked that one. It was his idea of good art.

CHAPTER

ELEVEN

Cullin had long admired the old knight's air of suave nobility and the weight of legends about him and was even more impressed to see how deftly Sir Dalbry slid into his role as officious art critic. He was versatile when it came to executing their complex schemes, and the knight had learned hard lessons, having lost his own lands, title, and fortune to noble grifters.

Cullin recalled how he first met Dalbry and Reeger when he was no more than a feral orphan. The two were dressed as itinerant monks selling splinters of the True Cross (home-made ones, fashioned out of splinters from dead trees). Before that, Reeger and Dalbry had gone from town to town selling the "genuine skull of the revered Saint Bartimund"—skulls which Reeger replenished from convenient local graveyards.

The young man had joined them in their adventures, building Dalbry's reputation, earning a good living. He liked it even better now that the former princess had joined them.

But the group had gotten used to soft, flea-infested beds at local inns, and Reeger felt they were getting spoiled. That night, after leaving King Longjohn and his fabulous art collection, Cullin and his companions made a rough camp in the middle of the woods, for old times' sake. They made their camp in the open air under the trees at the base of one of the protruding rocks, with a campfire, a cookpot, supplies from the town, and a comfortable bed of mounded leaves.

As the four of them sat in front of the big rock, Reeger roasted a large salami he had bought from a butcher in the town. It was called a special "surprise salami," because no one would reveal what sort of meat had gone into it. Reeger found that intriguing. The rest of them found it edible.

Affonyl had a shine in her eyes as she sat next to Cullin. "I've already got big plans for this one, Squirrel. As an artist, I have to be audacious and memorable—and these rock pinnacles give me an idea."

"Diggers were excavating them around the hills," he said, "though I don't know what for."

"We will use them for artistic purposes," said the former princess.

Reeger cut off a hunk of the smoking salami. "As long as I don't have to rustin' lift 'em."

"We will let Longjohn's anticipation build for a day or two, then I'll introduce our reclusive artist to the king. He's already hooked on the idea, like the giant pike that chomped on the sheep carcass." For dessert, Dalbry munched on dried apricots from his sack. "He's convinced himself he wants to invest in sizeable art."

"And I'm the one to provide that," Affonyl said. "First embroidery, then caricatures—and now gargantuan landscape art!"

"Quite an artistic progression," Cullin said.

Dalbry seemed content with the current plan, though it was different from their usual routine. "A fool and his gold are soon parted, and our job is to find fools for fun and profit."

Affonyl chuckled. "Yes, for fun!"

"For profit," Reeger said, chewing on his roast salami.

"And justice," Dalbry said with a dark expression.

Cullin knew that unethical nobles had stolen not only his lands, title, and treasury, but his apricot orchards as well.

"I can't get justice for those who conned me out of everything, but if we make our scam sting enough, the wiser nobles will learn a valuable lesson. We are, in fact, promoting critical thinking."

Reeger grumbled. "I hope we can also put those charlatan

wyvern slayers and basilisk slayers out of business for stealing our schtick!"

Even as their plans moved ahead, Cullin had a nagging question in the back of his mind. He enjoyed being part of the team, but most of the time he was just running errands. He spoke up, "I'm thinking about my part in this business. What do I actually ... do?"

"Plenty of room for advancement, lad," said Reeger.

Dalbry paused in chewing a leathery apricot. "Why, Cullin, you are an invaluable part of the team."

Although he felt warm satisfaction, the question came back. "Yes, but what do I *do*?"

"Why, you're a gofer," Dalbry said. "A respectable profession."

"You perform all the little tasks that hold us together," said Affonyl.

"Yeah, a sidekick, lad," Reeger said. "You're in charge of the crap that even I don't want to do. Like Dalbry said—invaluable."

Cullin rummaged in his pack until he pulled out a battered copy of the Knight's Manual, which he had picked up at a used book shoppe. "I already slew a dragon and won the hand of a princess, even if I ran away from the wedding...."

"Which was an excellent decision," Affonyl assured him.

Cullin could have been a king by default, but that hadn't felt right to him. "What if I want to be a brave knight?"

"Bravery is the stuff of legends," said Dalbry. "But it is rarely the stuff of reality. I've known many a knight who pissed his codpiece when confronting peril."

Cullin paged through the Manual, looking for answers. "I'm trying to learn where I fit in. This was written by brave Sir Tremayne, or perhaps his father. Rules to live by."

"No, just rules to control other people," Reeger said.

"We make our own rules," said the former princess. "That's what freedom is all about."

Dalbry peeked at Cullin's book. "That's an early edition of the manual—I remember when it came out, caused a lot of controversy. No longer considered canon. Tremayne updated it later."

Cullin returned the Manual to his pack and pulled out Ye Olde Journal instead. He had taken notes on the first few pages, but the rest of the book was blank. "I could act as our scribe and chronicler. If I write about our adventures, we'll have a permanent record. Future generations will know what is true and what isn't."

Reeger laughed. "Just because it's written down in a journal doesn't make it true."

"It is preserved in a fixed form, though," Affonyl pointed out, "and therefore eligible for copyright. That helps establish historical fact."

"Maybe we could sell the intellectual property to minstrels." Cullin tapped the cover of the leatherbound book. "This could inspire a wealth of songs."

"Just don't waste it on those three avant-garde minstrels," Dalbry said with a sour expression. "Find a real classic lute performer like Nightingale Bob."

Reassured again, Cullin felt motivated and happy. He could provide an important service—not just for history, but for the reputations of charlatans everywhere.

"I'm going to need your help." He looked at Affonyl and Dalbry. "I want to do this right."

"You can't remember events yourself?" the old knight asked.

"I can, but I'm not sure about the spellings, because so few of them are standardized yet."

As we climb the winding stone stairs to Prince Maurice's tower bedroom, I wrap up that section of my story because I am breathing too hard to continue. I hope that my son thinks they are "dramatic pauses."

Maurice is spoiled, no one disputes that. The boy has his own game room, a personal garderobe, and his own bucket of water. The window in his main bedchamber has a good view overlooking the kingdom, although the only thing currently visible is the pouring rain outside.

Drafts whistle around the room, but a fire has been laid in the hearth. Servants have set out snacks, a plate of fruit, carafes of water and apple juice.

If the prince were a normal young man, I might have expected posters of jousting teams on the stone walls, music from some of the more popular rap minstrels. But Maurice has taken up painting as another hobby, and framed still-lifes or landscapes hang in prominent places.

Maurice sets his lute on a shelf and grabs some grapes and fresh cheese to munch on, since he was not satisfied with the "turkey" sausage Reeger roasted for him. Like a typical teenager, he flops down on the four-poster bed. I know he's only half interested in my story, but half interested is better than not interested at all, and I count that as a victory.

"Are we almost to the orcs?" he asks. "It's been a very long lead up."

"You don't know how long the total story is," I point out. "It could be a thousand-page tome, and in that case we've barely begun our introductory scenes."

"Tell me it's not a thousand page tome," Maurice groans, "and not a trilogy. Or worse, a series. Some authors never finish their series."

"And some authors do," I say. "Relax, this is a short enough tale, and I'll get to the orcs immediately after we finish this interlude."

Maurice lies back on the goose-down comforter. "Don't you think saying 'interlude' sounds pretentious?"

"It's a way to break up the narrative." I really must scold the boy's literary tutors and insist that he get a greater understanding of commercial fiction. "We've come to a point-of-view shift so I can give a different perspective. I'll introduce the antagonist."

Maurice stares at the ceiling, where water is dripping. "In other words, you're going to tell me parts that you could never have seen with your own eyes."

"It's for dramatic effect," I insist. "Let's turn to the orcs."

TWELVE

The tavern's great room was filled with hickory smoke and the smell of roasting meat. A blazing fire spread an orange glow throughout the crowded hall, and other fires outside could be seen through the inn's smashed windows. Black smoke curled up into the sky.

The orcs were loud and rowdy, crammed into the tavern. They had knocked over tables and slid benches aside so they could all fit inside for the celebration.

Borc, the leader of the uncouth band, had once been told they numbered fifty, although he had never counted to such a high number. The other orcs took his word for it, and that was why Borc made such a good leader. None of them had administrative skills, so nobody noticed he wasn't good at admin either.

His band were close comrades, many of them blood relatives, many interbred. They had square teeth, smashed noses, and skin the color of rotted meat. They wrought a great deal of mayhem together as they crossed the countryside, living off the land, going wherever the winds of fate blew them. The orcs were like circling carrion birds looking for a fresh battlefield massacre.

Borc had brought his band to this village, and they had chosen the cozy tavern as their place to wind down and relax for TGIA, or Thank God It's Anyday.

From the inn's store room, the orcs had cracked open kegs of ale and barrels of wine. A few brutes with more refined palates guzzled grog or brandy. The tavern had crystal wine glasses, but the orcs grabbed tankards instead, because they were larger and universally appropriate for ale, wine, or hard liquor.

An uproar rippled through the crowded room, voices loud enough to rattle the smoke-stained rafters. It sounded like a challenge or a shouting match, but it was just the favorite orc drinking song, which consisted of more drinking and belching than actual singing (which was why it was so popular among orcs).

The orc leader refilled his tankard from an open keg and drained the sour ale. Some of the slimmer orcs added dishwater to their ale to create a sort of light beer. Two orcs—Jerx and Goil-—guffawed so loudly they spat in each other's faces and began shoving each other.

All the orcs wore studded leather armor, thick belts, and iron spikes in appropriate places. Their metal helmets could also double as stew bowls or chamber pots, depending on need. Because orcs were renowned for the thickness of their skulls, the helmets didn't provide much extra protection, but they enjoyed how shiny the metal was out in direct sunlight.

"When's dinner?" shouted one of the brutes, triggering a resounding echo of similar questions.

Over the rank odors of so many close orcs, Borc could smell savory meat, hear fat sizzling on the fire. "Yup, check it, Utz!" he bellowed, and one of the orcs strode to the fireplace and pulled out his dagger to test the meat.

The portly innkeeper and his wife both roasted on spits over the fire. The orcs occasionally turned them in order to ensure that they cooked evenly. By now, the skin was blackened and cracked, but Borc liked his meat slow roasted.

"Another ten minutes," said Utz, then licked off his blade.

But hungry orcs were impatient orcs, and none of them knew how to tell time. Borc couldn't stop them as they rushed to the fireplace a few moments later and cut off servings for themselves. Borc shouldered his way forward and cuffed a few heads to make sure he got a good prime cut of buttock.

The innkeeper and his wife were soon stripped down to bones, and then the bones were charred in the coals as crunchy snacks for later.

Outside, the whole village was burning, many of the cottages already up in smoke. Some peasants had managed to flee, but the orcs struck down the remaining ones with axes and pikes, or just balled fists. The band of brutes had plenty of meat for an extended party.

After the successful invasion, several orcs had painted crude graffiti around town, but on each wall they hit, they gave up after a few letters since none of them knew how to spell.

Restless and bored, Borc's orcs amused themselves by ransacking small towns, even if it was all just busy work. They believed in pillaging as a way of life. The uncouth band would stay here for a while, burn a few more buildings, and then move on. They were content with their ambitions.

The inn's front door smashed open with such force that the iron hinges shrieked and the wood crashed. The startled orcs whirled about, and the raucous noise fell to a grumbling silence.

At the threshold stood an ominous man in a long red leather robe accessorized with a black belt. A fierce-looking red metal helmet covered the top half of his head, leaving only a gray cadaverous chin below and perfectly straight but yellowed teeth, implying expensive orthodontia but lack of regular dental hygiene. Bright eyes blazed like coals through the eyeholes in the helmet. He seemed to ripple with energy as he extended his gauntleted hands.

The orcs muttered in confusion, annoyed by the intruder.

Borc strode toward the door. "Private party."

"The party is just starting," replied the cadaverous red-robed man. "I am Ugnarok, the wizard-mage. You must have heard of me? Now, you will tremble with fear."

The orcs looked at one another, whispering. Many shook their heads. Borc said, "We don't read many newspapers."

"Then you *will* know me!" Ugnarok's voice boomed through the tavern's main room like a cross between a serpent's hiss and a thunderclap. "Afterward, you will tremble with fear."

The orcs drew their spiked maces, battle axes, clubs, spears, and swords. They had just stuffed themselves with a good meal, but the tavern still had kegs of ale, and there was always time for a dessert course.

Borc's band became a threatening army. "Orcs don't tremble," he said.

The brutes pressed closer, but Ugnarok didn't flinch. Borc took that to mean that he was stupid.

Before the first battle axe or spiked club could reach him, the wizard-mage reached out a black gauntlet, curled his fingers, and blue lightning skittered around the tips. He tossed the lightning at the nearest orc—Utz— as if flicking a booger off his finger.

The crackling spell surrounded Utz like a net, sparking and snapping, cooking him from inside. The orc's biceps bulged, as did his eyes. Spittle burst from his mouth, and he let out a roar of agony that sounded like a belching duck. Cracking skin sloughed off his bones, and Utz fell to the tavern floor in a steaming pile.

A second orc jumped toward Ugnarok, swinging his battle axe, and the wizard-mage flung another lightning spell toward him. The axe grew red hot, and the orc dropped it on the floor, cursing. A follow-up spell cooked him in his tracks as well.

Ugnarok hadn't even moved from the doorway. Finally, he said, "Now that I have your attention, I need to recruit some orcs. An entire orc army."

"Like a military academy?" Borc asked.

"Like violent marauding invaders!" Ugnarok said. "I need you to ransack and pillage, cause mayhem, and swarm through the castle gates."

The orcs snorted and sniffed, some nodding. The two piles of cooked orc flesh slumped off the bone, and fluids dribbled across the floor.

"Yup, sounds good," Borc said. "Why didn't you just ask?"

Ugnarok continued, "I intend to take over an entire kingdom, usurp the throne, and seize a legendary treasure."

That sounded like a lot of steps to Borc, but he did like the idea. Besides, his orcs had nothing else to do.

"You will be well compensated," said the wizard-mage. "This is no joke."

The orcs cheered, even though the decision hadn't been finalized yet.

"Where are we going?" Borc asked.

"I must have my revenge against King Grog, but alas he died before I could have satisfaction. Fortunately, his son Longjohn has a huge treasure hidden in his castle. In order to seize it, I need some muscle."

"Muscle?" Borc was glad the evil sorcerer wasn't looking for brainpower. He flexed his arm to show off huge muscles under his leprous green skin. "Yup, take a look."

His band of orcs showed off their biceps as well.

Ugnarok strode the rest of the way into the inn. "Good." He gestured for two orcs to straighten a bench and a table so he'd have a place to sit. "Fetch me a glass of wine, and let me discuss with you the net worth of Longjohn's kingdom."

CHAPTER

THIRTEEN

Though she had always been fascinated by natural science, art was Affonyl's other passion. While raising her to be a marriageable bargaining chip, King Norrimund had unwittingly encouraged her artistic pursuits.

The independent young princess had flat-out refused to learn courtly dances, and her corpulent father did not press the matter because he himself was not light on his feet. A royal princess also had to engage in witty court conversation such as "Oh, look at that nice cloud" or "The weather turned cool yesterday" or "The flowers will be blooming soon." Affonyl had mastered that skill early on and grew bored with it.

Several years under the tutelage of Edgar, the court wizard had taught her much about science, chemistry, alchemy. Affonyl learned practical chemistry from him, and she wished Edgar had never left to take a higher paying job with an evil wizards' conglomerate. She knew he would be proud of all she had accomplished since fleeing her royal responsibilities.

Science was not considered a proper princessy thing to do, but art was another matter. Sitting with her vapid court ladies, Affonyl had spent hours embroidering, remarking on the colors of various threads, complimenting the other designs. She could show her independent streak with embroidery patterns, some of which might better be described as tangles. Because it was not proper to criticize the stitchery of a real princess, everyone celebrated her bold technique. Next, she had tried her hand at caricatures, and the rest was history.

"A princess is a princess," her father had hammered into her. "Don't go thinking of yourself as a person."

Now that she was free and roaming the land, building an independent career, she had a new purpose. She thought of herself as more than just a person, but as an *artist*.

She embraced her role in their new scheme, enjoying the mystique that Dalbry and Cullin had built about her. *Affonyl NoLastName.* King Longjohn was well primed, and she would make it work.

The former princess changed into a new peasant dress and pinned up her hair in an unusual fashion. Cullin and Dalbry had gone ahead to prepare the way, and Affonyl would arrive by herself for a grand entrance. She could hold her own in the haughty department.

The two guards at the castle gate celebrated her arrival and fell over themselves to usher her inside. "I am Guard Captain James Johnson," said a man with a thin mustache and a thinner beard. He wore a helmet with the visor up, and she could see his bright blue eyes.

Next to him stood a nearly identical man who rapped his pike staff on the flagstones, then bowed his head. "And I am Guard Captain John Jameson. Follow us. The king is eager to discuss the fine arts with you."

She walked with grace and confidence behind Johnson and Jameson, glancing at the yarn dream catchers and the macrame hangings. Some of the framed paintings were in the pop art category, depicting only a stack of soup pots or repeated pictures of King Longjohn's face in intense gaudy colors. It wasn't her style of art.

When the crier announced her, Affonyl stepped into the combination throne room and banquet hall. Dalbry and Cullin were already there, and the old knight, now art critic, stepped forward to introduce her. "King Longjohn, this is my client, Affonyl NoLastName."

Longjohn rose from his throne on his lanky legs. "And I hope to become her client, too! I can't wait to have an original work from such a famous landscape artist."

"*If* I decide to do it," Affonyl said, still playing hard to get.

The king's gaunt expression filled with worry. As she approached the throne, Cullin smiled at her, but she ignored him.

She decided to win the king over to her side. "I am kindly disposed toward any true patron of the arts, Your Majesty." She gave a polite curtsey, and Longjohn was impressed by her skill in important matters.

Deep in thought, Affonyl paced in front of the throne. "My muse speaks to me, Sire. As I walked onto your castle grounds, the fog lifted and I could see hills all around. I imagined the power of nature and how a new creation of mine might fit in."

Longjohn was like a kettle boiling over with excitement. "Something large! Something impressive that I can show all the neighboring lords."

"Once my work is unveiled, they will come from miles around to see it. I developed a concept that is perfectly appropriate to your greatness, but it will take a great deal of labor."

The king nodded. "We will provide all the support you need."

"As well as funding," Dalbry said.

"Yes, of course. And laborers."

Affonyl lifted her chin. "Art itself is work—that's what makes it so valuable. Take me to the placement site. I need to envision it more clearly."

Affonyl and Dalbry followed the king out to the side courtyard, while Cullin stayed behind to meet with castle staff and made preparations, as part of his job as executive assistant. The former princess flashed him a smile as she passed. This was all going well.

Once outside, Longjohn proudly indicated the courtyard. The bandstand had already been removed, and the open lawn had been cleared of the rows of folding chairs.

Affonyl put her hands on her hips and scanned the area, measuring with her eyes. "I see you have given this much thought. The art itself is important, but a prominent venue for a true masterpiece is just as important. It will be a truly substantial piece." She turned slowly around. "Massive."

The king liked the sound of that. "Massive!"

"I noticed those distinctive rock pinnacles in your nearby hills, like snaggly teeth from mountain giants. If I decide to do this work, I will need one of those. Once I choose the appropriate item, I must have it delivered here. Is that possible?"

"My kingdom is renowned for those stones," said Longjohn. "Our excavation engineers remove and transport them regularly."

Dalbry asked, "For what purpose, Sire? There is a market for giant rocks?"

"Yes, quite a demand. It's nothing like the customer base for my peanut shipments from the New Lands, but many Druid movements commission our famous rocks to make local Stonehenge homages."

Affonyl let the creative juices flow, and Longjohn held his breath, flushed with anticipation, until she said, "Yes, I will take on the commission."

King Longjohn couldn't have been happier.

Meanwhile, Cullin continued to lay groundwork. This plan was more complicated than faking the existence of a dragon, but far less dangerous.

Captains Johnson and Jameson led him to the castle's receiving rooms, where he pretended to take notes in Ye Olde Journal, whilst keeping his eyes open for useful details. "Once Affonyl's artwork is completed, we must have a grand unveiling. It is part of her artistic process."

"The king would insist on it," said Jameson.

"The grander the better," said Johnson.

Cullin learned that the two nearly identical guards were not related, but even the king could not keep James Johnson and John Jameson straight. He had promoted one of them for exemplary service, then couldn't remember which, so he ended up naming both Jameson and Johnson captains.

While Dalbry and Affonyl were outside inspecting the courtyard, Cullin met with the castle staff and was surprised to bump into Sue-Pam. The scullery maid recognized him and brushed aside the two guards. "I'll show him around, Captains."

Johnson was taken aback. "But you aren't licensed as an escort service."

"I know this castle better than anyone," Spam said with a huff. "And that's that."

Cullin suspected that the girl was more likely to give him the information he needed. He stepped forward. "It's all right, Captains. Affonyl NoLastName is an artist of the people, who understands the way commoners think. This scullery maid will be adequate for what I need."

"Adequate!" Spam muttered with an extra huff.

Dismissed, the guards left him in the girl's company, and she took him to the back larder opposite from the main ovens. When they were alone, Spam wrinkled her nose. "Your artist friend seems full of herself."

He felt he had to defend Affonyl's honor. "She's actually a very nice person."

"Sure." The girl wiped a smudge on her left cheek, distributing the grime down her face. "I never pretend to be important." Then she added with a twinkle in her eye, "That might all change though, if my cottage industry takes off."

"A cottage industry ... from a castle?"

"Innovative, isn't it?" She gave him a sly smile. "After working in the kitchens, I saw so many scraps of perfectly digestible meat going to waste—leftovers from dinner plates, animal pieces and parts like snouts or nipples. It all just gets thrown away! So, I realized that when life gives you scraps of worthless meat, you should make a delicious and shelf-stable potted meat product, my own special recipe."

The scullery maid led him to the back of the larder, moved aside barrels of apples and baskets of dirt-encrusted potatoes. There, hidden from prying eyes, she had stacked up tins of her chopped, processed, salted, and preserved scrap-meat product. "I've been selling it down in the village market." She seemed very proud of herself. "It's an acquired taste, but it's catching on. With all the preservatives, it'll last for centuries in storage."

"I like the blue label on the cans," Cullin said, though he wasn't sure he wanted to try any of it.

"I named it after myself," said Spam. "Right there, in bright yellow letters."

Cullin looked at all the tins labeled SUE-PAM. "You're going to be famous if it's successful."

"I've got cans hidden throughout the castle in case of emergency. And this castle has countless hiding places. That's one of my other special skills. I know how to sneak around. Let me show you."

Cullin agreed that was a very useful skill.

As they left the larder and moved along a torchlit corridor, Spam counted the stone blocks, then stopped to push one of them with her palm. A latch clicked, revealing a gap and another secret passage, like the one that had taken them to Longjohn's hidden art grotto. "How many secret corridors does this castle have?"

"Hundreds! The castle is a maze, but I've explored them all." She giggled. "They make good places to hide when I don't want to do chores." She snatched one of the torches from a wall sconce and led him into the passage, closing the hidden door behind them.

They moved down cobwebby tunnels, ducking into cramped corridors. They wound their way up to the living quarters, where she showed him peepholes into Longjohn's guest rooms, then she brought him to the large mess hall where the guards and workers ate lunch. Peeping through tiny slits, they watched the castle staff preparing the day's meals.

"Why does the king need so many secret passages?" Cullin asked.

"His father had a lot of off-book activities, and his crew needed shortcuts to get from the tide line up to the shipping department."

"What's down at the tide line?" Cullin asked.

"The sea caves where King Grog's smugglers brought in barrels of moonshyne. There are caverns and tunnels down there, so he could hide the product."

"But if he was the king, why did he need to hide the moonshyne? Can't a king do what he wants?"

Spam rolled her eyes as if the young man knew nothing about

laws and tariffs and trade arrangements. "King Grog didn't want to pay moonshyne taxes to the Inter-Kingdom Revenue Service. That's how this kingdom earned so much wealth." The girl continued to lead him along the winding corridors. "By now, though, King Longjohn has spent most of it on his private art collection."

"I thought the kingdom was wealthy because of Longjohn's successful merchant fleet and his peanut trade from the New Lands."

Spam found another secret doorway, and they emerged into the main corridors again. "Moonshyne is what funded that merchant fleet in the first place."

The pieces started to fit together as Cullin followed the girl back to the courtyard. "I thought it was only art that I didn't understand."

CHAPTER

FOURTEEN

R eeger didn't mind getting his hands dirty. In fact, he preferred them that way, because he had a superstitious aversion to cleanliness. He refused to bathe on religious grounds, since he had once sworn to God that he would never get into a tub again. Mucking out noble latrines or digging up valuable bones in grave-yards was acceptable labor, although not his favorite.

This time he had a more artistic part to play.

The former princess had sketched out her artistic design, which Longjohn enthusiastically approved. While looking over Affonyl's shoulder, Cullin had also approved. Reeger thought it was point-lessly complex landscaping, but the lanky king embraced the vision, and it was his money.

Today, Reeger's hands were covered in dirt up to the elbows, and his trousers were caked with mud. Affonyl had named him her personal "artistic engineer," and Reeger went out with Longjohn's ditchdiggers, rock haulers, and Stonehenge-component specialists to excavate just the right slab of rock. The labor crew would haul the rock across the hills, up the oppressively steep road to the castle, then erect it out in the side courtyard.

After the former princess had chosen a specific rock spire for her landscape art project—and Reeger wished she had picked a more convenient one—he supervised the crew as they shoveled a trench around the base, then used levers and ropes, mule teams, and wedges to wiggle the huge rock out of the ground. It reminded Reeger of a brown, aching tooth he had recently twisted out of his mouth.

Once the distinctive rock was properly uprooted, Affonyl walked around it to inspect every lump and cranny before pronouncing it perfect. King Longjohn watched the process with tears in his eyes, profoundly impressed.

"Now the rustin' fun part begins," Reeger muttered.

The wagon teams used sturdy palace mules, not Reeger's personal mule, which would have been offended to be pressed into such pointless service. They created a massive sledge to transport the giant slab, along with ropes and rollers. Reeger managed the operation, since life had prepared him to lift heavy things, although this exceeded his previous experience.

Affonyl, Dalbry, and Cullin accompanied the slow journey across the landscape. With shared glances and quick smiles to one another, they communicated that everything was on track for the plan.

A rainstorm came in, dousing the giant rock, which Affonyl called "a good rinse in preparation for my final creation." Unfortunately, the rain also muddied the ground, and the sledge and rock got stuck numerous times on the way up to the castle.

In addition to the rock slab, Affonyl's design required a thick tree to prop the rock at a precise angle. The earnest king sent word across the land and found the proper trunk—originally grown to be the main mast of one of his trading ships, but the sturdy pine suffered a kink, which made it unacceptable as a mast.

Affonyl inspected the slightly bent trunk and pronounced it perfect, however. "It's artisanal and rustic, adds drama to the work."

A separate crew hauled the rejected ship mast up from the harbor construction yards and reached the castle at about the same time as the laboriously dragged rock.

In the bandstand courtyard, the lawn had been cleared, the dirt leveled and raked, awaiting Affonyl's new work. The mules grunted as they dragged the slab through the side gates into the prepared area. Dirt-encrusted ditchdiggers and laborers also grunted against the ropes. Reeger shouted officious artistic-engineering instructions to the labor crew. "Remember, art work is *hard* work!"

Meanwhile, the artisanal ship's mast was sawed to exactly the correct length, per Affonyl's instructions, then it was raised with pulleys and a block-and-tackle, until the log hung at a 45-degree angle—meeting the giant rock slab that was also lifted at the same slant. The giant rock rested against the thick wooden strut, shading a large open space under the rock.

"After some decorating, I'll install a nice bench under the rock to experience the masterful work from its core," Longjohn said.

"Looks like a mousetrap," Cullin said.

"It is a poignant work of art," Affonyl corrected him with a sniff, but she was speaking for the king's benefit. "See how the powerful stone rests at exactly the right angle, held in balance by the sturdy majestic tree, symbolizing the interaction between forest and mountain, in perfect harmony. I shall call it ..." She drew in a breath, stretching out the suspense. "Rock in Its Natural State."

Dalbry nodded. "Rock in Its Natural State—I see! It is brilliant, Affonyl. Your finest work yet."

"Unless you count the embroidery," Cullin said.

"And when you tilt it like that, it looks different from any old Stonehenge pillar," Reeger said.

Putting on his art critic hat, Dalbry had already begun his erudite analysis. "It represents the power of nature, the potential energy of the looming rock. The tree trunk shows how living things can stand against enduring stone and resist the weight of nature. Such primal power! I've never seen anything like it."

Cullin agreed. "This is completely unique."

"And I am the only king who has one," said Longjohn. "It simultaneously shows the unpredictability and the stability of the natural world."

"And it was damned heavy," Reeger said.

Taking on his role as the artist's representative, Dalbry got down to business. "If you are satisfied with the piece, Sire, there is the matter of our contractual payment. As a critic in great demand, I must be on my way to neighboring kingdoms to inspect and criticize other collections."

"Well, ahhh, my treasury is a bit lean right now in liquid cash, until I sell the new shipment of peanuts." His happy mood would not be changed, though. "But we're not finished yet. We must have a gala unveiling! I shall invite prominent nobles from across the land. I'll send out printed invitations. It'll be a legendary event for the most discerning art lovers."

He called to Captains Johnson and Jameson, "Send riders to spread the word. We'll need RSVPs by dawn. But no one should see this masterpiece beforehand!" He clapped his hands together and called for his castle workers to bring an enormous canvas, originally designed as the mainsail for the largest merchant ship in his fleet. They spread the tarpaulin over the enormous landscape art to cover it up.

Cullin asked, "But hasn't everyone already seen it? We've spent days bringing it here and hours erecting it."

"It lacks formality," Longjohn said. "And panache."

Dalbry reluctantly agreed to stay. "Very well, so long as we are paid immediately following the festivities. To enhance her reputation, Affonyl NoLastName will present her newest and greatest work in a grand unveiling ceremony."

"And a feast!" said King Longjohn.

"A feast is always good." Reeger waggled his eyebrows at Cullin. "Since this kingdom is on the coast, maybe he'll even serve oysters. Real ones, this time."

The boom of thunder outside is as loud as a drunken two-headed dragon falling on a house. Startled, Prince Maurice jumps off of his bed, jangling the strings of his lute (which doesn't sound much different from his actual playing).

The rain is pouring down. I hope Reeger and Wendria have made it back to the Scabby Wench. No doubt many travelers will rush to the tavern for shelter, and Reeger will have a "downpour special" of leftover bratwursts; they'll be wet and cold but offered at a bargain price.

Water drips through the ceiling, splashing on the prince's down comforter. "I need to call the castle warrantee service," I say.

"Mother already filed a work order," Maurice says. "But our monthly plan doesn't cover leaky roofs during the rainy season."

"*Living in a dank castle is one of the burdens of royalty,*" *I say.* "*You'll learn that when you're a king yourself.*"

A flare of lightning illuminates the bedroom, brighter than the scented candles or the torches burning on the wall. Jittery, the boy looks up, as if imagining the tall castle turrets. Maurice has always been fragile and flighty, despite my efforts to toughen him up with tales of truly frightening things.

"*According to legend, thunder and lightning are caused by warring titans in the skies.*" *I hope that calls visions to his mind so he'll paint something other than flowers or still lifes.*

The boy scoffs. "*Lightning is caused by the release of positive and negative charges between a cloud and the ground, and thunder is created by the sudden increase in temperature accompanying a lightning bolt, which produces rapid expansion in the air, and that expansion creates a sonic shock wave.*"

I'm surprised. "*Couldn't have said it better myself. I know you're well educated, considering all the money we spend on tutors.*"

Another flash of lightning outside makes Maurice flinch again. "*The reason I'm worried is because of our tall towers. In such a severe thunderstorm, those turrets will attract lightning.*" *He glances at the drip coming down from his ceiling, then at the floor where the rugs are already damp.* "*And the leaking water conducts electricity.*"

"*Nothing can be done about the rain,*" *I say.*

"*We should install lightning rods on the highest towers in order to ground the castle. That'll protect us from lightning strikes.*"

I give an earnest nod at the suggestion. As a king, I'm supposed to know about all these things, and as a wise king I pretend *that I know all these things.*

"*I'll have a team of knights gird themselves in full plate armor to protect them from the rain, then I'll send them to climb the highest towers in the middle of the thunderstorm. They will install lightning rods with all due haste.*" *I can rally my knights for the task because they have all read the Manual and they know their chivalrous obligations.* "*No time to lose.*"

The next bolt of lightning is so powerful that the candles and torches flicker and go out, then relight themselves from the backup wicks.

"*Maybe not right this instant, Father,*" *Maurice says, worried.*

"The castle has weathered many a storm over the centuries. It can last for one more. The knight-installers can do it on a clear, sunny day."
"The men-at-arms will appreciate that." The boy might make a good king after all. *"Meanwhile, I'll keep telling you my story to while away the hours and make you forget about the terrors of the thunderstorm."*

CHAPTER
FIFTEEN

Seeing the king's excitement for Rock in Its Natural State, Reeger was at first scornful, but then he felt inspired. He had an imagination, too. If this giant rock on a stick was a "masterpiece," and if the eccentric sculptures in the statue garden were also considered great works ... well, then he could be just as artistic.

While preparations were underway for Affonyl's gala unveiling that night, Reeger tried his creative hand. Remembering everything he knew about art, which was nil, he would do something new and innovative with familiar materials.

He found three old boards in the castle's midden heap. Chuckling to himself, he twisted out bent, rusty nails in the first plank, but decided to leave them in place in the other boards, because art was often dangerous. At the back of the castle, he propped the three boards against the wall, then fetched a wooden bucket from the stables, which he filled with horse manure and watery mud to give it the right consistency.

He stirred the mixture with his hand, imagining it as his paint. As curious guards and castle staff watched what he was doing, Reeger scooped out a handful of his mixture and slathered the front of one of the boards. Next, he splattered globs on the top, then used two fingers to draw a smear and a squiggle.

"It's my own work." Reeger raised his voice, encouraging others to have a look. "The raw material of the earth mixed with a fresh fecal palette from the king's finest horses." (Actually, the dung came from the mule's stall, but no one would know the difference.)

He stepped back to admire his work, noting the audience's visceral reaction.

But he wasn't finished yet. He scooped a second handful of muck and splattered and smeared the next board, careful to avoid the rusty nails. "This brings out the sky elements, the power of the air around us, as conveyed by the terrible fumes wafting up."

He created a similar, yet entirely unique work of mess on the third board. He bent down and grabbed some soft dirt and threw it like a snowball to cover more of the plank.

Before the audience lost interest, he said, "I call this first piece Manure on Wood, One." He pondered the second board and pronounced, "And this is Manure on Wood, Two." For the third creation, Reeger drew out the pause for so long, the people were on tenterhooks. "And finally, Manure on Wood, Mud Variation."

Captains Johnson and Jameson stepped closer, presumably to admire the work. Reeger would have preferred compliments instead of nauseated muttering from the audience.

Reeger was unable to match Dalbry's erudite manner, but he spoke quickly. "I don't expect most people to truly understand these. I am the artistic engineer for Affonyl NoLastName, and this work is drawn from my experience and, of course, my innate skill."

He spread his brown-smeared hands in a magnanimous gesture. "King Longjohn has his personal art collection, but here is your chance to buy a new piece for your quarters! Own a piece of Reeger's imagination right here. Two gold coins each!" He blinked his cock-eyed eyes. "A bargain price, believe me."

No one in the crowd, not even the highly paid castle guards, seemed interested.

"All right then, as a special, because you were here to witness the birth of these great works—one gold piece each."

The staff decided they had important preparations to make for the evening's grand banquet and unveiling ceremony. Looking at his smeared planks, squinting with one eye and then the other, Reeger could not understand why his work was less desirable than Longjohn's other exhibits.

Dressed in his pompous garments, Dalbry strode up to him. "Reeger, there you are!" The knight ran his eyes up and down the filth-spattered jerkin and trousers. "Why are you out here smearing poop on planks? You must get cleaned up. The unveiling ceremony is tonight."

"Rust, I'm trying my own hand at creating art!" He indicated the three boards. "Quite successfully, as you can see."

"It's time to create cleanliness instead of art. As Affonyl's artistic engineer, you are one of the honored guests at the banquet tonight. Go wash yourself off!"

Reeger felt defensive. He wiped his manure-stained palms on his trousers. "I thought artists were supposed to be eccentric."

"Wear green socks if you want to be eccentric," Dalbry chided. "We have a large fee depending on this. If I can pretend to be knowledgeable about artwork, you can at least put on a clean shirt."

Reeger grudgingly agreed. Since he didn't know where to put his smeared boards for safekeeping, he decided to hide them back on the midden heap. If someone stole the pieces, that would be evidence of their worth as collectibles.

After Dalbry went to check with Cullin and Affonyl, Reeger trudged to the castle stables to find a horse trough wide enough to dunk himself in.

King Longjohn's riders had raced across the land with urgent, last-minute invitations, requesting immediate RSVPs. He invited any neighboring noblemen and noblewomen who were also art aficionados.

Under normal circumstances, the unveiling of such a grand masterpiece would have been planned for an entire season, but Longjohn was too eager for that (and Affonyl and her companions wanted to get paid sooner rather than later). Given the short time frame, the king would make the unveiling like a flash mob event, although with a full banquet beforehand.

A barrel of imported peanuts was brought in from the recently arrived ship, and special bowls were set out for snacking, while the kitchen staff created recipes that used peanuts in all the main dishes. The castle was a flurry of activity.

By contrast, the side courtyard was a place of quiet refuge. The big tarp covered the towering landscape art like a great tent, staked down so that stray breezes wouldn't flap it up and reveal the masterpiece.

Under the tarpaulin, Affonyl had a cozy, private place where she could prepare for the big event and stay out of the public eye. As an eccentric, reclusive artist, she would wait here for the great reveal after the banquet.

In the hot and steamy kitchens, the ovens baked bread, and the cauldrons were filled with bubbling sauces. Dishes clattered in washtubs.

Despite all the frantic work, Cullin pulled Spam away from her chores to ask a special favor. The harried girl wiped her wet hands with a filthy rag. "Not now, Cullin. We can sneak through the secret passages later, maybe when I'm supposed to be doing dishes."

"I just want some food to take to Affonyl—a special treat. She won't be attending the banquet herself, but she should be well-fed."

"Isn't it traditional for artists to be starving?" said Spam.

"Affonyl is a different sort of artist. She prefers an alternative to starvation."

Happy to help, the scullery maid grabbed a basket and ran around the kitchen, dodging the activity while somehow remaining unnoticed. She snatched a meat pie, an apple, some bread, and other supplies for a nice meal.

A matronly cook shouted, "Sue-Pam, don't forget to scrub out those meatloaf pans!"

"Right away, ma'am," she said, but ignored the instructions as she hurried with Cullin out to the side courtyard. The evening fog was rolling in again, thick and chilly.

Together, they worked their way under the tarp and surprised Affonyl, who relaxed in her peasant dress on one of the folding chairs previously used for outdoor concerts. Cullin introduced the former princess to Sue-Pam and described how the scullery girl had shown him the hidden passageways throughout the castle.

He thought Affonyl looked lonely sitting there under the tarp. "Don't you wish you could go to the banquet? I'm an executive assistant—I can pull some strings." His voice held rising hope. "Maybe you'll sit beside me near the king."

Spam pulled off the towel on her basket of treasures to reveal a picnic instead. "Those banquets are long and boring."

Affonyl smiled. "You are right about that." She pulled out the apple and a meat pie, looking at him with real gratitude. "Thank you so much for this, Squirrel. Don't worry about me. I like it out here, where it's quiet and private. In my previous life, I had my fill of inane, princessy things. You've been to one of my father's banquets."

Cullin nodded. King Norrimund the Corpulent was renowned for interminable feasts.

She continued, "I don't need the courtly finery, the uncomfortable clothes, the marital expectations. A princess is a princess, but I'd rather be a person—my own person. And you've helped me make that possible."

Cullin felt a warm flush in his cheeks. His stomach growled as she gobbled the meat pie, but he needed to save his appetite for the long feast.

He wondered if the last course, then the dessert and coffee would be over before midnight. At least the lunar charts showed there would be a bright, full moon to provide the proper ambience for a grand unveiling of Rock in Its Natural State. Unless the fog was too thick.

Spam reached into the basket to pull out three slices of white bread. "Here, I brought something special." She took out a knife and a pot, which she opened with reverence, then whispered, "I snitched some fresh butter made from the imported peanuts."

Using the knife, she spread a wide smear across the bread and presented it to Affonyl, and prepared the other two slices for Cullin and herself. The three sampled the exotic concoction.

Cullin tried to say how much he loved the sticky sweetness, but his tongue stuck to the roof of his mouth. He took some time to work it clear again.

"I've never eaten anything like this," Affonyl said, delighted. "Next time could you sneak a little pot of jam?" She smacked her lips. "I imagine that some grape jelly would be the perfect accompaniment."

CHAPTER
SIXTEEN

Thanks to his penchant for preplanning, Wizard-Mage Ugnarok had three fearsome dragon ships tucked away in a hidden cove down the coast.

Borc and his unruly orc warriors followed the evil sorcerer to the narrow, foggy cove. The three war vessels were camouflaged with a "nothing to see here" spell, but once Ugnarok waved his gauntleted hands to reveal the ships, the orcs ooohed and ahhhed. They were particularly fond of the carved figureheads, snarling reptilian beasts with long wooden fangs.

Goil poked his thick head next to the figurehead and grinned to show teeth almost as monstrous as the carved dragon's.

Standing at the end of the dock, the wizard-mage glowered through his skull-like helmet. "You orcs will lead the invasion. We will crash these dragon ships into the harbor town, then rush up the road to the castle. We will conquer the kingdom and take its great treasure for ourselves, and I will finally get my revenge on King Grog."

The orcs jostled each other as they scrambled aboard the open dragon ships, trying to get a good window seat, although everyone had plenty of fresh air.

"Yup, we're ready to conquer, Master Ugnarok," said Borc with an obsequious grunt.

"It's *Wizard-Mage* Ugnarok," the evil sorcerer corrected.

"Orcs don't use titles— too hard to keep track," Borc said. "And if we're your personal conquering orc army, shouldn't we be on a first-name basis?"

The powerful wizard agreed to be addressed as Ugnarok. By way of introduction, Borc had his people belch out their own names, which sounded like a holiday party at a slaughterhouse.

The wizard-mage paid little attention, turning his fierce helmet and blazing eyes forward. "Prepare to launch! The tide is going out, and the fog is coming in. The perfect setup for an evening of conquest!"

The orcs hooted, grunted, and cheered, pounding the butts of their weapons on the deck boards; when there was no room on the deck, they pounded the helmets of the nearest orcs.

"Yup, ready to sail, Ugnarok." Borc stomped his boot on the creaking wooden boards. "But could you show us ... *how* to sail? Orcs usually avoid the water—and don't expect us to swim."

The wizard-mage let out a fiery exasperated sigh. "So, no nautical prowess? But you do have muscles, correct?"

"Yup, lots of muscles." Borc once again flexed his bicep.

"Good, then you can row. That's all you need to become sailors."

As darkness closed in and mists thickened, the orcs settled into their places, argued over who got to hold which part of the oars. Ugnarok told them to hurry before the fog covered up the cove's narrow opening.

The orcs needed practice to coordinate their movements. Since they all knew how to count up to three, they began a rhythm, chanting in unison, "One! Two! Three!" Eventually, they figured out how to row in reverse, and the dragon ships backed out of the cove and into the misty darkness.

Once they reached the open water, they had to retrain themselves to row forward instead of backward, and the dragon ships wandered in circles until the orcs got it right.

Before full darkness, they were making good speed. The curling wake looked like spittle behind the attack vessels. Because he was in command, Borc climbed onto the prow next to the fierce wooden dragon. He waved back at the orcs. "I'm on top of the world!"

"Don't fall into the water," said Olugg. "I'm not jumping in to get you."

Borc took a firmer grip on the carved figurehead and held onto a rope.

They couldn't see through the fog, although the dragon ships were close enough that the orcs could hear the nearby grunts of effort. "One! Two! Three!" Borc yelled out.

Ugnarok manned the tiller to steer the flagship, but the other two vessels had no navigators. As the dragon ships pressed onward, their hulls bumped and caromed off each other, accompanied by shouted insults.

"Straight ahead," Ugnarok bellowed. "Don't deviate from your course."

Two ships bumped into each other again. The offended brutes, juiced up on orc testosterone as well as the promise of blood and conquest, yelled, complained, and threatened. They lifted their oars and started whacking the warriors on the opposite ship.

As the conflict developed into an all-out orc oar battle, the disgusted wizard-mage summoned lightning and sent crackling bursts onto each ship, just enough to frazzle the unruly orcs. Muttering, the crew settled down and pulled the oars again.

As they moved onward, Borc looked at the wizard-mage. "Do you know the way?"

"I have detailed directions," Ugnarok said. "In another five hundred feet, turn right and we'll enter the harbor. Soon the treasure will be ours."

The orcs salivated over the thought of jewels, gold, pearls, and more treasure. Only one orc, who had chosen a middle seat because it was less work, voiced his confusion. Qwol had always been a slacker for an orc, and Borc even considered him a bit girly. "But why do we want treasure? I've tasted gold. Broke a tooth trying to eat a coin once."

"You don't eat a coin," Goil sneered.

Qwol snarled back, "What good is treasure if you can't eat it?"

"With treasure you can buy whatever you want to eat."

Qwol sulked, pulling on the oar. "Seems like an unnecessary step. We could just raid the castle pantry instead of looking for treasure to buy the food that's already in the pantry."

Ugnarok was impatient. "You orcs need lessons in economics."

The brutes grumbled, mainly at the unhappy idea that they might have to take lessons.

The orcs continued to row, and the dragon ships glided ahead. When the shadowy mouth of the harbor appeared in the mist, the dragon ships careened into each other again, splintering hull boards. Two of the figureheads smashed together like snarling cats, their wooden teeth catching and then breaking apart.

Finally, they made it into the harbor. At full speed the marauding ships slipped past the anchored merchant vessels, which were closed down due to the night fog. Borc knew that his companions were eager for the battle to come, and the spoils of war.

Ugnarok's eyes glowed with anticipation through the helmet holes. "Soon, this kingdom will be under my rule. I shall become King Wizard-Mage Ugnarok!"

"That is a royal mouthful." Borc was glad they had agreed to use first names only.

Finally the dragon ships reached the shore. The orcs were rowing too fast and had forgotten how to row backwards, so the vessels rode up onto the rocky beach. One smashed a fishing dock, which collapsed into the water. The orcs were thrown about from the impact, and Borc fell from his position at the dragon figurehead and sprawled on the deck.

Ugnarok gestured with his black gauntlet. "To the castle of King Longjohn!" He released a sparkling flurry of lightning bolts that crackled up the road to the headlands above.

The orcs boiled off the ships and onto solid ground. They adjusted their helmets, waved their weapons, and started to run up the steep path.

CHAPTER

SEVENTEEN

Although the peanut butter on bread was quite a treat, Cullin saved his appetite for the actual banquet. While on the road, he and his companions were no strangers to hunger, forced to eat shreds of meat from scrawny rodents. But he had also experienced the grandiose gluttony of royal feasts.

Before the appetizer course was due to start, Cullin cleaned himself up, put on a fresh executive-assistant jerkin, and used the garderobe. The night's unveiling ceremony was bound to be a memorable, although lengthy event.

Before the guests started to arrive, Spam darted into the banquet room and scurried around, tidying the corners, straightening the seats, before she disappeared again. Cullin knew it was castle protocol that scullery maids were neither to be seen nor heard.

He met Dalbry and Reeger in King Longjohn's throne hall. Dalbry did not seem comfortable in his fancy maroon outfit with lacy white cuffs and collar. Since the old knight had slept on the ground for much of his life, a formal wardrobe gave him pains in places other than his sore joints.

The neighboring lords, ladies, and art aficionados arrived in their own finest finery, the most expensive gowns and suits, the gaudiest jewelry. Being invited to such a soiree forced them to prove their own worth and, preferably, prove that their worth was greater than the others'.

101

King Longjohn was a gracious, even gloating host. He walked his guests along the corridors, pointing out the vibrant yarn dreamcatchers, the macrame flowerpot hangers, the decoupage samples, the portraits of various unattractive nobles (which he had bought for a bargain price at an estate sale).

Returning from a brief hallway tour, the king approached Dalbry, leading a couple dressed in such extravagant clothing they moved as if petrified. "I am pleased to introduce Sub-baron Darylking and his wife Lady Pattilane."

The sub-baron had a twisted sneer on his lips that was evidently meant to be a smile. Imitating the sneer out of respect, Dalbry bent to kiss Lady Pattilane's knuckles. Because she and the sub-baron had been married for such a long time, Pattilane had an identical sneer.

Longjohn introduced Dalbry and his executive assistant to the next guests. "And this is Lowduke McCowan and Highduke Lessa."

"Shouldn't it be Highduchess, my Lady?" Cullin asked.

The dusky Lessa frowned enough that some of her dark lipstick flaked off. "Ridiculous waste of syllables. I'll stick with the masculine title."

Cullin took out Ye Olde Journal to make a proper notation.

The king darted to his next guest. "And Midduke Blande, with an E at the end to make his name less bland."

Dalbry shook the man's limp hand. Cullin wrote down the name in his book.

The lanky king grinned with pride, reveling in his position. Dalbry moved smoothly among the nobles, true to form, though the guests were more curious to meet the mysterious Affonyl than her representative. They were especially uninterested in meeting her representative's executive assistant. Sub-baron Darylking and Lady Pattilane, however, seized on Dalbry's status as a renowned art critic, and they debated the merits of metaphors and imagery in bird paintings.

Reeger strolled around, grumbling and prickly, which guaranteed that he did not have to engage in conversation. He had soaked his jerkin and trousers so that the mud and manure stains were less obvious, and his oily dark hair stood up in clumps, still damp.

Cullin knew that Reeger felt most comfortable when he was

miserable, and thus able to complain. Therefore, the present banquet gave him an opportunity to be very comfortable indeed.

Barrels of peanuts-in-the-shell had been set out as finger food for the attendees while they conversed about art and practiced their criticism. They reached into the barrels, pulled out the fresh peanuts, cracked them between thumb and forefinger, and tossed the shells right on the floor in a display of disdain for the scullery maids who would have to sweep up afterward.

At last, ready to begin the festivities, Longjohn strode up onto the dais to his throne at the head of the banquet table. He clapped his hands for attention, but the conversation droned on. At the other end of the hall, Captain Johnson crashed his sword against his metal shield, which served as an effective dinner bell.

Longjohn shouted into the waning conversations. "I brought you all here because you are connoisseurs of fine art."

"Or at least connoisseurs of peanut dishes," said Highduke Lessa, close enough for Cullin to hear.

"We will begin with a small banquet, merely seven courses. You will enjoy the delicious and delicate flavors of imports from the New Lands."

In involuntary commentary, Reeger's stomach growled like an angry bear.

"But that is merely a warmup for the main event!" Longjohn continued. "We are here to celebrate not the culinary arts, but the fine arts. The landscape arts! After the banquet tonight, we will unveil a tremendous masterpiece, a towering new work by the famed artist, Affonyl NoLastName."

The noble guests applauded, to show that they, too, had heard of the eccentric artist.

Servants escorted the patrons to their assigned seats at the table. Dalbry had an honored position near the king, but Cullin was relegated to a satellite table at the back reserved for executive assistants. As a mere artistic engineer, Reeger sat at the end of the table as well. Other guests chose to leave vacant seats on either side of him, on account of his unappetizing odor.

The banquet began with tureens of fish-head soup with floating peanuts, followed by fish-fin soup (sans peanuts), trays of oysters (to

Reeger's delight), roast fish smothered in peanut sauce, then steamed crabs, and other treats.

Cullin ate, and ate, and ate, and the courses kept coming. Captains Johnson and Jameson took turns sneaking a quick bite in the midst of their guardly duties before going back to their positions outside the banquet hall.

Reeger shoveled plateful after plateful of food into his mouth, but his stomach continued to gurgle. He grimaced and stood up. As servants entered with even more courses, he looked over at Cullin. A sheen of sweat glistened on his forehead. "I'm going to the garderobe."

Knowing the protocol at royal banquets, Cullin was alarmed. "You can't leave until the last course is served!"

"My intestines say otherwise."

Cullin was worried that some of the nobles and monarchs might consider this an insult. "But why do you have to go now?"

On his way out, Reeger bent down and whispered urgently, "I have to go now, lad, because something is coming out whether I want it to or not!" He stalked down a side corridor in search of the nearest garderobe.

Throughout the meal, the nobles discussed art in scornful and insulting tones, sneering at the works of creators who had become popular. Some critics derided commercial art that was so simple even mere commoners could understand it. Highduke Lessa and Lady Pattilane nearly came to blows over a disagreement about the use of grapes in still-life paintings.

At the head of the table, King Longjohn squirmed with anticipation for the grand unveiling.

Just as the dessert course began, but before the coffee could be served, a clamor arose in the hall, a clatter of weapons and armor, screams of terror, and a clash of swords.

The orc army charged in.

CHAPTER

EIGHTEEN

C ullin nearly choked on his crab-and-peanut cakes when the monstrous invaders boiled into the throne hall. The orcs roared, smashing heavy clubs against the stone walls.

The brutes had broad chests, studded leather armor, and tight metal helmets that made their rounded greenish faces look squished. Some of them swung spear-tipped pikes; others wielded spiked maces. They bellowed out an incomprehensible challenge, revealing mouths full of crooked teeth and thick, purple tongues.

Cullin knew something was wrong as soon as the first burly orc charged into the throne room. Jameson, or maybe it was Johnson, drew his flimsy-looking sword to defend his king, and the orc's battle axe cleaved the soldier in two, armor and all.

The lords and ladies rose from their chairs and began to scream. One orc tore a colorful yarn dreamcatcher from its display on the stone wall and stomped it under his feet, but his boots became tangled in the yarn, and the orc sprawled on his face. Mortally embarrassed, the brute tore the yarn to shreds. He climbed back to his feet, then decapitated the nearest man-at-arms who had witnessed his clumsiness.

A serving woman had just entered the dining hall with a tureen of hot chocolate chowder. She dumped the soup onto a charging orc, making him sputter and claw at his singed face. Behind her, another servant tried the same defense, but she carried only a tray of finger peanut-butter sandwiches, which proved less effective than the hot chowder.

King Longjohn lurched up from his throne. "But tonight is our unveiling!"

Captain Johnson, or maybe it was Jameson, and other men-at-arms rushed forward to face the orc onslaught. They were mowed down.

At the far end of the table, near the throne, Dalbry pulled Subbaron Darylking, Lady Pattilane, Lowduke McCowan, and Highduke Lessa behind him as he mounted a brave defense. But he was dressed as an art critic rather than a knight in shining armor, and although the pen was said to be mightier than the sword, Dalbry clearly wished he had a sword.

Longjohn snatched up a fork and a butter knife and attempted to hold his own. Meanwhile, the castle servants retreated to the kitchens.

Another round of the king's guards rushed into the throne room, closing their helmet visors and raising their shields and swords. Spiked enemy clubs smashed into cuirasses, shields, and shoulder plates, leaving large dents. Several dropped to lie in pools of blood like half-opened cans.

Cullin ducked under his side table and huddled next to the chair legs. He could hear shouts and war cries echoing through the halls as more invading orcs surged into the castle. Though his instinct was to run, he changed his mind when two of his table companions scurried to a nearby side entrance, where orcs minced them up, as if preparing yet another banquet course.

At the far end of the hall, Cullin spotted Dalbry fighting to the best of his ability with all the cutlery at hand. The knight managed to stick the tines of a fork into an orc's cheek and followed with a soup spoon down the enemy's throat. Alas, he was woefully underweaponed. Dalbry hurled a gravy boat filled with peanut sauce, then swung a dining chair back and forth to drive away the orcs, but the army surrounded him.

Cullin scuttled away from the side table and pressed his back against the stone wall, trying to find a defensible position. He had fought dragons and he had performed legendary (and imaginary) feats that were sung widely by minstrels. But right now he doubted he would survive his first art unveiling.

He wanted to protect Affonyl outside under the tarpaulin, but he couldn't do that unless he escaped the massacre. This was sure to be his last banquet.

Unexpectedly, he felt the stone wall shift behind him, and he stumbled backward into a hidden doorway that opened to reveal shadowy tunnels behind it.

Spam was there, her expression urgent. "Squirrel, come with me! I'll get you out of here."

"Only Affonyl gets to call me Squirrel. It's her pet name for me."

The maid huffed. "You want to wait out there while I think of another rodent nickname? Or do you want me to save your ass?"

Cullin watched an orc decapitate one of the last remaining guards.

"Squirrel is fine. You can save my ass."

He had seen no sign of Reeger since he'd gone to the garderobe. Dalbry and the rest of the nobles were swarmed by orcs, but at least they remained alive. The brutes seemed intent on taking them prisoner.

Suddenly, the orcs let out a gasp of awe, even a shudder of fear. In the midst of their mayhem, an ominous-looking man entered wearing a red leather robe, pointy shoulder pads, and an ugly skull-like helmet with blazing golden eyes.

"Ugnarok!" one of the orcs yelled, and the rest of them took up the chant. "Ugnarok! Ugnarok!"

Cullin turned to Spam. "In fact, let's go right now." They ducked into the passageway and were swallowed up by the dank shadows.

The girl shoved the door closed and fastened the latch. "Come on, we'll be safe enough here."

"Then we have to save the castle and rescue the captives," Cullin said.

Spam huffed. "I'll let you figure out those details by yourself."

CHAPTER
NINETEEN

Huddled under the tarp next to Rock in Its Natural State, Affonyl had time to think. She was satisfied with the meat pie, apple, and peanut butter—which made her wonder if peanut butter would go well on an apple.

Knowing the banquet was going on, and on, inside the castle, the former princess waited for her big debut, a little lonely and a little bored, but she would have been much more bored if she had to make chit-chat and endure noble conversation. She wished Squirrel could have stayed out here with her, but since this extravagant scheme was her idea, she wanted it to go off as planned.

By now, as Dalbry's executive assistant, Cullin would be pretending to be interested in the prattle of noble art snobs. Perhaps, the young man was wishing he was out here with her under the tarpaulin.

During her father's banquets, she had killed time by imagining how different her life might be if she were a person instead of a princess. When Cullin and Dalbry had come to court as brave dragon slayers, they inspired her to follow her dream. She wanted to be a naturalist, an alchemist, or at least a footloose explorer—rather than being forced to marry the evil Duke Kerrl. So she had rigged up a dragon-like blast with explosive powder and escaped her turret bedchamber, running off to find her fortune....

Now, under the tarp, she looked up at the looming slab of rock balanced on the artisanal mast, waiting for Longjohn's big reveal. Her first unveiling!

After dark, when the thick fog rolled in, Affonyl undid one of the ropes to raise the canvas and get a breath of fresh air. She could smell salt and seaweed, and the night chill raised goosebumps on her skin. Her peasant dress wasn't terribly warm, and she thought it would be nice inside the castle by a roaring fire. Maybe she could sneak some of the banquet leftovers or at least one of the dessert offerings—chocolate mousse or cheesecake.

She knew Cullin would save her a plate, hoping she would smile at him, or ignore him, or tease him. He considered any interaction at all from her was flirting. Even though he knew she was a princess, he thought of her as a person, and she liked that in a young man.

When Affonyl looked out at the fog-shrouded castle now, though, she heard an unexpectedly furious clamor, stomping boots, the metallic clang of weapons. An army of ugly helmeted creatures charged up the road and crashed through the castle gates.

Orcs! She remembered the hideous skeletons in the graveyard that had devalued the property in Longjohn's new subdivision, Serfdom Sunrise Acres.

Roars and screams erupted from inside the castle, but she was trapped out here. Behind the orc army came a dangerous-looking sorcerer who strode along, accompanied by smoke and crackling sparks. He passed through the arched doorway and into the mayhem, as if he already owned the castle.

Affonyl suddenly thought about her friends Reeger, Dalbry— Cullin! She ducked back under the canvas and secured it until she could figure out what to do. Fortunately, none of the invaders decided to explore the side courtyard. She hoped the orcs were not here to attend the great unveiling.

CHAPTER

TWENTY

After spending half an hour of quality time in the public garderobe down the hall, Reeger felt light on his feet again. He had added to the general miasma that roiled up from the deep pit beneath the sturdy wooden seat, but he was glad for a few moments of peace away from the interminable art talk. Although he was disappointed they hadn't served those interesting inland oysters, Reeger had discovered a fondness for peanuts.

Sitting in the uncomfortable banquet chair and listening to the drone of conversation, Reeger had endured each course, without the benefit of training in etiquette. His clothing was still damp and itchy, but no one could say he hadn't properly bathed for the event. The extensive choices in silverware and cutlery baffled him. Rather than risking the incorrect implement, and thus drawing a reprimand from stern protocol practitioners, he had decided the safest course was to eat with his hands.

Etiquette or no etiquette, however, he had needed to answer an urgent call of nature. Finally, Reeger used the double-ply corncobs to complete his business and clean up.

He wasn't anxious to get back. Dalbry, Cullin, and Affonyl had the plan under control. Cullin was a good kid, eager to do whatever chores he was assigned, even the scary ones, even the dirty ones, and Reeger was helping him become a well-rounded young man of the Middle Ages.

He had grown fond of the former princess, too, though she'd been annoying at first, with an air of princessy arrogance about her. But now that she was part of the team, her upbringing offered new opportunities beyond the usual dragon business schtick—even larger con jobs, such as this one with King Longjohn. Reeger was willing to try new things.

When he'd diverted himself in the garderobe for as long as he could justify, Reeger decided that the smell in the closed garderobe was enough to drive him out into the open hall. He pulled up his still-damp and still-stained trousers, tied the rope belt around his waist, and opened the door. He braced himself for court finery again.

He was not prepared for an invading orc army.

The ugly brutes stormed through the castle like drunken bears armed with dangerous weapons. They careened into one another, grabbed torches from sconces, smashed fists against the stone walls, or victims when they could find them. Servants ran away screaming. One lord bolted into a side passageway with his hair on fire and an orc lumbering after him, waving a torch.

Reeger cursed under his breath. "Bloodrust and battlerot!" He grabbed his hip, but he had left his dagger with the cutlery at the banquet table.

At the entrance to the banquet hall, two of King Longjohn's men-at-arms tried to defend themselves, but the orcs used maces and battleaxes to smash, splinter, and destroy the flimsy shields. Then they ran the defenders through before stomping on them.

The orcs laughed as blood squirted out the victims' ears and noses to make random patterns on the stone walls. This discovery led to other artistic endeavors, stomping and watching the spray, but the orcs soon grew bored of their colorful projects and got back to overthrowing the castle.

Before any of the invaders saw him, Reeger ducked back into the garderobe and pulled the door shut. It was a small confined chamber with a wide wooden seat and a hole down into the shit pit and sewer tunnels. He decided he was more likely to survive the pit than an orc army.

The wooden seat covering the hole was fixed tightly in place. He groaned and struggled, trying to tear it off so he would have enough room to slip down the hole. Finally, he stomped on the garderobe seat until the wood splintered and broke. He pried away the sharp pieces, leaving a jagged hole.

Reeger had a burly chest and square hips, but he swung his feet down into the hole, squirmed until his waist passed through. Gripping the splintered edges of the seat, he lowered himself down to where the stink was even stronger. He held on by his fingers, bracing himself for the long drop.

Above, he heard the garderobe door slam open, kicked in by an orc's thick boot—and that was enough incentive for Reeger. He let go and dropped down into the muck far below.

He had done many vile things in his life, but this ranked among the most rank. At the last moment, he pressed his lips together and covered his face with his palm. He squelched into the muck, which came to just above his waist, but it was thick enough to make movement slow and laborious. At least it broke his fall.

Looking up, he saw the jagged circle of light from the splintered toilet seat, and heard a groaning, wheezing orc in the chamber. The sound was not an angry war cry, but rather like intestinal distress.

"Urrr. That's a big hole," said the orc. "At least it has splinters."

To his horror, Reeger watched the light above eclipsed by fleshy greenish cheeks. He urgently sloshed away from the direct line of the garderobe above, desperate to escape before the bombardment began.

Beneath the garderobe, the sewage tunnel opened into other drainage passageways, and Reeger followed the path of least excrement. After paying attention to Affonyl's talk about natural science and his own understanding of engineering concepts, Reeger was well aware that shit flowed downhill.

He made his way in search of an escape, fleeing from the ominous plops behind him.

CHAPTER

TWENTY-ONE

The winding secret passages took Cullin and Spam away from the banquet massacre. He was still shaking after his near-orc experience. Even through the stone walls, they could hear the sounds of the melee, the clash of weapons, the bellowing grunts of orcs, and the screams of victims.

Carrying a lone torch, the girl rushed him along, but he pulled her to a stop. "We've got to do something!"

Spam gave him a quizzical look. "We're doing the only thing we can—we're escaping."

"But the orcs are killing everyone! We've got to save our friends."

Spam huffed. "I don't have any friends—except maybe you. You're nice to me."

"What about all the castle staff, the kitchen workers, the servants?"

"Just work acquaintances. They don't include me in social activities outside the castle. They've never once invited me to Margarita Night or Taco Tuesday."

"You're only eleven," Cullin pointed out.

"If I'm old enough to spend all day scrubbing seagull poop off of statues, then I'm old enough to join them for tacos after work."

"All right, I can sense your resentment, but *I've* got friends. I need to know whether Dalbry is alive." He gasped. "Wait—Reeger! He went to the privy just before the invasion."

Spam huffed. "He'll have to take care of himself. This castle doesn't have very defensible toilets."

Cullin listened to the distorted echoes that came from various alcoves. "Please?"

She considered, then pulled him along. They climbed moss-covered stone stairs, chased a family of evacuating rats out of the way, and finally reached a cramped alcove with two small holes drilled through the stone blocks. Spam peeked through. "This gives a good view of the banquet hall. I often watch from here so I can tell when it's time to clear the dishes and bring in the coffee." Her voice held a hint of pride. "We know everything going on in King Longjohn's throne room. It's a matter of national security."

"Would have been better to have security on the *outside*, in case an orc army charged up the road."

He stepped up to the second peephole, squinting through, and realized that these holes were drilled through the eyes of the ornately framed noble portraits.

The throne room was a disaster with smashed chairs and bodies strewn about—like the aftermath of a drunken fraternity-house brawl in a local tavern. Guards, castle staff, and art critics had been slain. Only three guards were still alive; they had been disarmed and pressed up against the stone wall. A few kitchen workers and serving maidens hid under the heavy table, unnoticed by the invading orcs, who did not tend to look anywhere but the obvious places.

Cullin turned to see the opposite end of the banquet table. A few lords and ladies had been taken prisoner, and he let out a sigh of relief when he saw Dalbry among them, alive and apparently uninjured. The old knight had been captured along with the sub-baron, the midduke, the highduke, and the lowduke, as well as their noble significant others.

If Sir Dalbry had been wearing his armor and carrying his sword, he would likely have fought to the death, hoping to inspire another dramatic verse in Nightingale Bob's songs. Cullin was glad to see he was a prisoner instead.

He didn't think orcs would hold hostages for ransom, though. The complexities of sending letters of demand to adjoining duchies and baronies, along with delicately hacked-off fingers or ears as proof of life, were clearly more steps than they could handle.

But the brutes were commanded by the evil red-robed sorcerer with blazing eyes and skull-like helmet. "Ugnarok, Ugnarok!" the orcs chanted as the wizard-mage approached the throne.

On his great seat, King Longjohn pulled his long legs and knobby knees up against his chest like a dying insect folding itself up.

"I will take your throne, son of Grog." Ugnarok loomed over him. "And I will take your treasure."

"I will never surrender," Longjohn said with quavering defiance, "not while I still have loyal men at arms who will fight and die in my name."

Against the far wall, the three disarmed guards struggled to break free. With a sneer, the wizard-mage reached out his gauntleted hand and flicked two fingers. Lightning bolts shot out, heating the breast-plates and helmets red hot until the poor guards fell dead on the flagstones.

"Perhaps you should reassess your situation, Longjohn," the evil sorcerer said, "now that the parameters have changed."

Ugnarok strode about the ransacked banquet hall. He was half a head taller even than the lanky king, and his fearsome helmet added an inch or two. He spoke in a voice that made Cullin's skin crawl. "You are renowned for your appreciation of art, King Longjohn—much more cultured than your father. Now, I can appreciate art, too, and there's a special piece I'd like to commission."

He gestured to the orcs, who seized the gangly ruler and dragged him off his throne. The wizard-mage considered the wall behind the throne. "Yes, a perfect place. Bring manacles! Hang him up there."

Longjohn squirmed and struggled, but the muscular invaders kept him under control. Two orcs balanced on wooden stepstools as they pounded manacle anchors into the stone blocks above the throne. Once the chains were in place, the brutes suspended the king high on the wall, where he dangled, his wrists and ankles bound in iron, his limbs spread out. No matter how much he twitched and squirmed, he was going nowhere.

With an evil laugh, Ugnarok regarded the new piece on the wall. "Excellent! This is my unveiling tonight." He pointed toward the wall behind which Cullin and Spam were hiding. "That painting! Bring it here."

The two ducked away from the peepholes, terrified that they had been spotted. Orcs tore down the portrait in its ornate frame, then stomped out the canvas before carrying the empty frame back to where King Longjohn hung miserably. As Ugnarok watched, they hoisted the frame and squared it around Longjohn's head. Though it didn't fit properly, the frame did provide a clear artistic boundary.

"The first work of art for my new kingdom!" said the wizard-mage. He turned away from the pathetic king and gazed toward his orc soldiers. "Now, we begin the subjugation."

"And the treasure!" shouted one of the orcs. "Find the treasure!"

Ugnarok nodded his ugly helmeted head. "And the treasure."

CHAPTER

TWENTY-TWO

Dalbry missed his suit of armor. Over the years, his shining steel had been a reliable best friend. It was far more than just a costume to impress potential customers of his dragon-slaying abilities. He had a close relationship with his polished helmet, cuirass, greaves, gauntlets, gorget, vambrace, pauldrons, and other pieces whose names he couldn't remember. They fit him like a glove. Better yet, they fit him like a well-tailored suit of armor.

While traveling with his companions, he often slept in his armor on the ground, though the metal did transmit the cold on winter nights. He would buff the steel dry after a rainstorm, scour off any rust spots, and follow all the maintenance steps in the Knight's Manual. His trusty sword was also an important part of the ensemble.

He and his companions had practically invented the dragon business, concocting a convincing story that was little more than a figment of props and imagination. Now, however, surviving an invasion of bloodthirsty orcs led by an evil wizard-mage was an entirely different situation. As an art critic, he was far less impressively armed than a brave knight.

The rambunctious invaders smashed and murdered, getting out of hand even for orcs, even though Ugnarok commanded them to show restraint. They killed not only the king's guards—which was generally acceptable in a monster invasion—but also many of the castle staff, the very people who were needed to clean up the bloody mess.

Finally, to prevent them from killing more noble guests, the wizard-mage used a magic thunderclap to smash helmeted heads together. "Hostages! I need important hostages."

Thanks to his fancy outfit, Dalbry appeared to be an important personage, and he was herded to the "visiting noble" side of the banquet table. Sub-baron Darylking, Lowduke McCowan, Midduke Blande, and Highduke Lessa, along with an assortment of effete princelings and viscountesses, were gathered in a terrified clot of blueblood. They were overwhelmed.

Yes, Dalbry missed his armor.

To his relief, he noticed that Cullin was not among the hacked corpses on the floor, although he hadn't seen how the young man had gotten away. Reeger had also managed to disappear, so Dalbry assumed they were safe. Therefore, he was on his own, and without his trusty sword he could do little more than fling sharp criticism at the orcs.

After Longjohn had been hung on the wall in a frame, Wizard-Mage Ugnarok loomed with eyes glowing through his fierce helmet. He raised both hands and clenched his gloves until evil lightning crackled from his fingertips.

"I have already usurped the throne of King Longjohn, and with these hostages I will subsume all the local kingdoms and queendoms and principalities. I will force those leaders to surrender to my bloody and benevolent rule." He chuckled. "No joke!"

Following suit, the orcs rumbled with laughter. Their burly leader grunted, "Yup, so we'll just hold them here, and not eat them."

"No, don't eat them," Ugnarok chided. The orcs shuffled their booted feet on the bloody floor. "At least not yet. We will ransack the castle until we find the great treasure. In the meantime, we will send letters to the neighboring kingdoms and secure our victory."

"And eat them later?" Borc asked.

"That depends on how fast we receive the ransom," said Ugnarok.

Midduke Blande's lip was trembling as he whispered to Dalbry. "The art world would be devastated by your loss, sir."

"I'm not lost yet," said Dalbry, "nor do I plan to be."

"Take them to the dungeons!" the wizard-mage commanded.

The orcs surrounded the hostage nobles, bumping them along, arguing over which corridor to use and which door led to the lower levels. Since none of them knew the layout of the castle, they dispatched scouts until finally one of them located the dungeons and came back to lead the way.

The captive nobles were led away. Dalbry kept a low profile, glancing from side to side as they were herded down steep steps and into tunnels. The lords and ladies were dismayed to see the rat-infested cells with rock walls covered in dripping slime. Only a few low-wattage torches flickered in the wall sconces.

The orcs shoved them all into the largest cell. McCowan groaned in dismay. "There's not enough furniture for all of us."

"Economy lodgings," snarled an orc as he slammed the cell door shut. Dalbry grasped the rusty iron bars and watched the brutes march away. Rats squeaked along the cracks in the floor, sniffing at the mold.

"Do you think we might have to eat rodents to survive?" asked Lady Pattilane.

"There are plenty of leftovers from the banquet upstairs," said Darylking, "but they'll go bad after a few days without proper refrigeration."

Highduke Lessa daintily sat on the wooden bench. "To be honest, I am glad to be here in a safe space. Did you see how violent those orcs were? Prone to tantrums and uncontrolled anger! Who knows what they might do if we were alone up there. These bars protect us—it's like a panic room."

"Yes," said Blande, "if we were running around without an entourage, we'd be in danger."

A pale, thin princeling agreed. "We'll make the best of things. We are nobility, after all."

"Yes, we'll make the best of it," Dalbry said, but he was already considering escape plans. He didn't know where Cullin, Reeger, or Affonyl might be, but he was sure his companions wouldn't abandon him. A bigger plan must be brewing.

Surreptitiously, he reached into his trouser pocket, found the magic sack of dried apricots. He worked the string loose and slipped out one of the orange fruits.

He had enough to eat for the time being, although the magic sack would need to be replenished. In the meantime, he just had to figure out how to trick and overthrow an orc army and an evil wizard.

CHAPTER

TWENTY-THREE

The clammy sea fog was like a noose strangling the headlands. In the harbor town below, the merchant ships, portside businesses and local school district declared a "fog day" and hunkered down. All daily business with the castle was suspended, because no one wanted to go out into the weather.

Thus, no one noticed that their kingdom had been invaded and the castle was under new management.

Hidden inside the secret passageways, Cullin and Spam kept watch through the peepholes. From their perspective, the entire castle had gone into lockdown, thanks to the orc invasion. Patrols marched up and down the winding corridors, frequently getting lost in the labyrinth.

Even though the thick stone blocks muffled any noise, Cullin kept his voice to a whisper. "What are we going to do now? We're trapped in here!"

"Plenty of emergency exits," Spam said. "We can sneak out anytime we like. I bet most of the staff have already headed out in search of alternative employment."

"You mean even with all these orcs, we can just ... get out and run away?" Cullin couldn't believe that was a viable option.

"If that's what you intend to do, Squirrel."

"Don't call me—" he said, then paused, deciding not to remind her of their tacit agreement on names.

"It's a big castle with lots of empty halls."

On the other side of a peephole, a lumbering orc strode down the corridor, plunking his spiked club on the floor in a delicate rhythm. *Bump, bump, bump.* He paused in his tracks, as if he had heard their whispered voices. His piggish eyes became alert and wary.

"Quiet!" Spam said, even though Cullin had already ceased talking.

The orc turned in circles, trying to find where the voices were coming from. Cullin watched through the peephole, ready to escape down the secret passageway in case the orc bashed through the solid wall to get to them.

Oddly, though, the brute looked not just stupefied, but frightened. He twitched at a faint noise from the other side of the hall, then scuttled away in the opposite direction, dragging his spiked club along the floor with a more rapid tempo. *Bump, bump, bump, bump.*

Cullin let out a sigh of relief. "He didn't see us. I think he was afraid."

"I doubt he would've been afraid if he *did* see us, Squirrel."

Cullin knew the girl was using that name on purpose, but now it made him think about the former princess, since it was her nickname for him. "Affonyl still must be hiding under the tarp for the great unveiling. I hope the orcs haven't found her!" Cullin felt the urgent need growing within him. "We need to rescue her! She's delicate, you know—a former princess. And she's a person, too."

"I know a side exit, and I just oiled the hinges last week, so it won't creak." Spam grabbed his arm and led the way. "But I'm not convinced she needs rescuing. Affonyl seems to know how to handle herself—just like me."

They slipped through the lower door behind a hedge and emerged into the side courtyard. The thick, gray tarp covering Rock in Its Natural State looked like a big tent. Ducking low, even though no one could see him through the mist, Cullin hurried forward and called in a loud whisper. "Affonyl! Are you in there?"

The tarp rustled, and the former princess poked her head out from underneath the canvas. "I'm assuming the unveiling ceremony is postponed?"

"Indefinitely," said Spam.

Feeling exposed even with the fog, Cullin and the scullery maid ducked under the tarp to join Affonyl. "I saw the orc army coming up—I counted fifty or so—then I heard the battle. King Longjohn's soldiers fought bravely, I assume? How many orcs survived?"

Cullin thought fast. "Um, about fifty, I think."

Affonyl sighed. "What about Dalbry? And Reeger? Are they all right?"

"Reeger disappeared, and we haven't found him. Dalbry and the other nobles were captured. Wizard-Mage Ugnarok is holding them hostage, expecting a large ransom."

"And Dalbry's with them?" Affonyl's face was troubled. "Who's going to pay a ransom for an art critic?"

"All those snarky reviews are going to come back to bite him," said Spam.

Affonyl looked up at the slab of rock balanced above them, making their shelter like a cave overhang. "We can't stay here, even though we have a solid roof over our heads."

Spam had a good suggestion. "We can run away to the town, catch a ship to the New Lands, and make a new life for ourselves. As a scullery maid, my skill set is in high demand."

Cullin shook his head. "We can't leave! Our friends are in there. Dalbry needs to be rescued, and nobody's even seen Reeger."

The ragamuffin girl blinked her eyes at Cullin. "Then I guess I should stay here with you and make myself useful."

"We'd appreciate the help," he said, suddenly wondering if she was flirting with him. "You're the only one who knows all the castle passages."

"I can take us back inside the castle, easy as pie," said Spam. "We can spy on Ugnarok through the peepholes, keep track of the orc movements."

"But what about Sir Dalbry?" asked Cullin.

"He's probably in the dungeons. I know the back door there, too."

"Time to make a plan, then." Affonyl still had half the apple left from before and some scrapings of peanut butter from the jar. She divided the apple, and they spread the sweet goo on the slices of fruit, agreeing that apple and peanut butter was also an excellent combination.

The young man felt determination rise within him. "Yes, we'll save Dalbry, find Reeger, overthrow the wizard-mage, and defeat the orc army." He squared his shoulders. The peanut butter had made him feel brave.

"I don't like to get involved in politics," Affonyl said. "The art world is already malicious, full of backstabbing and sniping. Once we find our friends, maybe we should just get away and forget about steps three and four above."

"Sounds like a plan," said Spam.

CHAPTER
TWENTY-FOUR

E ven if the castle was infested with orcs, Affonyl decided the dank secret passages sounded preferable to the chilly fog and the constant drip of water from the underside of the tarp. Tonight, for a change, she might even have preferred her old princessy quarters, but she would settle for staying behind the scenes.

Spam hurried them through the hidden hedge entrance. Cullin moved ahead, pushing cobwebs out of the way. "We need to make sure we're not discovered. The wizard-mage can zap people with lightning. He cooked three men-at-arms right in their plate armor. And he hung King Longjohn on the wall like a piece of art!"

"Art is subjective," Affonyl said, letting out a sigh. "I can't believe an orc invasion spoiled my first grand unveiling."

"It doesn't look like we'll get our payment either," Cullin added. "I doubt Ugnarok values landscape art as much as King Longjohn does."

Affonyl said, "If we could liquidate his art collection, we could cover all our expenses. Longjohn is rich in assets."

Spam huffed. "If the king is so rich, then he could afford to pay the kitchen staff more than minimum wage."

Cullin remained fidgety and anxious to do something. "I'm more worried about our friends."

"Friends are worth their weight in gold," the former princess said with a sage nod. "And proverbs are often quoted by people who have no gold."

"Our first step is reconnaissance." Spam led them on with her torchlight. "Let's see what Ugnarok is doing in the throne room before we plan our next move."

At the observation alcove, they took turns peering through the peepholes. Tall and fearsome, Ugnarok loomed in front of the throne, gloating. His golden eyes blazed through the eye holes of his scary helmet, and his thunderous voice boomed out. "The castle is mine now, King Longjohn—mine! I will settle into your royal bedroom, as soon as I have the orcs change the sheets and comforter."

The orcs grumbled and snorted at the prospect of being assigned mere housework, but Borc lashed out in his guttural voice. "Only the bravest orcs are chosen to change the royal sheets!" This mollified the brutes, and soon they were fighting over who would be picked for the assignment.

By now, the orc invaders had dragged away the banquet victims, leaving long smears of blood on the floor. They carried body after body to the main balcony and dumped them into the lower court-yard, where the carcasses could ripen in the fog until they were ready for eating. The three spell-sizzled guards were kept in the pantry, because they'd already been steamed in their armor, and the precooked meat would do for a late-night snack. Two orc soldiers came into the room with a broom and a mop to clean the blood-stains and sweep up the cracked peanut shells scattered throughout the hall.

Jittering in his manacles on the wall, Longjohn moaned. "Please don't take my artwork!"

Ugnarok's ghastly mouth twisted in a sneer. "*You* are the artwork, now—no joke!" Arrogant and victorious, he walked down the cluttered banquet table. The leftover dishes were cold now, but Cullin knew the wizard-mage could always heat them up through the use of magical thermodynamics.

"I'll seize everything you have, your riches, your merchant fleet. I will take your imported luxury items from the New Lands." He scooped a handful of whole peanuts from the bowl at the king's seat.

"Including your peanut gold!" He cracked the shells and spilled the nuts into his palm. "They are mine now, Longjohn. Everything is mine!" He tossed the peanuts into his mouth and crunched away. "Interesting taste."

Behind the peepholes, the three watched, holding their breath in fear and horror.

Gloating as he stood before the dangling king on the wall, Ugnarok tauntingly ate another handful of peanuts, shells and all. His vengeful laugh grew louder.

Borc and the orcs joined in the laughter, grunting and chuckling. King Longjohn whimpered.

Ugnarok coughed.

He choked and spat out all the peanuts. He coughed again and clutched his throat with a gauntleted hand. His mouth opened and closed. "Can't ... breathe!"

The orcs imitated him, thinking it was part of the performance.

The wizard-mage thrashed, wheezed, and coughed some more. He made a *gakking* sound, with an undertone of gurgle. Drool ran from the corner of his mouth. He staggered backward, crashing into a chair. His blazing eyes seemed to bulge inside the helmet.

"What's happening?" Cullin whispered to his friends.

Affonyl squinted through the hole. "He's dying horribly, I think."

Spam snickered. "I've heard rumors about deadly peanut allergies, but I thought they were just old wives' tales."

The orcs backed away, frightened, not knowing what to do. A few bashed their spiked clubs against the floor, as if that would help. It didn't.

In his manacles, Longjohn yelled, "Get him some water, you fools!"

The orcs scrambled about. One yanked the mop out of a bucket and poured dirty water onto Ugnarok's head, but it did no good. The wizard-mage writhed and choked, grabbing his throat. He fell backward onto the banquet table, knocking the noodle and fish dishes aside.

Mouth open and tongue lolling out, he gasped a gurgling death rattle that went on and on.

"You could try giving him mouth-to-mouth resuscitation," said King Longjohn.

The orcs recoiled, sniveling and whimpering. "Poison!"

"A curse!" said another.

None of the orcs dared approach the wizard-mage, even after he lay still. "A curse," two more orcs said, building a consensus.

"Poison," repeated the first, but as the mutters increased, the vote tally tilted in favor of curses.

In the secret alcove, Affonyl's eyes held an impish gleam. She whispered in Cullin's ear, telling him what to say.

"I'm not going to say that!" he retorted. "You do it. It's your idea."

"I need a male voice, and you're the closest thing we've got."

"But what will that do?" Cullin asked.

Affonyl jabbed him in the ribs—endearingly, he thought. "Just say it, Squirrel! And watch what happens."

Cullin cupped his hands around his mouth. In as loud and haunting a voice as he could manage, he said through the observation hole, "This castle is cursed! You will all die if you remain here."

His voice cracked at the end, and he hoped the orcs would attribute that to supernatural terror rather than lingering puberty.

After hearing the unexpected ominous voice coming from nowhere, even King Longjohn wet himself in terror.

The orcs fled the throne room in a panic, making such a loud clatter that no one heard Affonyl chuckling from behind the peephole.

CHAPTER

TWENTY-FIVE

After a night in the crowded and cold dungeons, Dalbry and his fellow captives contemplated their future.

"King Longjohn never skimps on decoration," said Lowduke McCowan, "but the miserability index down here is quite high."

"Certainly up to code, though," said Sub-baron Darylking. "Exceeds the minimum requirements for clamminess, slime on the walls, and rat population. Standards accepted throughout the many kingdoms and principalities."

"Aren't there rules for how prisoners are supposed to be treated?" asked McCowan. "Three meals a day, plus tea and maybe a midnight snack."

"I didn't even bring a change of clothes," sighed Highduke Lessa.

"Maybe the brutes will deliver fresh sheets," said Blande.

Dalbry surreptitiously chewed on a dried apricot. "You'd better hope the orcs don't get hungry," he said. "Because when they do, they'll want a light meal of human flesh."

"Ewww," said Pattilane.

"They are orcs after all, my dear." Darylking patted her hand.

Sir Dalbry wasn't worried about that just yet, though. After the bloody invasion, the orcs would have plenty of fresh meat for quite a while.

Blande rattled the iron cell door. "The bars will protect us from those monsters."

"The orcs have the keys," the knight pointed out, which created an anxious murmur among the prisoners, until Highduke Lessa reminded them that orcs often had trouble using keys.

Dalbry didn't think his dungeon companions grasped the situation at hand. Wizard-Mage Ugnarok clearly intended to use them for ransom, and that protected the captives somewhat—at least until the invaders realized that Dalbry the art critic wasn't worth much.

"If only there was a way for you to use your critical art skills to get us out of here," said Blande.

The other nobles had raised Dalbry to a level of critical acclaim that he had never before experienced, but in his heart he was still a brave knight and legendary hero. His responsibility was clear, according to the Knight's Manual.

"I have a confession to make, since these may be our last hours." He leaned back against the slime-encrusted dungeon wall. "I'm not actually an art critic. I am, in fact, a knight in shining armor, a brave dragon slayer. Perhaps you've heard of me? Brave Sir Dalbry?" He raised his eyebrows. "I'm featured in many songs by Nightingale Bob and other minstrel cover bands."

The nobles conferred with one another, but being art snobs, none of them listened to popular music.

"Very well," he sighed. "I most recently defeated the monster pike in Queen Amnethia's lake, but word hasn't spread far and wide yet. I've been a kraken hunter, and I've scattered the bones of many dragons across the land. I slew an ogre once, and that's a tale that could entertain a group for many hours."

"Ever killed any orcs?" asked Blande.

He lowered his head. "No orcs ... not as of yet."

"Maybe you could break us free and battle your way out of here, slaying orcs right and left," said McCowan.

"You could kill that wizard-mage," said Lessa. The other captives agreed wholeheartedly.

Before Dalbry's To-Do List got any longer, he said, "At present, we must content ourselves with the tale of my ogre encounter." He settled back. "I usually have a band of helpers, you see, and I seem to be short staffed."

Just then he was startled to hear a whispered voice through a chink in the stone wall by his ear. "Dalbry, it's Cullin! And Affonyl's here with me, too."

A younger girl's voice said, "And Spam."

Surprised, he turned to face the slimy stones, pressing close to one of the cracks. "Cullin, lad! And the former princess! What are you doing inside the wall?"

"Behind the wall, actually. This castle has many secret passages."

The nobles in the cell muttered in surprise and asked so many questions that Dalbry couldn't hear the faint voice. He raised his hand for silence, then pressed his ear to the crack. "Are you safe, or are you trapped? Where is Reeger?"

"Haven't seen Reeger. The orcs have taken over the castle. King Longjohn is hung up on the wall."

The captives gasped and moaned. "The wizard-mage hung King Longjohn!"

"Hung in a decorative fashion. Even put a frame around him," answered Affonyl. "But there's even more good news."

"My, it's been a very busy day," Dalbry said. The prisoners crowded around the whisper hole to listen.

"The evil Ugnarok is dead," Cullin said. "He suffered an allergic reaction from the peanuts that he seized as spoils of war. The orcs are spooked, and they won't go near the body."

"Now is our chance!" said McCowan. "Brave Sir Dalbry, break us out of this cell, then rush through the castle, defeat all the orcs, and everyone can live happily ever after."

Dalbry frowned at the lowduke. "That's not a workable plan, given our current circumstances." He turned back to the wall. "Cullin, could you possibly let us into those secret passages? Surely there's room."

Whispers were exchanged behind the wall, and Cullin came back. "This particular dungeon cell doesn't have an emergency exit. We'd have to snatch the keys from one of the orcs."

"And that's not going to happen!" said the scullery maid's voice.

"Then, lad, we must rely on you and your companions," Dalbry said. "It's up to you to drive the orcs out of the castle."

The sounds behind the stone wall were less than enthusiastic.

Cullin's voice asked, "And how do we do that? There's fifty of them!"

An idea took shape in Dalbry's mind. "We must make an organized, step-by-step plan. Wizard-Mage Ugnarok was a fearsome enemy, but now you are merely facing an army of orcs. The odds are more in your favor."

"Merely!" Spam's voice scoffed. "Still fifty to one!"

"Fifty to three," Affonyl corrected.

Dalbry spoke more earnestly. "Regardless, the end result is that we must get rid of the orcs. Cullin, you made a good start after Ugnarok died, and we can build on that. Remember the key thing about orcs."

Silence held for a few moments as the companions conferred. "That orcs are stupid?" Cullin asked.

"True, but a more important detail is that orcs are *superstitious*, and they are particularly terrified of ghosts, because they can't *bash them*."

The voices whispered behind the wall, and Cullin said, "So, you want us to haunt the castle?"

"Yes, scare the orcs away. That would be quite acceptable," Dalbry said. The noble prisoners agreed.

Spam's voice interjected, "There are whisper holes and spy alcoves throughout the castle. We can use them! It's not a design flaw —it's a feature."

"Glad I could help," Dalbry said, feeling much more confident. "I shall be available for any further advice you require. Meanwhile, commence with the haunting."

All this talk about secret passageways and hidden catacombs inspires me.

The dripping water from the ceiling, the cold draft through the window casement, and the rain rattling against the glass makes me think about the remodeling I've done in my castle. It is a king's right, after all. A man's home is his castle, and a king's castle is his home. I can have whatever architectural design or embellishment I like.

"*Maurice, let's continue this story in a cozier place—my private den. We can relax together. Father and son.*"

"*What's wrong with my own room?*" *The boy looks at the still-life paintings on his wall, his lute, his comforter, his snacks.*

I rise to my feet. "*No, it's time I brought you into my private club.*"

"*You mean like a lodge? With funny hats and initiation ceremonies?*"

"*Nothing so special. Just a little place I call my own, where I can ponder kingly matters and do the special things that men consider so dear.*"

I walk along the bedroom wall, running my fingers against the stone blocks. I don't often use the passageway from the prince's private quarters, but I know it's here. Finally, I move aside one of his paintings —a watercolor with yellow sunflowers and a brown bunny. "*Ah, here it is!*"

I press the little keystone. When I hear the latch click, I push against the block. The secret stone door swings inward, grinding on the floor because the hinge is out of alignment from disuse.

Maurice springs off the bed. "*Wait! There are secret passages in our castle?*"

"*Son, there are secret passages in every castle. It's part of the design standards.*"

Curious, the boy comes over to join me. "*But I never knew about that.*"

"*Hence, the reason the passages are called secret. But there comes a time in a young man's life when his father must share secrets and teach him the facts of life.*" *I take a torch from the wall, leaving the lavender scented candles behind. I duck into the dank shadows, pausing a moment to get my bearings.* "*Follow me to my own special place.*"

Maurice is light on his feet, maybe from the court dance lessons the kingdom paid for. I trudge down the sloping corridor, find the left-hand passage and steep stairs. We head deep into the bowels of my castle until we arrive at my special den.

I open the creaking wooden door and step inside, shining the torch to make sure that everything is ready for us. I use the flame to light several candles. "*Here it is, son. My man cave.*"

Maurice notes the two leather overstuffed chairs, the card table where I have become an expert in playing solitaire, a humidor filled with the best cigars from the New Lands, a side table with a crystal decanter of imported brandy. A cubby shelf displays gaudy curios, keepsakes, and kitschy doodads that the queen won't let me display anywhere the public might see them.

"A man cave fit for a king," I say.

"But you are a king."

"Indeed I am, and I can do whatever I want."

I light a fire in the hearth, and soon a cheery orange glow fills the den, supplementing the smoky torchlight. Extra candles make the entire room feel welcoming. "Here, I can be my true self. You'll need to remember that, once you feel the true burdens of the throne."

"I'll have other people to manage the burdens of the throne," Maurice says, sounding too confident. "My tutors are giving me extensive lessons on delegation."

"Sometimes, a true ruler must bear the burdens himself." I sit back in the overstuffed chair and let out a sigh of relief. I make a show of pouring a goblet of brandy for myself and a smaller one for Maurice. The prince doesn't particularly like alcohol, but that is another one of the burdens of being a king. He will have to learn.

"I'll help make you a man, Maurice. I had to learn, and so must you." With great reverence, I open up the humidor and remove two cigars, thrusting one at the young prince.

"What do I do with this?" He gives it a quizzical look. "Eat it?"

"Have you never seen a cigar before?" I am astonished at his lack of education.

"I've ... heard of them."

"You stick it in your mouth, light it on fire, and inhale the smoke," I explain. "It's manly."

Maurice doesn't see the charm, but I help him go through the motions. He mumbles, "So, it's like a pipe, but without the intermediary equipment?"

"A far more efficient delivery mechanism for harmful substances. Our court naturalists have studied it extensively."

With one of the candles, I light the end and inhale deeply, but the tobacco is moist and doesn't catch fire easily, so I'm forced to use the more substantial flame of the torch. Finally, I have our cigars lit, and we sit puffing away, blowing blue-gray smoke into the confined man cave.

Maurice coughs and retches. His eyes water. His face turns green.

"Now you're getting it, son!" I draw another long breath, filling my lungs, and it is all I can do to suppress my own coughing fit. I won't embarrass myself in front of the prince.

"I feel sick," Maurice says.

"That's how you're supposed to feel." I draw another deep puff, then sip the brandy and let it burn inside my mouth.

Maurice asks in a miserable tone, "Does it ever get better?"

"My son, this is as good as it gets." I exhale a long curl of the reeking smoke. "We do it because we're not supposed to do it. Believe me, your mother would have a stern lecture for us if she knew."

"But you're the king," the boy says. "You can do whatever you want. Just issue a royal decree."

I swallow another sip of brandy, letting it burn all the way down. "Tell that to your mother."

I lounge back in the overstuffed chair. Maurice reluctantly takes the opposite seat. "Now then," I say, "back to our story."

CHAPTER

TWENTY-SIX

The big castle was an orc's dream come true, even though orcs didn't have extravagant dreams, thanks to their thick skulls and limited imaginations.

Borc the orc was now king. He had a throne and a little crown to prove it ... probably a treasure somewhere, if he could find it.

Not long ago his highest aspiration had been to pillage the land, burn a few villages, and have a good time with his friends. Then, in short order, he and his band had been recruited by an evil wizard-mage ... and through unexpected circumstances, Borc now found himself in possession of an entire castle, maybe even an entire kingdom. Now, that was a level of fame and power he had never imagined!

He just wished the castle wasn't cursed. That put a damper on the whole party.

After Ugnarok died horribly eating a mouthful of peanuts, the terrified orcs evacuated the throne room, leaving the bloodstains unmopped on the floor and banquet remnants scattered across the table. The wizard-mage's corpse sprawled where he had died, his ominous helmet staring up at where King Longjohn dangled on the wall, surrounded by a gilded but poorly sized frame.

The disgraced king tried to attract attention. "Don't forget about me!"

But the orcs retreated to the staff mess hall near the kitchens—a much more comfortable, dark, and smelly place. The orcs gathered, uneasy, their square teeth chattering as they whimpered about ghosts and poisons and curses.

They huddled around the long wooden table, reminiscing about their glory days and how much they had enjoyed roasting the innkeeper and his wife in the recently overrun village. Now, many of the orcs whined that they should have just stayed there. Jerx lamented the fact that they had left a lot of perfectly edible goats and sheep back in the village.

But Borc was their leader, and now he had to step up. At the head of the mess hall table, he smashed down his spiked club like banging a gavel to call a meeting to order. He roared at the top of his lungs, "We are orcs, not sissies!"

His companions flinched, but no one disputed the statement.

"We conquered this castle. Yup, Wizard-Mage Ugnarok tried to keep it for himself, but now he's dead—and good riddance!" Borc hawked up a wad of phlegm and spat on the table.

The orcs spat a hailstorm of mucous onto the splintered surface. "Good riddance!"

"Yup, this is my castle! I rule here now!" He pounded his chest with one fist and pounded the table with his spiked club. He easily riled up the other brutes.

They cheered and called out his name. "Borc! The orc! The king!"

"Borc! The orc! The king!"

"And a king needs a throne room." Borc jabbed a fat finger at three orcs. "Goil, Olugg, and Qwol—go in there and drag out Ugnarok's body. I don't want my throne room cluttered up."

The other orcs cheered, relieved that they hadn't been chosen for the job. Peer pressure worked on the three assigned to wizard-mage removal duty, and they trudged back to the banquet hall.

For quality-control purposes, Borc followed them to watch, and more orcs trailed after him, clattering and clanking their armor and weapons, scuffing their thick boots on the stone floor.

The Ugnarok disposal crew tiptoed into the banquet hall, nervous. When they were not immediately struck down by residual evil lightning, they approached the twisted corpse.

Longjohn called from the wall, "I'm glad you came back. I was getting lonely."

The three orcs ignored him, daring one another to pick up the hideous wizard-mage corpse. "Where should we take him?" Goil asked.

"Throw him out the window," said Qwol.

Olugg whined, "It'll contaminate the other meat we stored there."

Goil offered a better alternative. "Then throw him out a different window."

Longjohn interrupted in a pleading voice. "There's a storage chamber just off to the left of the throne room. Armor and swords and such, but it's only half full. Plenty of room, and most conveniently located. You could put him there."

The three orcs discussed the options and opted for convenience. Worried about being turned to stone or blasted into ashes, Goil, Olugg, and Qwol grasped Ugnarok's body and, moving with the speed of terror, they carried the evil sorcerer's tall form out the side door.

When the orcs found the promised storage chamber, which was cluttered with spare armor, swords, helmets, and boxes of holiday decorations, they dumped the wizard-mage's corpse on the floor. The skull-like sockets of the metal helmet were dim, and his mouth hung open and slack, showing bad teeth. The orcs scrambled out and swung the heavy door shut, then rammed a thick crossbar in place, so Ugnarok wouldn't get any ideas about walking around the castle with the other ghosts.

Relieved, King Borc reentered the hall with great fanfare, lifting his square chin high. At last he took his throne.

Through the peepholes, Cullin, Affonyl, and Spam watched as the dead wizard-mage was dragged out of the banquet hall. The young man let out a sigh of relief. "That guy made me uneasy, and being dead doesn't make him any better."

"In my studies of natural science, Wizard Edgar explained how twists of fate can be caused by dietary incompatibilities," Affonyl said. "This particular one is called *peanut ex machina*."

Spam was anxious to get started. "We need to be even scarier than Ugnarok if we're going to haunt the castle and chase the orcs away."

Cullin vowed, "We'll be so terrifying that they'll run screaming like little girls into the night."

"Hey, even I don't scream like a little girl!" Spam sounded indignant.

Affonyl mused, clearly imagining what else they might do with it, "That helmet is a nasty piece of work."

"It's stuck on his nasty head right now," Cullin said.

"Then let's go get it." Spam stepped away from the peepholes and gestured them to follow her. "I know a secret entrance into the armory and holiday-decoration storage room."

Cullin was impressed. "Whoever designed this castle thought of everything."

A rat scuttled in front of them, darting at their feet, and then vanishing into a chink in the wall. "This castle needs a lot more cats," Affonyl said with a frown. "I could go down to the harbor town and find some, sneak them in the back door. Cats tend to follow me."

Spam sniffed. "That's been a point of discussion among the scullery maids for some time. Castle cats would certainly control the rodent population, but King Longjohn is severely allergic, and he's forbidden them."

The former princess sighed, definitely disappointed. "Allergies can be very inconvenient."

"Ugnarok would agree with you," Cullin said.

The scullery maid found the right spot on the wall, dug her fingers into cracks until she found the latch, and swung open the hidden door into the storage room. They pushed aside a crate of crocheted doilies, can coozies, and ribbon banners for the annual Saint Bartimund's Day parade.

Ugnarok's body lay sprawled in the middle of the floor.

"He's not going anywhere. First things first—we'd better arm ourselves." Spam ran to the weapon racks and snatched knives for each of them. After a quick whispered discussion, they decided not to take big swords, because clattering blades and scabbards would be inconvenient in the narrow passages.

"But those crossbows are nice," Cullin said, lifting one and checking the nut, string, and trigger. "And plenty of spare quarrels." He pulled the string back, locked it in place, then clicked the trigger with a satisfying snap.

"I want one of those!" Spam said. "We used to shoot pumpkins out in the courtyard."

"And orcs are even bigger than pumpkins," Affonyl said. "We can stash several of them throughout the tunnels for the most convenient user experience."

Cullin felt as if they had made significant progress, but he remembered they had come here for the wizard-mage.

Affonyl squatted in front of Ugnarok's body for detailed analysis. His impressive demonic helmet was tilted to one side. She grasped the metal horns and sharp ridges, trying to wrench it from the sorcerer's head. "Squirrel, help me. Pull down on his ears."

"His ears?"

"For leverage."

They wiggled, pulled, and twisted until finally the helmet came off with a pop. Beneath the mask, Ugnarok's face was gaunt and gray with sunken glassy eyes, hollow cheeks, and wrinkled gray skin.

Cullin scowled at the no-longer-threatening wizard-mage. "He looks ghastly in death."

"He was probably ghastly in life, too," Spam said.

Affonyl tucked the scary helmet under her arm. "Quick, back into the passageways. Carry the crossbows, so we can be ready. Spam, is there someplace we can scheme? Like a secret conference room?"

The scullery maid grinned. "I know just the place."

CHAPTER
TWENTY-SEVEN

The sheer cliff beneath Longjohn's castle was riddled with tunnels that wound from the dungeon levels down to the tide line. They descended one flight of stone steps after another, then down rusty iron rungs pounded into the walls.

"So many shafts and tunnels—was this an old dwarven mine, by any chance?" Affonyl asked.

Spam laughed as she kept lowering herself down the shaft. "Most of the dwarves in these parts signed on as crew for the merchant ships —they like working down in the dark, crowded cargo holds. No, these tunnels were for something else."

The girl dropped down the last few iron rungs and waited for Cullin and Affonyl to join her in a large sea cave, which opened to fresh air and foaming waves that curled along the rocky shore.

At the back of the cave, Spam pointed out a stack of barrels and storage pallets for illicit cargo. "Moonshyne. Smuggler boats would row in and unload secret shipments of grog here. Then King Grog would sell the moonshyne to the neighboring coastal towns and subkingdoms. Made a huge profit, with no taxes taken by the Inter-Kingdom Revenue Service."

The girl shook her head in disappointment. "These are all left-overs. The current king doesn't have the devious heart for it. Longjohn stopped the moonshyne running and thought he could make a greater profit by investing in rare works of art."

"Has his collection actually earned him any money?" Cullin asked.

Spam snickered. "Most of the kingdom's liquid cash goes straight into buying new artwork, which he hides in his private gallery." She gave Affonyl a skeptical frown. "Including the money he was going to invest in that giant rock on a stick you built. I can't believe he fell for that."

"Rock in Its Natural State is a perfectly innovative work that's integral to the landscape in the castle," said the former princess. "In a collector's market, it could be worth quite a bit."

"Now you sound like Dalbry." Cullin suddenly felt a flicker of concern for the old knight in the dungeon.

"What a crock of rustin' bullshit!" said a loud voice. "You're not supposed to believe your own scam, Princess! Goes against the rules."

Reeger emerged from behind the storage crates and moonshyne barrels. He was rumpled, his hair greasy and matted, his face grizzled, and his clothes more stained than usual.

"Reeger!" Cullin cried. "What happened to you? Where have you been hiding?"

Reeger grudgingly accepted their delight upon finding him unharmed. "I was down here, obviously." He glanced at Spam. "Didn't know the backstory about the moonshyne running, though. Good to have historical context. Now it all makes sense."

"How did you get away from the orcs?" Cullin asked. "I saw you leave the banquet hall just before the invasion."

"Aye, most providential crap I've ever taken. When the monster army arrived, I locked myself in the garderobe. But the orcs came pounding—no respect for privacy! There was only one emergency exit, so I had to take it. My pa always told me you don't look a gift outhouse in the mouth."

"You crawled through the garderobe hole?" the former princess asked, looking queasy.

"I had a soft enough landing," Reeger said. "Good thing I decided not to dive head first. Would have been a different story. I was safe as shit, you might say. I followed the sewage downhill through the tunnels. Rust, it's like a dwarven mining complex down here."

"I mentioned that," Affonyl said.

"By the time I found these sea caves, I was covered in enough effluent that even the rats didn't mind me. I washed myself in the tide pools, used seaweed as a scrub brush, so now I'm clean as a whistle."

Looking his friend over, Cullin decided he never wanted to put a whistle like that in his mouth. "So, once you were safe and cleaned up, you were making plans to come find us? And rescue Sir Dalbry? He's in a dungeon cell."

"We've already found the solution," Spam announced. "We're going to haunt the castle."

"And how are you going to haunt a castle?" Reeger asked.

"By using our imaginations," Affonyl said.

"And the gullibility of orcs," Cullin pointed out.

The sea breeze blew into the mouth of the grotto, carrying sounds of the crashing surf. The wind whistled and rippled through the tunnels, letting out a ghostly fluting sound. The eerie noise gave Cullin a chill.

"Hell of a draft," Reeger said in a matter-of-fact tone. "Watch this." He went to the back wall of the cave, where boulders and crates blocked air holes that led into the rock and up above. "An old ventilation system. The whole bluff is honeycombed with air shafts."

When he rolled away the rocks, fresh air whistled through the previously clogged tunnels, and as the tide came in and the sea wind picked up, an eerie moan crawled through the castle.

"That's the start of a ghost right there." Reeger chewed over the possibilities. "Rust, sounds like it could be fun. Count me in."

TWENTY-EIGHT

B orc slouched on the throne, trying to find a comfortable position. He even had Longjohn's crown, a pointy affair that he balanced on his bald, warty head. It was much too small for him, but Borc considered it a trophy. Orcs were legendary for their lack of fashion sense, and he had a reputation to uphold.

He hadn't considered that being a king was so boring, though. He growled orders, found busy tasks to keep his people in line, but it was a distraction, because orcs had short attention spans.

They had roasted and eaten some of the banquet victims, which kept them content for the moment, but they would get restless soon enough. Orcs were footloose by nature, wandering the earth in search of adventure, victims, and treasure. Over the years, Borc had led his marauding band on much pillaging and mayhem, which was a good bonding technique.

None of them liked the ghosts and the curse that came with the castle, but the treasure provided inspiration. Search parties marched through the corridors, pounding on walls, breaking down locked doors, ransacking storerooms, desperate to find the fabulous hoard, without success.

The castle had a lot of empty places—bedchambers, hallways, closets, storerooms. The orcs had dug into the castle larders. They had combed through the courtyards and the statue garden, even looked under a gray tarpaulin that covered a rock slab propped up by a thick tree trunk. Still nothing.

Borc knew that the sooner they found the treasure, the sooner they could leave and go back to the business of ransacking and pillaging again. None of them wanted to settle down.

Two of his followers, Goil and Skeez, stumbled into the throne room to make their report. "We looked everywhere, Borc," said Goil. "No sign of any treasure."

"And what happens if we find the ghosts first?" asked Skeez.

"Don't look for ghosts. Find the treasure instead," Borc said. "Then we can leave."

The orc scouts marched back out, unable to remember which places they had already searched.

Hearing a sound from behind him, he looked up to see King Longjohn dangling on the wall. "When you orcs depart, could you please let me down from here? It'll just take a minute."

Borc had a flash of insight. "Only if you tell us where the treasure is."

"The treasure is there for all to see—but only if you appreciate fine art," said Longjohn. "My fortune is well invested, but alas my treasury is rather lean in liquid assets at the moment."

"Then stay up on the wall." Borc crossed one thick leg over the other and squirmed in the seat. With a long, bored sigh he looked across the hall to the vaulted fireplace, where a large fire was burning.

Suddenly he heard a bloodcurdling moan, followed by maniacal laughter. The flames in the fireplace surged in a flare of haunted energy. Green and purple fire blazed up, and noisome smoke curled into the room.

A deep, terrifying voice boomed out of the fireplace. "This castle is cursed! Leave here!"

Borc lurched out of the throne and ducked behind it, afraid that some supernatural army of murderous ghosts would swoop down the chimney. With a crash, something skull-like and fearsome dropped onto the fireplace grate, smashing the burning logs.

As the colored flames and reeking smoke boiled away, Borc saw the blackened skull helmet of Ugnarok. Flames burned through its eye sockets, and the moaning voice curled out of the hearth again. "This castle is cursed!"

On the wall behind him, Borc heard a jittering clank and looked up to see Longjohn shivering in his manacles. "I didn't know about any curse, honest! It wasn't in the disclosure when I inherited the castle."

After the delightful pyrotechnic scare, Cullin and his friends agreed that the helmet was the star of the show, with or without Ugnarok inside it.

The young man couldn't stop grinning. "That worked like magic!"

"Not magic, Squirrel—simple chemistry," Affonyl said. "A great wizard once said that any sufficiently advanced technology is indistinguishable from magic."

Cullin gave her a solemn nod, to pretend that he understood.

Down in their hideout in the smuggler caves, Affonyl placed her bag of necessary items on the battered and stained table. "Just a little chemistry that Wizard Edgar taught me." She poked around in her sack, which was mostly empty. "If we want to do more spectacular parlor tricks, I'll need to replenish my supply."

Feeling safe, they celebrated their first haunting victory with a feast that was quite different from King Longjohn's last banquet. From a stockpile hidden in the catacombs, Spam had retrieved four blue tins of her Sue-Pam potted meat product. "We have enough provisions to last us a long time." She passed the cans around. "These'll never go bad."

Reeger peeled off the top lid and dumped out the gelatinous, pinkish block, which he prodded with the point of his dagger. Affonyl and Cullin looked closer, sniffing. After the numerous peanut-laced courses served at the last banquet, Cullin hadn't thought he would ever be hungry again, but his stomach was growling ... although less so, now that the Sue-Pam cans had been opened.

"It looks a bit like pâté," said the former princess.

Reeger took a bite and smooshed it around in his mouth. "Tastes good. Could use a bit of salt, though."

"We might be eating it for every meal. This haunting could take quite a while," Cullin said. "Orcs aren't exactly fast learners."

Reeger took another bite and talked with his mouth full. "Rust, a good scam takes proper setup and careful orchestration."

The former princess said, "Dalbry would want us to make ambitious plans, without delay. He's in a miserable situation right now."

Spam sat cross-legged on the cave floor, enjoying her own processed-meat product. "I know. I can't remember the last time those filthy dungeon cells were mopped and aired out."

Affonyl frowned. "Actually, I mean being in prison with all those vapid nobles."

Cullin ate half of his Sue-Pam before he pushed the blue tin away. "We're going to need more food." He glanced at the scullery maid. "Do you think you could sneak us into the kitchen larders to steal supplies?"

"Get some of them peanuts," Reeger said.

The girl considered. "I know a passage not far from the kitchens. If the coast is clear, we could grab some apples and carrots."

"And bring peanuts," Reeger repeated.

Affonyl poked around in her bag. She seemed to be making a mental list. "You two fetch supplies, and I need to replenish my chemical stockpile. Reeger, can you gather a few fresh, unlit torches? I've got an idea for our next scary little prank."

CHAPTER
TWENTY-NINE

Thanks to her education in natural science, Affonyl knew many wondrous tricks of chemistry and alchemy—but she couldn't do anything without the right ingredients.

She'd used the last of her magical catalysts and reactants to make a spectacular show of sparkles and smoke with Ugnarok's helmet, but a thorough job of haunting King Longjohn's castle would require a lot more.

Since she and her companions were in a typical medieval castle, she knew exactly where to look. Slipping through the shadows, pausing to listen for any grunting orcs or plodding footsteps, Affonyl ventured down to the castle apothecary, which was dark and unoccupied.

Propped in the window of the closed door, a sign said, "Will return after the invasion."

Through the rippled glass, she could see the well-stocked shelves: pots, vials, bottles, boxes, and a separate section for greeting cards. Not known for their interest in herbalism, the orcs had not raided the apothecary stockpiles yet.

Affonyl was relieved to find the door unlocked, and she slipped inside, lighting one small candle so she could see well enough to inspect the drugs, chemicals, syrups, and unguents. High on a shelf she found the most interesting purified chemical compounds marked with strident warnings. She chose the substances with the most prominent danger symbols.

This was more fun than a candy store. The possibilities were endless!

By the light of her candle, she pulled down bottles and packets, filling her bag of necessary items. She found sulfur, potassium, salt-peter, magnesium salts, an abundance of digestive aids, though those would not be useful to her current plan. She hummed to herself as she gathered more vials and tinctures, careful not to let the sealed packets touch each other.

She smiled wistfully to remember learning under Wizard Edgar —the best days she could remember. Edgar had always treated Affonyl as his apt pupil, an apprentice rather than a princess. She thought the old, bearded man with kindly eyes and warm smile was lonely.

King Norrimund delighted in flash-bangs, colored smoke, and stink bombs as a demonstration of Edgar's dark powers. To learn astronomy and astrology, Edgar and Affonyl had studied constella-tions from the castle's highest turret; to learn taxonomy and zoology, they dissected all manner of insects, frogs, fetal pigs, and chickens.

When Wizard Edgar left her father's service for a better paying position at an evil wizard conglomerate, Affonyl had been heartbro-ken. But she continued her private studies, though her father insisted that Affonyl concentrate on embroidery in preparation for a royal marriage someday. Fortunately, when the time was right, the frus-trated princess had used what Edgar taught her, in order to fake her own abduction by a fiery dragon.

So, apart from being trapped in a castle full of orcs, everything had turned out for the best.

When she heard heavy shuffling down the outer corridor, she blew out her candle and crouched down, waiting as an orc patrol moved past in their fruitless search for treasure. After they were gone, she gathered the remaining items she needed to concoct a pyrotechnic mixture. Checking that the hall was empty, she darted back to the secret doorway in the stone wall and made her way down to the smuggler caves....

As instructed, Reeger had gathered half a dozen fresh torches. "I hope you didn't want me to get the lavender-scented ones from the king's bedchamber," he said, dropping the torches next to the work table. "Borc is already moving in there. Changed the sheets and everything."

"These torches will do just fine, once I add my special ingredient."

She spread out the supplies she had taken from the apothecary and organized them into categories of catalytic danger.

Outside, the waves crashed as the tide came in, and the breezes made the regular torches flicker on the cave wall. Reeger went to adjust the boulders covering the ventilation shafts, and the mournful moaning sound rose and fell as it wandered through the castle. "That'll put the orcs on edge!"

"It definitely builds up the agitation."

Affonyl found an adequate mixing bowl. Concentrating on her work, she emptied appropriate powders into the bowl, added a dash of chemicals from the kitchen spice cupboards and the scullery maid's cleaning closet, and stirred them together into a delightful grayish paste.

Reeger bent close, sniffing. "Smells foul." It didn't sound like a criticism.

"That's not even the best part," she said.

She hoped to have everything ready by the time Cullin and Spam returned from raiding the pantry.

Despite the danger of the assignment, the ragamuffin girl led Cullin through the maze of passageways. He was obviously disoriented, and Spam seemed glad that he needed her guidance.

For protection they each carried a crossbow from the armory and holiday-decorations closet, but since they would need both hands to carry any food they pilfered, they left the weapons just inside the secret passage entrance. After surveying the area, Spam sneaked him out of a hidden doorway not far from the kitchen larder. Cullin wasn't surprised no orcs were around, because it was brunch time, and orcs rarely did brunch.

The girl left the door ajar for a quick escape in case a disaster happened.

The dim pantry larder just off the kitchen was much like a dungeon cell, only cleaner and filled with more food. Barrels and small kegs were stacked on the floor, and baskets held stored produce. "An apple or two would be nice to go with our cans of Sue-Pam," she said.

"And peanuts," Cullin said, starting to fill his burlap sack. "Don't forget the peanuts."

The two of them dumped wrinkled apples and dirt-encrusted carrots into their sacks. After considering, she also stuffed in a head of green cabbage that was starting to grow smelly and soft.

When their sacks were full, Spam said, "Sling it over your shoulder, Squirrel, so the two of us can carry this keg." She indicated a small barrel marked with the universal symbol for peanuts.

Once they had gathered their emergency provisions, Cullin ducked out of the larder, glanced from side-to-side, and nodded that the way was safe. With the sacks slung over their shoulders, they scuttled down the hall with the keg of peanuts. Cullin was delighted with how smoothly the operation had gone, when a bellowing roar came from the kitchens.

A burly orc lurched out, brandishing a rusty pike that was taller than he was. "Hey!"

Spam whirled. "Hey, yourself!" She turned back to Cullin. "Hurry! Get to the door!"

The orc bounded toward them on thick legs, his iron-shod boots thundering on the tiles. Cullin scooted ahead and almost lost his grip on the peanut keg. If only they had time to open it, they could scatter shells on the floor to make the clumsy orc slip and fall.

They kept running toward the hidden door, and Cullin could see the gap in the wall. The orc charged closer, swinging his pike. The axe blade whistled through the air as if decapitating invisible victims.

The girl dropped her end of the peanut keg. "Go! Open the door, Squirrel!" She snatched out the soft, green cabbage just as Cullin pushed open the hidden entrance. She hurled the cabbage, and it smashed the orc full in the face, flattening his ugly nose.

The brute grunted and staggered, losing his stride. That gave the two all the time they needed to whisk the peanut keg and their vegetable sacks inside the passageway. Spam slid the door shut.

Their safety lasted only for a second. With heavy fists the cabbage-smashed orc pounded on the wall until powder fell from the ceiling. He bellowed and smashed at the doorway.

"He's going to break through," Cullin said. "We'd better run."

"All that noise is going to bring more orcs, too," she said.

The young man caught his breath. "Wait! If they find these tunnels, they'll root us out. We've got to stop him."

Spam cocked an eyebrow. "I'm open to ideas."

He snatched up one of the crossbows they had left beside the door. "Time to make a stand."

"Against that? You know I'm only five foot, two inches, right?"

"I've got three inches on you," he said, as if that made him sound more intimidating.

She picked up the second crossbow as the orc continued to hammer on the wall. The latch rattled, weakening with every moment.

"We have the element of surprise." Cullin drew a breath, bracing himself. "Let's use it."

They both raised their crossbows, nocked quarrels, and cocked the strings. With a silent count to three, Cullin reached forward and flipped the latch.

When the orc pounded again, the hidden barrier sprang inward, and the startled brute lurched forward.

"Surprise!" Spam said.

Cullin and the girl both launched their crossbow bolts. Both quarrels sank into the orc's throat beneath his fat double chin. He staggered back, dropped his pike with a clatter on the floor, and clutched at his neck.

Cullin used both hands to shove the dying orc backward. The brute gurgled as he toppled over onto his back, bleeding all over the floor.

From down the hall, they could hear other orcs storming forward in response to the shouts. Leaving the dead brute sprawled in his own blood, Cullin and Spam quickly closed the hidden door and secured the latch. The secret barrier would be invisible against the stone wall.

Spam was defiantly giggling. "They'll find one of their band murdered, with no one around!"

"Ghosts!" Cullin smiled.

On the other side of the wall, the orcs bellowed in alarm as they discovered their slain comrade in a pool of blood. "It's Skeez! He's dead!"

The girl snickered. "Quick, to the whisper hole."

In his harshest voice, Cullin rasped out, "The castle ghosts demand vengeance! Orcs must leave!"

Without discussing the matter, the orcs fled down the hall.

CHAPTER

THIRTY

Relieved after their close brush with death-by-orc, Cullin sat in the smuggler caves, writing more of their plans in Ye Olde Journal. "I'm documenting all this, just in case others need to know how to haunt a castle."

"Careful, those are trade secrets, lad!" Reeger said, snacking from a can of the Sue-Pam potted meat. The scullery maid preferred to munch on the fresh peanuts they had taken from the larder. She tossed the shells out into the crashing surf.

The windy moan picked up again, blowing like a haunted draft through the ventilation system.

Reeger sharpened his personal dagger against the stone wall. "Hidden in these tunnels, we can spy on the orc patrols, spring out at them when they're alone, kill off the brutes one by one. You two made a good start today. Handy with a crossbow, but you could slice a few throats if you like."

"I'll leave that dirty work to you," Cullin said.

Reeger tossed the empty blue can out into the surf. "You know that's what I enjoy best, lad!"

Affonyl arranged Reeger's five unlit torches on the smugglers' table. Each one was smeared with a glittery gray paste. "There, these are finished. Ready for our next big scare tactic?"

Late at night, Spam led them to a side corridor that was due for an orc patrol within the hour, though the invaders were notoriously bad at telling time. They emerged into an empty passageway carrying the slathered unlit torches, which they swapped for the original ones in the wall sconces. One by one, they removed and snuffed the burning torches, and the corridor grew darker, more sinister.

"In my father's castle, we called this mood lighting," Affonyl said.

With the special, unlit torches in place, they ducked back into the hidden passage and settled in to wait until they heard the thump of heavy boots.

Cullin pressed his eye to one of the peepholes, and Spam crowded next to him to get a look. He would rather have been close to Affonyl, but the former princess had claimed her own spyhole two stone blocks down. Reeger moved further along the passageway to watch through a different hole.

After what seemed like hours, two orc sentries prowled into the gloomy corridor. The pair hesitated when they saw that the wall torches were not lit. "Maybe the king didn't pay his torch bill," said one.

His partner shivered. "Or maybe a ghost snuffed them out. Ghosts like creepy shadows."

They each carried a candle, which provided the only illumination in the shadowy hall. Moving hesitantly forward, the first orc said, "We better light them again. A good fire drives ghosts away."

They each went to a wall sconce and touched the candle flame to the waiting torches. With a sudden unexpected fury of sparks, smoke, and hissing flares, Affonyl's chemically coated torches roared to life. The explosion of bright colors was more spectacular than when Ugnarok's helmet had dropped into the throne hall fireplace.

The first orc sounded like a weasel stepped on by a mule. The second dropped his spiked club, and both fled in terror from the chemical fires.

Cullin, Spam, and Affonyl covered their laughter as the terrified invaders blundered away at top speed. Reeger, though, burst into action. He snatched his crossbow and four quarrels and yanked open the secret doorway. "Rust, now it's time for me to have some fun!"

"They'll see you!" Cullin said, but the man barged into the corridor, raising the crossbow.

Reeger loaded one of the quarrels, drew back the string, cocked it against the nut, then fired at the bellowing orcs. The projectile whistled past one brute's blocky head, clipping his ear. He yelped and put on a burst of speed.

Reeger loaded another quarrel and fired, stomping his foot on the floor as if that would improve his aim. It did not, and the second bolt missed as well.

By now, the first orc had reached the far end of the hall, ready to turn left into an intersecting corridor. Reeger fired his next shot, and the crossbow bolt whistled through the air and sank deep into the second orc's back. He squawked and belched, flailing behind him in a vain attempt to reach the projectile. He staggered forward, then collapsed face-first on the floor, bubbling blood.

Now that the orc was no longer a moving target, Reeger launched his last crossbow bolt, scoring another direct hit.

Running ahead, the first orc skidded to a halt, turned, and looked in horror at his dying comrade. He bleated and bounded around the corner.

Reeger ducked back into the shadows, chuckling as he rejoined the others. "Not as personal as I'd like, but now we've killed two of the orcs."

"Good," Spam said with a huff. "Only forty-eight more to go."

CHAPTER

THIRTY-ONE

L ocked in the dungeon with terrified nobles and art aficionados, Dalbry was about to eat the very last dried apricot from his magic sack, which had not yet replenished itself. The worn leather bag seemed to be more sack and less magic.

Sub-baron Darylking rested his chin in his large hands. "It's been days. Who's going to rescue us?"

"Do you think we should just escape?" asked Midduke Blande.

Highduke Lessa rattled the rusty iron bars. "And how are we going to do that? The orcs have the keys."

"You'd think even invaders would have the courtesy to empty our chamber bucket," said Lowduke McCowan.

"I can't recall the last time I've been so bored," said Pattilane. "Did anyone bring playing cards?"

Two of the effete art critics were snoring against the wall.

Dalbry considered cutting his last dried apricot into tiny bits so each of them could have a morsel, but after listening to the conversation, he slipped the whole apricot into his mouth. "I've been in far worse situations. I could tell you tales of horrific peril."

"That would at least reduce our boredom," said Pattilane.

"Please do, Dalbry," said Blande. "It can't make our situation any worse."

"Does it have a happy ending?" asked Lessa.

"I survived, so it was a happy occasion for me." He sifted

through his repertoire and chose a story he hadn't told in a long time, one that was usually good for two rounds of drinks at a local tavern. Today, it would provide a brief reduction in misery, or at least in the complaints.

"Let me tell you about the pirate cyclops of Wit's End. You must have read about it in the history books. Sir Dalbry and the pirate cyclops?"

The nobles and art aficionados nodded uncertainly, took confidence from the indecision of others, and nodded more vigorously. "We know Sir Dalbry in the hallway," said Pattilane. "Is this one more exciting?"

The old knight began his tale without answering. "Up the coast at a strategic rock promontory called Wit's End, a surly cyclops built a citadel from which he could prey upon passing ships. The cyclops had hairy shoulders and a hairy back, and a face so ugly that only a blind mother smoking too much giggleweed could love. He had one eye in the middle of his forehead and warts all over his skin.

"The cyclops would stand in his rock citadel, pound his chest, and bellow down at the passing ships. He commanded them to pull up to the shore and pay a tax before he let them sail away. If they refused, he would hurl down boulders and spears made out of tree trunks.

"Some captains were foolish enough to stop and pay the toll, but that was unwise. You see, up on Wit's End, the cyclops could not hunt any game and he was too high above the water to fish, so the duped supplicants were his only food source." Dalbry gave a sardonic smile. "Most captains wisely tried to sail away."

"How did they escape the hurled tree trunks and great boulders?" asked McCowan.

"Though he had a strategic advantage from his high point, the cyclops had only one eye and, therefore, no depth perception," Dalbry said. "His aim was atrociously off. His boulders made a great splash in the water, the spears cut close to the hulls, but the cyclops rarely hit his mark. It was enough to make sailors terrified of the monster pirate, but not enough to cause many casualties."

He stroked his chin. "Nevertheless, the cyclops was a nuisance, and the queen in those parts put out a call through the minstrel network and also ran a classified ad in the monastery newspapers, seeking to hire someone who would take care of the problem." He drew a deep breath. "I, Sir Dalbry, stepped up to the task."

"Did you bring an army?" asked Lady Pattilane.

"I did not. I'm a brave knight, and I follow the Knight's Manual as a matter of honor. I chose to challenge and defeat him myself."

"That sounds very brave," said Lessa.

"Or unnecessarily overconfident," said Darylking.

"I rode up to the promontory on my trusty horse Drizzle and called out the pirate cyclops. The monster emerged to face me carrying a stack of tree-trunk spears under one arm. He hurled them directly at me one by one."

The dungeon audience waited in suspense.

"I stood as stoic as a stone, not flinching, because his aim was so bad. The spears crashed on either side of me and Drizzle. When this disconcerted the cyclops, I pressed my advantage. 'You are a lousy pirate! Passing ships are not the least bit afraid of you, sir. In fact, in the taverns they laugh about your poor aim. You aren't even a real pirate.'

"The monster hurled another spear, which crashed close, but posed no actual danger.

"'I am a pirate!' the cyclops yelled.

"'I don't believe it,' I said, and came forward, drawing my sword. 'If you were a pirate, I would challenge you to a duel to the death.' I laughed in his face, which further enraged the one-eyed beast. Even Drizzle snorted at him. 'But you don't even wear the proper costume of a pirate.'

"The cyclops bunched his biceps, clenched his fists, and stalked forward. 'What would make me a better pirate?' he demanded. 'Then I will fight you to the death!' He drew his long, curved scimitar and menaced me with it."

Darylking interrupted, "Where did the scimitar come from? You didn't say anything about a scimitar before."

"That detail should have been included in the character description. Apologies. Now, let's move on," Dalbry said. "My own trusty sword was much smaller than the monster pirate's, so I knew my best tactic was to focus on his wardrobe. I said, 'You don't have the simplest, most basic trappings of a pirate. No one will take you seriously without the proper costume.'

"'What do I need?' the cyclops demanded. 'I have my scimitar, I have my citadel. I hurl rocks and spears down at ships. If anyone pulls up to shore, I steal their booty and eat them.'

"'Excuse me, but it's obvious. You don't even have an eye patch,' I said. 'Every pirate needs an eye patch.' The cyclops was dumbfounded by this. 'And you don't have a parrot on your shoulder either.'

"'Where would I get a parrot?' the cyclops asked.

"'That's a secondary detail,' I said. 'The eye patch is far more important.'

"From Drizzle's saddlebags I pulled out a swatch of black cloth and folded it, then produced a leather string. 'Here, once you put on an eye patch, then you'll at least look the part, and I will take you seriously.'

"'Then I'll be a pirate!' The cyclops grabbed the eyepatch and tied it in place."

"I see where this is going," muttered Blande.

"I continued, 'Excellent! And now we can properly duel. Then I can say I defeated the pirate cyclops of Wit's End.'"

Dalbry saw the rapt expressions on the faces of the prisoners.

"Then what happened?" asked Lessa.

"Well, as soon as he blindfolded himself, I thrust my sword straight into his belly, then I thrust up into his heart and went round back to stab him in the kidneys."

The nobles and art aficionados were surprised. "That doesn't sound very sporting," said Pattilane.

"I precisely followed the rules of chivalry," Dalbry said, "which clearly state that the rules of chivalry are suspended when dealing with monsters and pirates. It isn't a very sporting world out there."

"So, what does the Manual say about invading orc armies that throw you into a dungeon?" asked McCowan.

"I'm still working out the details." Dalbry chewed the last of the apricot in the back of his mouth and swallowed.

"Perhaps you should go slay the orc king." Blande seemed partic-

160

ularly confident in the old knight's abilities. "Once you've done that, it should be a simple matter to take out the rest of the orc army."

"Yes, a ... simple matter," Dalbry agreed, "but in the meantime we will let my compatriots keep softening the enemy by haunting the castle."

With a sigh, Dalbry leaned against the slimy dungeon wall, waiting to hear more from Cullin.

Down in my secret man cave, I feel warmed by the expensive brandy. The memories of my glory days also bring a clear satisfaction, and sharing this story with my son makes it all seem priceless. Someday, Maurice will be just like me.

The prince is completely engrossed now, and he cannot restrain himself from asking questions. I pause in my tale so that he can speak what's on his mind.

"Do you have to keep smoking that cigar?" He rubs his eyes.

The air of the man cave is redolent with blue-gray smoke. Even my eyes are burning a little, and Maurice is a much more sensitive person. I take a long puff and exhale with a satisfied sigh. By twisting my lips and modulating the smoke with my tongue, I curl out a magical smoke ring, which dissipates and spreads out into the room.

"If you think this is bad, you should smell the smoke from a dragon's gullet, son."

The boy coughs and rubs his reddened eyes.

I waggle the cigar. "This is one of the pleasures and obligations of being a respected king. Tobacco comes from the New Lands, you know. A very expensive import—just like peanuts."

"Next time could we bring peanuts instead of cigars?" Maurice asks.

My heart swells with pride. The prince has asked for a next time! "Yes, next time we will bring peanuts—and cigars." I sip my brandy again, and Maurice touches the snifter to his lips, struggles to hide his grimace.

"Father-son bonding time," I say with a smile. "More importantly, king and prince bonding time."

"These stories ..." he says. "Were you there when Sir Dalbry battled the cyclops pirate?"

"No, that was one of his solo adventures. Like my two-headed dragon." I'm not certain I believe it myself, though I never challenged Dalbry because I didn't want to wound his pride.

"It seems a little preposterous."

Of all the things I've told him, that *seems preposterous? "Some of the details are lacking, which weakens the veracity."*

"But how do you remember all these details, Father?" The prince scootches his butt around the overstuffed chair. *"You must have a very good imagination."*

"Or a very good memory."

"Maybe ..."

"In fact, I don't need to rely entirely upon my memory, because I recorded the events first-hand, right when they were happening. Look here."

Above, we can still hear the boom of thunder muffled through the stone walls.

With a flourish, I bend over to open a small wooden chest beside my seat. From inside, I retrieve a battered leatherbound book. *"Here it is, Maurice—the original copy."*

I hold it up. *"Ye Olde Journal."* I open it to show the yellowed pages covered with my fumbling handwriting. *"Before I forgot anything, I jotted down these chronicles, adventure after adventure in the dragon business."*

The boy reaches out to take the book. *"I thought you were making it all up."*

"Careful, it's very old. A historical record."

The prince shows no particular respect for the journal's fragility and importance. He skims down some of the pages. *"You have a lot of misspellings."*

"Spelling wasn't standardized when I wrote it. And remember, I did grow up an illiterate, feral child before I found my true home with a band of con artists. Since that time, I've gone to night school."

When my cigar has burned down, I stub it out in the royal ashtray. Eventually the ventilation will waft away the smoke, and Maurice is already breathing more clearly.

"So, is it going to take much longer to scare the orcs out of the castle?" he asks.

"Do you mean, am I building toward a grand climax? Or am I still weaving storylines and planting plot threads that will become tangled in a crescendo."

"I meant how much longer?" he asks.

"Sit back and enjoy. Now, where were we?"

CHAPTER
THIRTY-TWO

Cullin slipped away to the banquet hall peephole to watch the brutes gather for supper, but he had another important mission: sitting on his ass and taking names.

The orcs were rowdy, boisterous, and offensive as always, but an undertone of tension simmered in the crowded room. He listened closely, heard them talking about the two mysteriously murdered orcs—Skeez and Urml. Goil, the orc who had escaped the haunted, sparking torches, kept telling his story about the ghosts, exaggerating the terror more and more.

Spam startled Cullin by whispering loudly in his ear. "Look how scared they are. He's doing our work for us!"

He jumped. He hadn't heard her come up. "There's plenty of work to go around."

He took out Ye Olde Journal and filled in the names he heard, keeping a list. It would help them make their hauntings more personal.

"I heard Goil, Jerx, Bofurt, and Olugg," Spam offered.

"I already have those," he said, but surreptitiously wrote two of them down.

The girl accompanied him constantly, chattering away, almost to the point of being a pest. With her waifish face, round eyes, and ragged mop of hair, the smudged kid seemed to have a crush on him.

Cullin wished Affonyl found his company so charming....

They could hear the orcs grunting, pounding, and slurping at the dinner table. Nauseating smells drifted through the peepholes. He saw the table covered with roasted human dishes cut from the defenestrated banquet victims. Not bothering with the salad course, the brutes ripped hunks of meat from the bones. While chewing, they compared notes about the flavor—the hint of perfume on a lady's roasted thigh, the tough gaminess of an older guard.

"Aged perfectly," said Bofurt. "Just this side of putrid."

"We've gone through the best parts already," said Olugg.

King Borc sat at the end of the table with the too-small crown propped on his head. "How much is left in the midden piles?"

"Maybe four days of meals," said Olugg. "Two days of feasts."

"Fewer mouths to feed now that Skeez and Urml were murdered by the ghosts," Nrguff said, looking on the bright side.

Borc pounded his fist on the table. "Find the treasure, and then we can leave here!"

"We're looking, Borc!" whined Qwol.

Goil challenged him. "You wouldn't know treasure if it was right in front of your face."

The two orcs rose to their feet, ready to bash each other with their spiked clubs. Cullin could only hope.

King Borc raised his scepter-club in one hand and a battle-axe in the other. "If I kill you two, there's even less mouths to feed!" He stared them down. "And more treasure for the rest of us." He slumped back down, plucking the fingers from a roasted hand and crunching on the bones. "We can always eat those prisoners in the dungeons. No shortage of food."

"Another feast!" yelled Ditto, and the orcs cheered.

Cullin wrote down more names, Otto, Ditto, Qwol, Nrguff.

An orc spilled a tankard of ale into the lap of another, and the crotch-soddened brute lurched to his feet, picked up a bowl of soup entrails, and smashed it into his companion's face. Naturally, this led to a retaliation.

Femurs and roast haunches were hurled through the air. Goblets, plates, and an untouched crudité platter went flying. Before long, the food fight was in full swing, leading to mayhem in the dining hall.

"They're just burning off nervous energy." Cullin closed the journal and looked at Spam. "We have enough for tonight."

Long after dark, armed with the names of numerous orcs, Cullin, Affonyl, and Reeger followed the scullery maid to a spot behind the wall of the crowded bunk room the orcs had taken over. These lower chambers had once been inhabited by castle guards and kitchen staff. Now they were a wreck.

Borc had moved into Longjohn's large, royal bedroom, so he didn't sleep with the rest of the orcs. While the new king enjoyed his fancy digs and fresh sheets from the royal linen closets, the rest of the brutes slept in communal barracks.

When Cullin and his friends peered into the crowded, smelly room, Spam was incensed to see that orcs had commandeered her own bunk. One orc—Otto—had used her patchwork comforter as a handkerchief, and the frayed swatches of cloth were caked with green goo. Now, more than ever, the girl wanted revenge.

Affonyl reassured her with a grin of anticipation. "Time for the next-stage haunting. This is going to be fun."

Some of the brutes slept on the floor, some on sturdy bunkbeds, others slouched in chairs. Ever since the previous prank with the sparking and hissing torches, the orcs were averse to burning too many lights. Only two guttering brands were propped in wall sconces, as nightlights.

Cullin and his friends listened as the sleeping orcs snored and stirred, farted, and whimpered with nightmares. One orc—Qwol, he thought—was sound asleep with his head lolling to one side; his leg twitched and twitched like a dog running in its sleep. Another orc elbowed him hard, and Qwol rolled over. When he was deep asleep again, he started twitching and running with his other leg.

Affonyl whispered loudly through a peephole into the bunk room. "This castle is cursed!"

At another hole, Reeger said in a deeper voice, "Beware of the curse!"

Cullin and Spam each took a turn, and the orcs awakened in alarm. Several whimpered, others grabbed for their weapons, but they saw nothing to fight. "You can't bash ghosts," Nrguff said, waving his club in the air.

Now it was time for the low blows to start. Affonyl spoke in a clear, husky voice, "Jerx likes to wear princess clothing!"

Hearing this, the orcs recoiled. Some chuckled at their companion. Jerx balled his fists and turned around, trying to punch something. Seeing no ghosts, he slugged the nearest orc.

Cullin rasped out, "Goil picks his nose ... and doesn't eat the boogers!"

Gasps of disbelief rippled among the invaders. They were agitated by the voices coming out of nowhere.

Spam called out the most damning fake secret of all, targeting the orc who had taken her blanket. "Otto wants to be a vegetarian!"

The orcs let out loud groans. One whistled in disbelief through a gap in his teeth. Otto was enraged. "I do not! I do not!"

"The ghosts know all your secrets," Affonyl said in a threatening tone. "Your deepest, darkest secrets!"

Their job finished, the companions retreated, already planning their next step, but Reeger wasn't satisfied. "Not a high-enough body count yet."

CHAPTER

THIRTY-THREE

A fter being cooped up in the secret passages for days, Cullin was going stir crazy. He wanted a breath of fresh air.

Affonyl agreed. "I need to check on Rock in Its Natural State. I hope the orcs haven't damaged it."

"It's a rustin' rock on a stick," Reeger muttered as they followed the scullery maid to the emergency exit by the hedges. "How could you tell if it's damaged?"

"They could deface it with graffiti," Affonyl said.

"Except orcs can't spell," Cullin pointed out.

The former princess crossed her arms and frowned at him. "They could still deface it with misspelled words. Orcs don't appreciate art."

Once they were outside, Cullin couldn't tell what time it was in the gloomy fog, and the garden sundial was no help. As usual, sea-gulls wheeled and shrieked overhead, and a white plop landed on the grass near his feet.

Affonyl hurried to the side courtyard where the tarpaulin was still draped over the enormous slab of tilted stone. The invaders had torn the anchor ropes and lifted up the edges, looking for treasure, but found nothing remarkable about the covered masterpiece. "At least it's intact," she said, relieved.

"I've got some artwork, too, over in the midden heap," Reeger said.

Rather than looking at the Manure on Wood sequence, Cullin suggested they check on the mounts in the stables. Drizzle, Pony, and the mule had been left alone for days. Dalbry had initially paid a stableboy to care for the animals, but the fine print of the agreement said that the terms were not binding in case of acts of God, natural disasters, or orc invasions.

When they entered the stable, Drizzle let out a welcoming whicker and Pony snuffled, while the mule just ignored them. Cullin was relieved to see that the water troughs were still full and plenty of hay had been piled up within the animals' reach. He suggested bringing the three large animals into the narrow secret passages for safekeeping, but the others objected that it would be impractical.

They returned to the castle by way of the statue garden, as a shortcut. As they walked among the artistically confusing exhibit, Spam was dismayed to see the sculptures covered with gray and white splatters. "Just look at all the poop! I haven't done my regular scrubbing for days. I should get a bucket of soapy water and my bristle brush, then sneak out here at night."

Cullin was glad to see that the girl took pride in her work. "After the orcs are gone, you'll get your chance. Let's concentrate on scaring them off first."

"Rust, we could just kill them all," Reeger suggested. "That's a nice, permanent solution."

Affonyl sighed. "At this rate it'll take half a year or more."

Smiling, Cullin muttered to the maid. "Affonyl's very good at math."

The former princess was deep in thought. "Unless we speed things up. I'd like to contribute to the reduction in orcs—not with a dagger or hand-to-hand combat, but ..." She smiled as an idea occurred to her. "Maybe I can think of a more princessy solution."

🐉

They reconvened in King Longjohn's hidden art gallery grotto, where they had gathered cushions and blankets to make the cave a more comfortable hideout. The group sat around the keg of peanuts, cracking shells and tossing the empties on the stone floor. Cullin had even trained one of the rats to sit up and fold its tiny front forepaws to beg for a treat.

Deep in thought, Affonyl sat cross-legged on the floor, a position definitely not part of her princess training. She looked at the king's private collection of driftwood carvings, jewel-encrusted ashtrays, gilded placemats, and painted porcelain figurines. "Even if the orcs found this grotto, they wouldn't recognize the treasure."

Cullin tried to appreciate the weight of artistic ambivalence, but the only work that caught his eye was the painting of tavern dogs playing cards. "I doubt they have any contacts in the art world."

Leaning back against a cushion, Reeger enjoyed the contents of an old jug of moonshyne. "I never imagined I'd be in a place like this back when I made grandiose plans for my life. My parents would be proud."

Cullin ate another peanut. "After all the adventures we've had together, Reeger, you never told me your backstory."

The man belched. "I usually require a tankard of ale before I give up my biography." He sipped from the moonshyne jug again. "But this'll do. I came from a well-respected peasant family, worked in the agricultural business: grooming fields, preparing the land for large-scale farming."

Affonyl's disbelief was plain. "You, a farmer?"

"He has a way with fertilizer," Cullin said.

"Field prep, yes sir," Reeger said. "I come from a proud line of professional clodhoppers."

"What's a clodhopper?" asked Spam.

"What do you think? We go out in the newly plowed fields and hop from clod to clod."

"But *why* do you hop from clod to clod?' the girl pressed.

"We smash the clods with a big mallet." Reeger's expression became wistful. "You've got to break up the lumps before a farmer can plant seeds! My parents, my sisters, and I would hop across the new fields, bashing clod after clod. It's respectable work." He emphasized his comment with another swallow of the moonshyne. "But I had dreams of bigger things. I used my experience as a clodhopper to apply for other jobs. On the strength of my resume, I got promoted to being a ditchdigger.

"One day, after a good heavy rain, I was clearing out an irrigation ditch, and the mud flowed back up to my knees as fast as I could shovel it, when a forlorn Sir Dalbry comes by, dressed in his suit of armor." Reeger sighed. "He was devastated from being conned out of his fortune." He cocked his eyebrows. "You've heard how a band of treacherous lords and knights tricked him out of his family lands, leaving him with nothing but disappointment. He needed a ray of hope—and there I was standing in the mud. A ray of rustin' sunshine, that's me! We exchanged our tales of woe and our secret aspirations and decided to set off together. I've never looked back. It's been a glorious life."

"I doubt Dalbry thinks so right now, locked in a dungeon cell," Affonyl said.

"Should we bring them food in the dungeons?" Cullin asked. "Feed Dalbry and the other prisoners?"

The scullery maid gave a skeptical huff. "Fancy nobles are picky eaters. With their delicate constitutions, what if one of them has a peanut allergy, too?"

Cullin sighed. "You're probably right. We shouldn't risk it."

Affonyl squared her shoulders, determined. "It won't be much longer now anyway. I've figured out how to get rid of a few more orcs."

CHAPTER
THIRTY-FOUR

S tuck in the dungeon cell, Dalbry was getting hungry enough that even the rats seemed like a viable menu option. By now the last of his dried apricots were gone, and his magic sack remained magically empty.

As a legendary knight, he had been feted at royal courts. Parades had been thrown in his honor, usually to celebrate the slaying of a dragon or some other monster. He had also spent a lot of cold nights sleeping on the hard ground. He'd eaten camp food prepared by Reeger, which was an ordeal in itself. The other man scrounged whatever animals he could find, whether they be rabbits, hedgehogs, garter snakes, even banana slugs (which tasted nothing at all like bananas).

Dalbry's stomach growled. Sooner or later the rats were going to sound delicious, but once the captive nobles and art aficionados ate all the rats, then perhaps they'd have to draw straws and eat one another. Dalbry hoped that his skulking companions could scare away the orcs before they reached that point.

"I miss the tyranny of Wizard-Mage Ugnarok," groaned High-duke Lessa. "At least he knew how to hold hostages. By now he would have sent demand letters to all of our friends and family."

"That's the civilized way to do it," said Darylking. "Half of us could have been set free already."

Blande said, "My family ran several successful crowdsourcing campaigns across the land. Right now, I could be sleeping in a warm bed with a cup of Earl Grey tea ... if only Ugnarok hadn't died and left us with these uncivilized orcs."

"Peanut ex-machina," said Lady Pattilane, and the other prisoners muttered amongst themselves.

"But who was Ugnarok in the first place?" Dalbry asked. "What was his origin story? And what did he really want here in Longjohn's castle?"

"It's too late to get to know him now," said McCowan with a rude snort. "He was a powerful wizard-mage. What more do you need to know?"

"He was evil, but he wasn't stupid," Dalbry said. "I can't believe he would fall for the old cliché of wanting to rule the world."

"Perhaps he appreciated fine art," suggested Pattilane.

"He certainly didn't come for the peanuts," Blande said.

"I read a profile on him once in a monastery newspaper," Darylking began. "Ugnarok was raised to be a court jester, and he dreamed of being the greatest clown in all the land. Alas, he wasn't funny. He got the bum's rush from court after court, but his worst humiliation came from Longjohn's father, King Grog." The nobleman nodded with grave seriousness. "Grog drank too much of his own moonshyne and heckled Ugnarok. Worse, his heckling was a lot funnier than Ugnarok's own attempts at entertainment, and so the would-be jester left the kingdom in disgrace.

"Later, in order to get his revenge, Ugnarok studied the dark arts. He got an internship at an evil wizard conglomerate, but even the most sinister spells couldn't make him funny. After he graduated as a wizard-mage, Ugnarok began wreaking havoc, terrorizing kingdom after kingdom. But his true revenge was reserved for this castle ... even if he was too late to get back at King Grog while he was still alive." Blande sniffed. "He possessed all the dark magical power imaginable, but not enough to make people laugh at his jokes."

"And now we're all paying the price for it," groaned Lady Pattilane.

Dalbry watched a rat scurry along the floor before it disappeared into a crack in the stone blocks. His stomach growled.

CHAPTER

THIRTY-FIVE

Mulling over the options, Affonyl decided that the most princessy method of orc attrition was to experiment with deadly poison. And that necessitated another trip to the abandoned apothecary.

She was no longer interested in explosive powders or pyrotechnic reactants. Instead, she went to the Assassin Supplies section in the back of the shop just behind the Get Well cards. Her mouth watered as she reviewed the possibilities: hemlock, nightshade, cyanide, toadstool poison. She even found a variety pack with different flavors, some to be mixed into a tasty drink, others to be used as a nefarious air freshener.

Affonyl wouldn't convince the orcs to imbibe a surprise drink, though, and judging by the way they smelled, orcs weren't inclined to use air fresheners.

No, she needed a general-purpose death powder, which she would have to concoct herself. She took the right ingredients with her, careful not to get any trace of the substances on her hands.

Back in the smuggler's cave, she dragged the worktable closer to the breezy sea opening for better ventilation, even if the stray winds swirled some of the dried petals and powdered toadstools. Not unexpectedly, Cullin offered to help, but for his own sake she didn't want him and his over-eager assistance anywhere near the poisonous ingredients.

She used a mortar and pestle to grind the mixture, wishing for the first time in years that she had a pair of her delicate ballroom gloves. When all the ingredients were prepared, she had a mixture that could be easily spread and easily inhaled—preferably by orcs, not her companions. She covered the bowl with a lid so the fine powder wouldn't spill or blow up into the air.

She held it up to show her companions. "A little treat for the orcs. Tomorrow morning, once they're all out of bed and back to searching the castle for the treasure—"

"Or ghosts," Spam interrupted.

Affonyl nodded. "Or ghosts. Then I'll have my chance."

Behind the orc bunkroom, they watched through the peepholes and waited for their opportunity. The brutes snorted and tossed and turned, restless and afraid they would hear more spectral insults coming through the walls. None of them were early risers, but eventually the orcs lumbered out of bed and went about their daily business.

Spam was still upset to see orc snot all over her faded patchwork comforter. "It's ruined."

Affonyl held up the covered bowl of poison powder. "This will make it worse."

Once the room was clear, with Cullin and Spam keeping watch, the former princess tiptoed into the bunkroom and made her way over to the girl's patchwork blanket. Bending over the bed, she held her breath as she sprinkled the deadly powder liberally over the fabric. She covered the biggest snot stains, which indicated where the orc slept with the blanket pulled up against his face.

She had enough spare powder to sprinkle on the pillow in the adjacent bunk. "Pleasant dreams," she said, then retreated to their safe hiding place.

They spent the day planning other stages of the haunting process, but they waited anxiously for bedtime. When the orcs finished another disgusting feast and finally went to sleep, Affonyl felt a thrill of anticipation.

The brutes piled into their bunkroom and claimed their favorite beds, lighting extra night-light torches. They debated setting sentries to keep watch against murderous ghosts, and although everyone agreed it was a good idea, no one wanted to give up sleep.

One of the orcs, Otto, slumped down onto the broken bed that had belonged to the scullery maid. With thick fingers, he pulled the stained comforter up to his face and tossed back and forth.

On the bed beside him, another orc, Ditto, smashed his face into the pillow and began coughing and wheezing, snorting, sniffling. His eyes watered. He hacked and retched.

The other orcs stirred, annoyed by the loud disturbance.

Otto pushed the comforter up against his nostrils and inhaled deeply. "Smells funny." Then he sneezed. And coughed. And gurgled, wheezed, and coughed some more. His eyes bulged. His thick purple tongue lolled out, and his lips swelled up.

"Keep quiet!" another orc snorted, but Otto and Ditto both continued to spasm, writhe, and choke. Finally, they died with a long, slow burble of phlegm and hemorrhaged blood. In his convulsions, Ditto ripped his pillow to shreds, and loose goosedown sprayed into the air.

The orcs in the bunkroom took a long time to figure out what was happening. "It's the curse! The same thing that killed Ugnarok."

The uproar redoubled, which Affonyl found immensely satisfying. Much better than fighting them with harsh words and insults.

"Two less hungry orcs to eat innocent people," Cullin said, writing down the score in Ye Olde Journal.

The scullery maid was particularly happy. "Now I can have my comforter back!" She peered through the tiny hole, pleased to see the horrific orc corpse sprawled on her blanket.

Affonyl didn't want to ruin the mood of grim accomplishment with disappointing news for the girl.

Reeger seemed the most pleased. "This haunting is building momentum." He patted Cullin on the shoulder. "But now we have to really up our game, lad. Raise the stakes! And I know exactly what to do next."

CHAPTER

THIRTY-SIX

Reeger coughed deep in his chest, then spat at the grassy
headlands, but he was grinning as they walked far from the
castle. "Just like old times, lad. You and me."

"Just like you, in ... personal hygiene matters?" Cullin wondered
if he, too, was expected to expectorate.

"Rust, not that! I mean doing real labor. We'll be the type who
need a shower after work."

Again, Cullin was perplexed, because Reeger never took a shower
at any time of day. The best he had seen was when the man had
dunked himself in the horse trough before Longjohn's banquet.

That morning, before they set off, Reeger had confiscated a
handcart from outside the stables. "This'll carry quite an auspicious
load." He glanced at his eager sidekick. "And to show how much I
trust you, Cullin, I'll let you pull it."

The young man was glad to be an important part of the dragon
business activities. "I'll write about it in Ye Olde Journal."

"You probably want to wash your hands first."

They trudged away from the castle into the gloomy mist, heading
toward the main road. "You'll be proud of this labor, lad. Your
muscles will be sore, your back will ache, your joints will swell up,
and you'll get filth under your fingernails." He laughed again. "True
dirty work! None of that princessy nonsense."

"Is that why Affonyl didn't come along?" Cullin asked, disappointed. "I thought she and Spam had something more important to do."

"Crotchrust, what could be more important than digging up graves and wallowing in the muck?"

"I couldn't imagine."

The two followed the rutted road for a while, then Reeger turned left on a side route. They were near the abandoned subdivision, where the hopes and dreams of those peasant homeowners had been shattered when the property values plummeted. Now Cullin realized what they were doing. "Oh, we're going to the orc graveyard!"

Reeger's cockeyed gaze brightened. "Some might call it a graveyard—I prefer to think of it as a resource stockpile."

Cullin smiled, too, though he did not look forward to aching muscles, sore back, swollen joints, or filth under his fingernails. "Shouldn't we have brought spades? We're not going to dig with our hands."

Reeger snorted. "Now you do sound like a princess. I think you're sweet on Affonyl."

Cullin flushed. He lamely responded, "That didn't answer my question."

"Efficiency, not princessy." Reeger snorted as he stomped along. "Remember, the contractors abandoned all their shovels and spades. Why haul our own tools out here? Too much extra work."

Cullin felt relieved as he parked the handcart. "You know more about management than I do."

In Serfdom Sunrise Acres, drooping ropes with colored flags celebrated the imminent grand opening, but only a few hovel foundations had been laid. The discovery of the orc graveyard had brought all work to a screeching halt.

Looking around the sad, empty subdivision, he thought that a proper marketing agent might make a tourist attraction of the orc graveyard, maybe raise the property values again. A nice hovel built on the edge of the bone repository could be advertised as having a graveyard view. *Live on the edge of legends!* He was surprised King Longjohn hadn't thought of that before he'd abandoned Serfdom Sunrise Acres. Maybe the king had no more insight into real estate than he had into esoteric artwork.

"With the right bones and the right staging," Cullin mused, "we can make the orcs flee in terror, just the way the construction crew did."

"All part of my plan," Reeger said with a deep-throated chuckle.

"*Our* plan."

"Rust, we can divide up the credit later. But there's a difference between mere bones and *cursed* bones. That'll take a little more doing."

Cullin knew that was something the former princess and the young scullery maid could help with.

As Reeger stalked around the abandoned graveyard, kicking at clods of dirt with his boot, he sent Cullin to retrieve the abandoned shovels and spades. By the time Reeger had identified excellent skeletal repositories, the young man came back with an assortment of digging implements.

With a shovel on his shoulder, Reeger strolled around like a livestock judge at the county fair. Out of old habit, he swung the shovel and smashed clods of dirt.

Cullin brought the handcart to the first likely site, and they both began digging. Fortunately, the fog and drizzle had kept the dirt moist and soft. The old orc flesh had rotted away from the corpses, so they were only digging up mud-encrusted skeletons. Putrid skin and drooping eyeballs had never been Cullin's favorite part of the grave-robbing business, although Reeger said he had a great aptitude for the work.

They dug down, throwing the soft earth into piles. Cullin used a narrow sexton's spade to probe his way carefully, but Reeger dug with great gusto. "No need to be delicate, lad. Just dig down! You'll know when you hit an orc skull."

"But if I smash and splinter the bones they won't do us any good—"

"Don't underestimate how dense orcs heads are, or their ribs or femurs."

Cullin worked harder, throwing dirt into a neighboring plot, and soon he hooked a ribcage. After digging around the edges, he pulled out the entire set of bones. A long ulna and hand bones ended with spiked knuckles and thick phalanges.

Reeger held up a prize of his own, a fully intact skull. "Now this is what we're looking for!" He tossed it with a thunk into the bottom of the cart. "The other bones will add fine peripheral details. For veracity."

Cullin agreed. "And make it seem more real."

Since the orcs had been killed by sword thrusts and hacked by battle axes, many of the bones were nicked, but that added to the fun as well.

"Here's a big one," Cullin said. "I think it might be a king."

The two dug around the bones and excavated a full, burly skeleton. "I like that one," Reeger said. "Needs a bit of cleaning up, but it'll make a provocative display."

Working alongside Reeger, Cullin recalled previous fun times raiding church graveyards or out-of-the way peasant cemeteries. Before their small band had joined up with Affonyl, he, Reeger, and Dalbry had profited from selling "bones of the saints" to gullible local church leaders.

Now, they had dire circumstances to face, a castle to haunt, and an orc army to frighten away. "You and I make a good team, Reeger," he said as they filled the cart with rib bones, vertebrae, and blocky orc skulls.

"We do, lad." Reeger spat another wad of phlegm to the side.

As a gesture of camaraderie, Cullin did the same.

CHAPTER

THIRTY-SEVEN

O rcs had thick hides and thick skulls, but they also wore thick helmets, thick breastplates, and thick shoulderpads studded with metal bosses. They viewed the helmets as a fashion statement, wearing them for all occasions, whether pillaging, in battle, or even lounging around.

After days cooped up in Longjohn's cushy castle, though, they realized how heavy and inconvenient the body armor was. King Borc commandeered a granary closet so they could store their spare equipment. After dumping out the sacks of grain—since orcs had no fondness for bread or pastries—the orcs piled up their extra helmets, breastplates, gauntlets, back supports, girdles, and misshapen codpieces. Borc told his crew to make themselves comfortable so they could keep searching for Longjohn's treasure. With the hauntings and the curse, though, the orcs kept their weapons handy.

Affonyl and Spam crept through the passages to the rear of the repurposed grain-storage room. The two watched the orcs disrobe, chipping away at the rust and dry blood, loosening laces and buckles, peeling off their breastplates.

Affonyl hadn't thought that the orc body odor could get worse, nor had she realized that unclothed orcs were even uglier than armored orcs. Once dressed in their casual armor, the invading brutes marched off.

Spam worked the hidden latch and swung the stone doorway open so they could enter the dim room, moving quickly.

Orc stench wafted up from the discarded armor. The former princess hefted a round metal helmet with crudely drawn fangs on the sides. "This will do nicely."

Spam wrapped her small hands around the handle of a double-bladed battle axe. "Should we take a broadsword or a mace to kill any orcs we might find in an empty hallway?" She grunted as she tried to lift the heavy weapon, raising it only a few inches off the floor before letting it clunk back down on the flagstones.

"You'd only manage to cut off an orc's toes," Affonyl said. "Best to stick with crossbows." She kept sorting the stored armor, knowing that when Reeger and Cullin came back, they would have all the pieces they needed. "Find complete sets if you can, an assortment of sizes."

As they identified acceptable helmets and armor components, the scullery maid dragged the pieces out into the hidden passages. Affonyl rummaged among the armor components, moved aside a breastplate, and found an excellent pair of scuffed boots. She felt determined to scare off the orc army and get back to business. "I really would like a grand unveiling for my landscape art someday."

Spam came back from the tunnels, covered in dust and cobwebs. "I thought Rock in Its Natural State was just part of a trick. Cullin said you were scamming King Longjohn into paying you for a worthless piece of art."

"Worthless is in the eye of the beholder." Affonyl felt a warm flush in her cheeks. "And a con artist is still an artist. I take pride in my creative work."

Spam dragged off the set of boots. "I wish I was a princess. Life must be so easy."

Affonyl coughed. "Don't underestimate being set up like a prize milk cow at the fair, expected to marry an evil duke."

"But you'd still be marrying a *duke*." Spam clearly did not see the downside.

"That wasn't the life for me." She regarded the waifish scullery maid. "Better to have adventures—and also a secure job. Just think of all the opportunities you have, Spam! Three meals a day, and you get to spend time around great art. And each time you go outside with your bucket and scrub brush, you know you've done good work."

The girl tried to look on the bright side. "I used to be content here. I had a cozy nook to sleep in and a patchwork comforter." She made a rude huff. "Before one of the orcs used it as a handkerchief."

They gathered all the orc armor they needed, and Spam pulled the secret door shut behind them. Farther down the narrow passage, one of their stolen torches guttered in a sconce, illuminating the shadows and cobwebs.

As they headed to their staging area, Spam showed clear resolve. "I'm a scullery maid hiding out in secret tunnels inside an overrun castle. The possibilities are endless."

CHAPTER
THIRTY-EIGHT

Once they had all the necessary components, the companions reconvened in the art gallery hideout. While Cullin and Reeger unloaded their treasure trove of excavated orc bones and skulls, Affonyl brought in the salvaged orc armor and piled it among the bones.

Spam earned a round of applause by sneaking back from the kitchen pantries with a stolen pot of peanut butter, a jar of jam, and some salvaged stale bread. "The castle bakery hasn't produced any fresh loaves since the invasion. Something to do with the yeast, and the murder of the kitchen staff."

They all snacked on the treat as they made their plans. Reeger complained that peanut butter and jam were too messy on bread, until Affonyl suggested that he contain the goop *inside* the sandwich rather than spreading it on the outside.

Cullin lounged against the old barrels. "It's nice to have a secret clubhouse."

Reeger rummaged among the bones and orc breastplates. "It'd be nicer to have the whole rustin' castle once we scare the orcs out of here."

"And I want to free Dalbry as soon as we can." Cullin helped him sort through the best skulls, matching them up with appropriate helmets. Affonyl and Spam began stuffing ribcages inside leather breastplates and footbones into the boots. They wrapped greaves around femurs.

"Enough for four complete sets," Reeger said.

Cullin did a count in the back of his mind. "Five, if we scrimp."

"Let's just use two for our first exhibition," Affonyl said. "Make the best impact."

Reeger had retrieved a full jug of the potent moonshyne. "Hate to waste this stuff, but it's for a good cause."

Spam spoke up. "I found the perfect hallway—just outside of King Longjohn's bedchambers. We'll have the chance to do our setup before Borc goes to bed."

"We need a bold warning painted on the stone walls to hammer home the message." Affonyl nodded to herself. "ORCS MUST LEAVE—in all capital letters for emphasis. Paint it in blood. That'll terrify them."

"I thought orcs liked blood," said Cullin.

"Not when used in a literary fashion. We can paint it in big letters."

"That'll take a lot of blood." The young man felt a lump in his throat. "Does it have to be blood?"

Affonyl's brow furrowed. "What else are we going to use, Squirrel?"

"Well ... red paint?"

"Where are we going to get red paint?"

He felt confused and defensive. "Where you always get paint—from the hardware store."

"And where are we going to find a hardware store?"

Cullin sighed in resignation.

"Blood it is, then," Reeger said. He jabbed his thumb with his dagger point. When red blood welled up, he pulled the empty jam jar close so he could squeeze out more blood. The leftover strawberry preserves added a bright flare to their paint.

Affonyl showed no princessy hesitation as she did the same. Spam had to jab twice with the dagger tip because her fingers had thick callouses.

Cullin, reluctant to show any less bravery than his companions, told himself he wasn't afraid of a little pain. He cut a small gash in his palm, which bled profusely into the community blood reservoir. They all took turns until the jam pot was full.

After using cloth scraps dipped in moonshyne as a disinfectant, they bound up their minor wounds, then moved the two armored orc skeletons, the pair of skulls in thick helmets, and the highly flammable grog.

The hallway outside the king's chamber was perfect, quiet and empty before Borc's bedtime. Cullin had to take down one of Longjohn's colorful dreamcatchers to clear the wall for their dramatic warning in blood and jam.

Reeger propped up the orc armor and helmets, positioning the skeletons inside. Affonyl inspected the display, rearranged the arm bones, and cocked the helmets *just so* for dramatic effect.

Spam volunteered to paint the message, but the girl was too short to reach the high part of the wall. Since Cullin had already proved his questionable spelling ability in Ye Olde Journal, the task fell to the former princess. Affonyl smeared out in dramatic dripping red letters ORCS MUST LEAVE. She considered for a moment and added an exclamation point.

Once the tableau had been set, Reeger wrenched the cork from the moonshyne jug and doused the two armor-clad skeletons. The companions looked at one another, drew a deep breath to brace themselves (Cullin coughed because of the moonshyne fumes), and then signaled with bandaged thumbs that they were ready.

The scullery girl had brought two copper pots from the kitchens, and now she banged them together with a loud clamor. Using a wall torch, Reeger lit the two alcohol-drenched bodies on fire, while Spam kept banging the pots. As the flames surged up, the four retreated into the nearest secret passage. Cullin dragged the hidden door shut just as shouting orc warriors bounded into the corridor with torches and battle axes.

The brutes staggered to a halt. One let out a high-pitched whimper. "It's ghosts!"

More orcs stomped into the passageway, staring at the blackened skeletons engulfed in flame. Fire licked out from under the helmets. "It's the castle curse!"

One orc noticed the writing on the wall and pointed. They stood together, squinting their piggish eyes as they concentrated, moving their lips.

Finally, King Borc strode up to investigate the commotion outside his bedchamber. "What's happening?" He saw the burning skeletons, the smoking armor, and the blood-red words. "What does it mean?" He stood with his companions as they all struggled to sound out the words Affonyl had painted.

Borc ponderously read aloud, "Orcs ... must ... leave."

"I think it means we're supposed to leave," said the nearest orc.

"I don't like this castle anymore," Nrguff said.

Borc cuffed him on the side of the head. "Then find the treasure so we can get out of here!"

The nervous orcs withdrew as the alcohol fires guttered out, leaving charred bones and smoking armor.

CHAPTER

THIRTY-NINE

O ne time in a gambling den, Cullin had watched Reeger lose all the gold they had earned from selling a fake dragon eggshell. The dice turned against him again and again, and afterward Reeger waxed philosophical about the odds of winning.

"It's all about probabilities, lad. Let me give you a literary example. If you have an infinite number of monkeys and an infinite number of goose quills, inkpots, and parchment, one of them will eventually produce an illuminated monastery-quality Bible. You just have to keep trying."

Cullin was dubious about that particular example. "Instead of gambling with our gold, maybe you'd be better off if you hired monkeys and took up writing?"

Using the last remaining coins they had for one final gamble, Reeger covered his eyes, hummed a silly rhyme, and rolled the dice across the table—and won. "That proves it, lad! There's luck—and there's dumb luck."

"That part I believe," Cullin had replied.

Now, after so many days of fruitless searches, as the orc's desperation built higher, the combination of dumb and luck finally paid off for them.

One orc, Jerx, accidentally blundered into an unlatched entrance to the hidden catacombs. He pushed open the secret panel and stared into the dark opening, baffled. The orc might have imagined the mysterious tunnels to be a lair of ghosts and run away in terror, but instead, because Borc had demanded they find the hidden treasure, Jerx bellowed his discovery to the whole castle, and the orcs came running.

Dozens rushed to the scene, peering into the dim passage and trying to work up the courage to explore. King Borc arrived, holding a mace in one fist and a torch in the other. "Yup, that looks like a treasure hiding place! Search these passages! Ransack every cobwebbed corner." He lowered his voice to entice his comrades. "I'll give *a gold coin* to the first orc who finds the treasure pile."

Never adept at mathematics or accounting, the orcs considered that a good deal. The whole band charged pell-mell into the catacombs.

From inside the tunnels, Cullin and Spam heard the commotion and peeked around the corner to see the invaders boil in. She grabbed his arm. "Come on, Squirrel! We've got to warn Reeger."

The girl darted off, and he ran panting after her.

Affonyl had gone exploring on her own to find more ingredients for their haunting, but Reeger had curled up for a nap in Longjohn's art grotto gallery. Now Cullin roused his friend. "The orcs are coming! Wake up!"

As Reeger snorted, blinked, and rubbed his eyes, they heard the nearby stomp of boots, the clatter of weapons and armor, gruff voices. "This way! Something up ahead."

After the previous night's flaming display, the remaining orc skeletons were piled against the side wall, but the bones needed sorting. Reeger had barely started assembling two partial skeletons and a few mismatched armor components before dozing off.

Cullin looked at the pile of leftovers. There wasn't time to arrange a spectacle as before, but even disorganized, it might make an impact. "Light them up, while we find a place to hide."

Reeger brought his ceramic jug and poured it all out. "This is the last of the moonshyne—better make it count."

As the clamor grew louder, Cullin touched his torch to the mound and followed his friends into a dark, narrow side passage as the flames roared to life. "Burning skeletons are always a good distraction."

Led by Borc himself, wearing his tiny crown, the brutes charged into the art gallery. They stared at the vault full of paintings, sculptures, vases, ashtrays, and decoupage—then recoiled in terror when they saw the jumble of burning skeletons against the wall.

"Somebody else got here first!" Goil said.

"The ghosts killed 'em!" yelled Olugg.

"This is the ghosts' lair," said Jerx. "Look how they've decorated it with pretty pictures."

Borc stood with his fists bunched, and one of the tarnished brass bosses on his leather breastplate popped out and hit the grotto wall with a *spang*. "Maybe there's treasure's inside that rare historical vase!"

Goil upended a tall urn, but found only a few dead spiders inside. He smashed the vase on the floor, while Borc knocked aside cute porcelain figurines, pulled down framed paintings, scattered enameled pottery across the stone floor. "It's got to be here!"

The burning bones and armor sputtered and crackled in a last, particularly flammable gasp.

"Nothing but ghosts," Olugg cried. "And they're watching us!"

Several of the orcs bolted out of the grotto chamber, and Borc was eager to follow. "Back to the throne room—where it's safe!" The orc king hesitated before fleeing. He glanced back at the paintings, especially the costumed medieval puppies playing cards.

He tucked the painting under his beefy arm and marched away.

When all the orcs had rushed away from the throne hall to another part of the castle, Affonyl seized the opportunity.

Poisoning the linens in the bunkroom had been a great deal of fun, but she imagined numerous other possibilities. In particular, she thought Ugnarok's sinister empty helmet still held a lot of potential. If only she could retrieve it from the ashes ...

When King Borc and his crew left the banquet hall, the former princess opened the secret door. Seeing no watchful brutes, she scurried to the great fireplace, which had burned out. The superstitious orcs were afraid to touch the embers after the sparking and smoking helmet had crashed down into the hearth.

On her knees she rummaged in the cold ashes, then pulled out the wizard-mage's ugly blackened helm. She brushed at the gray powder and smiled. The soot made it look all the more ominous.

Hearing an unexpected sound, she spun about and saw King Longjohn dangling on the wall. The lanky man was snoring, catching a nap in the brief respite now that the orcs had left the hall. He grunted in his sleep.

If her companions had been with her, they would have worked together to take him down. Affonyl doubted he liked being a work of art. Still carrying Ugnarok's helmet, she darted over to the throne, looking up to assess the situation.

"King Longjohn!" she said in a nervous whisper, then glanced back into the halls, listening for orcs.

He snorted and stirred, and the chains jangled, but he didn't wake up.

Manacles bound his wrists and ankles, but she couldn't see whether they required a key or worked on a more convenient latch system. "King Longjohn!"

Before he awakened, she heard gruff voices in the outer corridors, orcs hurrying back to the throne room. They sounded agitated, frightened.

She glanced up at the dangly, gangly king, and knew she wouldn't have time to free him. With a sigh, she ran back to the hidden door, carrying the hideous charred helmet.

Now, to figure out what to do with it....

CHAPTER

FORTY

Considering all the haunting they had already accomplished, Cullin felt it was time to give Sir Dalbry an update. He didn't want the old knight to be left out of the loop. "He deserves a progress report, since the haunting was his idea in the first place.

"Rust, he's got the easy part just lounging in a comfortable cell while we do all the work!" Reeger had peeled open a blue tin of Sue-Pam meat product and snacked on it along with some peanuts from the keg.

The scullery girl offered to go with Cullin. "While we're at it, we should bring the prisoners some food, after all. We have plenty of extra cans, even for soft-bellied nobles."

"Good idea," Cullin said, looking at Reeger's questionable feast. "They may even be hungry enough to enjoy it."

Affonyl was busy scouring the stained helmet of Ugnarok, using Spam's old scrub brush and bucket. The singed bones had been extinguished, and many of them were intact enough to be put to secondary use.

Cullin felt anxious to go, but Reeger put his boots up on an empty barrel. "I'll just wait here a bit. I'm taking my lunch break."

Cullin and the girl filled a sack with cans of Sue-Pam, then made their way to the dungeon levels. Since they could not deliver food through the chinks in the back of the dungeon cell, they had to emerge into the main prison tunnels, which were lit only by low-wattage torches. The cans in Cullin's sack clanked together as he hurried beside Spam. Both of them doubted the orcs would waste manpower guarding the prisoners, since they were far more interested in finding treasure.

When they reached the cell, Cullin was shocked to see how gaunt, haggard, and miserable the captives looked.

"Cullin, lad!" Dalbry said in a raspy voice. He moved unsteadily over to the bars, gripping them as if he needed the support to keep standing. "I could use some company." He lowered his voice, glancing behind him. "Their conversation is despairing, yet pretentious at the same time."

Cullin was eager to update Dalbry. "We're here now, and we've got a lot of good things to report."

"But did you bring any good things *to eat?*" asked a man Cullin recognized as Lowduke McCowan.

Spam took the sack and reached inside. "We brought a special delicacy."

Cullin was about to tell them to lower their expectations, but he could see how hungry they looked. He frowned. "Didn't the orcs feed you?"

The knight sighed. "Why would those brutes bother to feed us, lad?"

"Well, to fatten you up, if nothing else," the girl said cheerfully. "Poor planning on their part." She offered the blue tins through the bars of the cell door. "Here, this is very nutritious—packed with protein, fat, sodium, and preservatives."

Dalbry passed the cans to his fellow prisoners, keeping one for himself.

"Did you bring any napkins?" asked Lady Pattilane.

"You'll have to rough it," Spam said. "Think of it as a dungeon picnic."

Barely able to contain his enthusiasm, Cullin described the progress they had made in spooking the orcs over the past several nights. "We killed four of them so far, two by crossbow, two by poison. Affonyl retrieved Ugnarok's helmet, and we still have leftover bones—at least one complete skeleton."

"A most satisfactory start," the knight said. "But could you possibly pick up the pace?"

"Don't worry, we can always bring more cans of food if you get hungry," said the girl.

The nobles opened their tins and sniffed skeptically at the pinkish gelatinous substance.

"I wish we could get you out of that cell, Dalbry," Cullin said. "With your help we'd run the orcs out of the castle so much faster!"

The knight rattled the barred door. "I would dearly love to fight like a true legendary knight, rather than an art critic." He slumped back. "Alas, the cell is securely locked."

The nobles tried to tell their stories all at once, wanting to know if ransom notes had gone out, asking about the news headlines of the day. Cullin couldn't keep track of it all, and worse, the jabber distracted him.

Spam heard the noise first and let out a yelp of alarm. Cullin spun just in time to see a lumbering orc clutching a knotted club. The orc stomped forward, and his eyes blazed when he saw the two standing outside of the cell.

"Wrong side of the door!" He charged toward them, swinging his deadly weapon. He filled the passageway, preventing them from running back to the hidden door.

Sir Dalbry and the nobles backed deeper into the cell, but Cullin and Spam were trapped outside. They pressed their backs against the bars. Spam whipped out her little dagger and held it up, looking feral, while Cullin drew his own knife, but the orc was far too big and burly for them to fight.

"I'll try to slice his ear off, Squirrel," the scullery maid vowed.

"I'll go for his nose," Cullin said, realizing that it might well be the last thing he ever did.

"I'm gonna smash you through those bars!" Clearly, the orc could kill both of them with one blow of the massive weapon.

Cullin squeezed his eyes shut, waiting for the end.

Suddenly the brute staggered and lost his balance. "Urghk!"

Cullin opened his eyes to see that Reeger had pounced out from the hidden passage and jumped onto the orc's back. The ugly helmet had a convenient curved horn on one side, which Reeger used as a handle. Straddling the brute, he pulled back on the horn to tilt the enemy's head up and expose his thick neck.

With a grunt of effort, Reeger slashed his dagger across the orc's throat. Blood sprayed out. The brute grunted, gurgled, and then fell forward to crash onto the dirty dungeon floor.

In the cell, the nobles gasped in terror.

"Bravo, Reeger," said Dalbry. "We're very pleased to see you."

Pleased with himself, Reeger wiped his bloody blade on the orc's leather chest plate and stood up. "Rust, I've been keeping my eyes open for an opportunity like that."

Spam slid her dagger back into its sheath. "I would have sliced off his ear."

With a more important idea, Cullin dropped to his knees beside the corpse. Rolling the brute over, he was rewarded to hear a satisfying jingle. "And I've been looking for this sort of opportunity."

An iron ring and a set of keys hung on the thick belt. Cullin held them up in the dim torchlight, jingling them for Dalbry to see. "We can set you loose at last!"

"An excellent turn of events, lad," the knight said.

The young man stepped up to the rusty lock and worked the keys one after another, trying different ones.

The knight turned back to his co-prisoners. "Maybe we should all just slip away from the castle. Evacuation is sometimes the best plan."

The nobles were greatly concerned. "Sounds risky to me," said Sub-baron Darylking.

"We have been quite safe here," his wife said. "Apart from the lack of hospitality, the cell bars protected us. The brutes couldn't harm us."

At last Cullin found a key that worked. The lock clicked, and he swung open the barred door.

Dalbry hurried out, but the others remained where they were. "And whatever would we do hiding in dank, secret tunnels?" asked Highduke Lessa. "At least these cells have a bit of ventilation."

Reeger let out a skeptical snort and turned to his companions, lowering his voice. "She's got a point. If we took these fancy-schmancy nobles into hiding, they might accidentally alert the orcs to where we are."

Cullin understood how unruly some nobles could be in a situation that required competence, bravery, and discretion.

Dalbry stepped over the body of the orc lying on the floor, carrying his still-unopened can of Sue-Pam meat. "I, for one, would prefer to be a more active part of this haunting."

Cullin's heart warmed. "It'll be good to have the team back together again."

Blande called, "Best of luck to you, Dalbry. You always were at greater risk, because few people would pay to ransom an art critic."

After coaching the captive nobles to explain that murderous ghosts had killed the brute, if any orcs should ask, Dalbry wished his former cell-mates the best. Cullin locked the cell door again, pocketed the keys, and promised that they would keep trying to frighten the orcs out of the castle.

They ducked back into the hidden tunnels, which the old knight found quite satisfying. "Excellent. Part of the standard design for castles."

"Affonyl will be glad to see you," Cullin said.

"I look forward to a full debriefing," Dalbry said. "I had plenty of time to ponder ideas while in that dungeon cell, and I can't wait to implement them."

CHAPTER

FORTY-ONE

O nce he was well fed and cleaned up, Dalbry was eager to contribute to the haunting. He had a lot of catching up to do.

The young scullery maid had taken him to the armory and holiday-decoration storeroom, where he selected a fine sword of his own. The knightly blade restored and invigorated his confidence. He couldn't wait for the opportunity to use it.

Due to the unfortunate circumstances in King Longjohn's castle, though, he hadn't given a single orc so much as a fat lip from a well-placed punch. That didn't align with his legendary status.

Though he had made the best of his situation locked in the dungeon cell with stuffy company, he had a great deal of catching up to do. In the dragon business Dalbry always played a prominent role. He was used to being the front man, the legendary knight, the dragon slayer.

After learning the details of his companions' efforts, he wanted to ratchet up the tension, and the possibilities were endless. King Borc was already upset at not finding any treasure. The murdered orcs, as well as the supposed ghosts, the moaning wind, the whispered curses—all made the orcs uneasy and even more unruly than usual.

Dalbry picked up the retrieved helmet that had made Wizard-

Mage Ugnarok so terrifying, turned it over to study it, peeked through the empty eyeholes. Just dropping it into the fireplace had been their first act of terror inflicted against the orcs, but he felt it had much more potential. He could use it for a different scam. After all, Dalbry didn't want the others to think he wasn't contributing his fair share of the ghostly effort.

When he saw the one remaining orc skeleton, complete with all its body parts, a truly innovative idea came together in his mind. Reeger would help him implement the details.

Cullin thought it was a shame to let the leftover bones go to waste. While raiding the graveyard, he and Reeger had appropriated extra skulls and numerous spare body parts. Once Dalbry took what he needed, the mismatched skeletons and armor components weren't enough to make complete sets, but Affonyl pointed out that the orcs didn't know much about anatomy. Loose scattered bones might be just as frightening.

After scoping out the castle's empty corridors, Cullin, Affonyl, and Spam emerged with their baskets of bones. As the orcs continued to search amidst rising superstitious tensions, they would eventually stumble upon these grisly little reminders.

The three darted down the shadowy corridors late at night, flitting from one pool of torchlight to another, strewing leftover bones like flower girls at a wedding. Alert for blundering orcs, they tossed a femur here, a few rib bones there, rolled an old skull into a corner. The disconnected bones gave the impression of a total massacre.

"They want to find treasure, but all they're going to find are skeletons," Spam snickered.

Affonyl was more contemplative. "I wish there was treasure. Longjohn gave us the impression that he had chests of gold to pay us."

"For the next scam we should run a credit check," Cullin muttered.

"The king uses regular peanut shipments to fund his line of credit," the scullery maid said. "He writes checks and pays his bills, with very little left over to reward the staff."

"Or to buy more artwork." Cullin shook his head. "The orcs don't see the inflated value in the masterpiece collection. Longjohn's money is all tied up in assets."

Affonyl sounded discouraged. "Well, the orcs won't leave unless they have some treasure, no matter how scared they are." She tossed a fibula down the hall, and it rattled and clanked against a suit of armor in an alcove.

"I know where to find one chest of gold—the king's petty-cash fund," the scullery maid said. She discarded the last of her bones, then shook out the basket, rattling loose a few more metatarsals.

Now she had Affonyl's complete attention. "Petty cash? Where is it?"

"Around the corner in a doorway under the stairs. But we're not supposed to use it unless we write out a receipt."

The former princess's eyes were bright. "Show us!" She distributed the last of her spare bones, and they hurried along with empty baskets.

Spam led them to a door tucked under a side staircase. "This special financial storeroom is known only to the king, his treasury department, and a few selected scullery maids."

Cullin was surprised. "Selected scullery maids? And you're one of them?"

"I keep my ears open." She swung open the low door, and they all ducked to enter the cobwebbed chamber, which was empty except for a single wooden chest on the floor. Spam opened the latch and lifted the lid to reveal that it was filled with gold coins. "This is King Longjohn's walking-around money, the spare cash he takes with him into the harbor town for shopping."

"Oh," Cullin said, "his mad money."

The girl looked around, reticent. "We're supposed to leave a receipt if we take this."

Affonyl decisively closed the lid. "We'll take care of the paper-work once we resolve the invasion situation. Besides, the king promised me a down payment for Rock in Its Natural State—which is completed, even if it's still un-unveiled."

Cullin picked up one side of the heavy chest. "What are we going to do with it?"

"It's a chest full of gold, Squirrel," Affonyl said, taking the other side. "We'll figure out something."

CHAPTER

FORTY-TWO

After another day of fruitless treasure hunting in the confusing castle, King Borc retired to his royal bed chambers—formerly Longjohn's suite—to take a load off his feet. He was no longer enamored with his usurped kingdom and the responsibilities of high-level royal management.

Being a king, especially one without a treasure, was not as exciting as it had sounded. Borc wasn't sure why he stayed here anymore.

One more orc had been found murdered by the ghosts, this time in the dungeons. In addition to the burning skeletons he and his comrades had found in Longjohn's junk grotto, now loose bones were strewn all over the halls. Dead orcs were unhappy orcs.

And Ugnarok's scary helmet had vanished from the fireplace! Part of him was glad the ugly thing was gone, since the other orcs had been afraid to touch it or move it ... but did that mean the dead wizard-mage had taken it back to continue his vengeance? Was Ugnarok's ghost now roaming the halls?

That wouldn't be good.

Borc had never wanted to rule the kingdom in the first place. He didn't understand why the evil sorcerer had been so hell-bent on having this castle, although he definitely had some personal issues.

When he was just an ugly little child, Borc's mother gave him a lot of maternal wisdom, emphasizing each lesson with a hard smack to his head. (One such lesson was that he learned to wear a helmet from an early age.) His mother had said, "Don't ever get too big for your breeches," and she punctuated the wisdom with another hard smack. "If you split your butt seam, it's damned hard to mend." She held up her fat hand. "Especially with fingers like blood sausages."

Borc realized that Ugnarok had grown too big for his magical breeches—and he had died choking and writhing in the throne hall. That was worse than splitting a butt seam, no matter how difficult it was to mend.

"Big drafty castle, too many ghosts—not enough treasure!" Borc grumbled to himself. "We never needed that nonsense before. Yup, we were happy orcs, lived a contented life."

He plopped down on the king-size bed (Extra Long in this case). The mattress was overstuffed with straw and feathers, and the bedspread and blankets were made of fine fabrics without any satisfying prickliness. As far as he could tell there weren't even any bedbugs!

He had slept in this chamber for several nights now, after his crew had changed the linens and replaced them with fresh bed coverings from the royal linen closet. The rest of his orcs slept in the bunkroom, close enough to smell one another, to hear the snores and grumbles like lullabies. Although there was the downside of ghostly insulting voices coming through the walls and the risk of horrible death by poisoning.... Maybe he was better off here.

With thick fingers he worked at the clasps and laces of his boots, until he pried them free. He pulled off the boots and wiggled his toes. The powerful smell of his feet wafted up strong enough to drown out the sickly-sweet bowls of potpourri that King Longjohn kept on the royal dresser.

Before turning in, Borc checked under the bed, but saw no ghosts. The wooden door of the closet that held all of Longjohn's fancy garments—none of which fit Borc—was closed securely. Now he could get a good night's sleep.

He took one last look at the colorful painting of dogs playing cards, which was mounted on the opposite wall so he could see it from his pillow. The funny picture made him smile.

He blew out the candle and slumped back in the darkness. The eerie moaning sounds drifting through the walls made it hard for him to doze off, but he did manage to dream of roaming the countryside, bashing things, ransacking villages, enjoying life....

With a loud clank of iron chains followed by a rattling boom, his closet door smashed open. "This castle is cursed!" said a deep, terrifying voice.

In the closet with Longjohn's kingly garments stood a tall, terrifying skeleton—and the skull wore Ugnarok's helmet! Fire flared in the eyeholes. At first he thought the small flames were merely candles, but his terror transformed them into demonic blazes.

The skeleton's arms raised up, threatening—or warning? Ugnarok's helmet caught fire, and blue sparkles and smoke gushed from the empty ribcage. The skeleton moved and flailed. "Orcs must leave!"

Borc leaped out of the king-sized bed, yelling as he bounded for the door. He thought he saw a shadow, some figure moving behind the skeleton, but he wasn't interested in understanding. This was not a time for dangerous curiosity!

He bolted out of the royal bedchamber, bellowing for his orcs. He'd had enough! Borc had been too stubborn to give up, but now he realized the error of his ways. No treasure was worth this.

It was time to get back to a much safer pillaging routine.

On his way to the banquet hall, he tripped over a loose femur lying on the floor. He sprawled on his face and slid forward into a broken skull in the corner. It gave him even more incentive to hurry to get out of there.

Standing on the dais, Borc called his disorderly orcs to order, but they were more skittish than ever. "Yup, it is time to cut our losses!"

"Have there been even more losses?" Olugg asked. The other brutes looked at one another, as if trying to take attendance. Some were seated on the banquet table benches, others leaned against the stone walls.

"I miss pillaging and burning," said Qwol.

"Me too," said Goil. "Free to wreck and roam wherever we please, all the townspeople we could eat."

"And treasure whenever we wanted it," said Olugg.

"We never needed treasure before." Borc slouched on the throne. "Yup, we were happy orcs."

The brutes pounded their spears and axe handles on the floor in agreement.

Borc wished orc culture had a more parliamentary way of replacing leaders who no longer wanted the job. Sure, some orc could always challenge him to trial by combat and kill him to take his place, given enough dumb luck—but that wasn't the way Borc intended to retire.

He raised his fat chin. "There's no treasure here, and it's not worth fighting the ghosts. Time for a new adventure."

The orcs looked at him with expressions of hope. Goil asked, "Are we leaving? Should we all pack?"

"Yup, it's back to the good old days of raiding towns, burning taverns, and scaring off flocks of sheep."

The band of orcs cheered.

On the wall, a miserable King Longjohn rattled his chains as he tried to clap his hands. "Thank you for visiting. Please come again soon." The manacles stopped his wrists, so he couldn't actually bring his hands together.

"Not so fast," Nrguff interrupted. His stomach growled like a mastiff that had been too long on a fasting diet. "We ate up all the snacks that were left from the invasion, but we've still got those tasty nobles in the dungeon larder. Shouldn't we have a going-away feast? One for the road?"

Borc remembered yet another lesson that his mother had taught him. "It's stupid to waste food."

He stood up, adjusted his too-small crown. "That'll be our treasure. Build up the fires, mount the spits!" He assigned two of his orcs to the kitchens. "And prepare some nice sauces. When it's all ready, bring up those nobles from the dungeons. Once the fires are hot, we'll roast them alive."

"Somebody set the table!" Qwol shouted.

The orcs quickly forgot their superstitious terror.

FORTY-THREE

Panting hard, Cullin and the young scullery maid ran back from the peepholes behind the banquet hall. "The orcs are leaving!" Spam cried.

Dalbry drew himself up as if he had found his legendary role again. "Excellent. Our flaming skeleton and Ugnarok's helmet served as precisely the catalyst we intended." He reached out and gave Reeger a high-five.

Without context, the scullery maid's report sounded like cause for celebration, until Cullin explained the rest of the alarming news. "And they're going to eat the prisoners before they go! The captive nobles are about to become hors d'oeuvres, main dishes, and desserts. The orcs are firing up the kitchen ovens right now."

Reeger grunted. "I wonder if they found more peanut recipes."

Affonyl cracked her knuckles—which her princessy advisors had told her never to do—and got to work. "No time to lose."

Dalbry nodded. "Fortunately, the rest of our castle-haunting plan is ready to be implemented. We have our separate duties, and it's time to get started." The old knight had assumed a leadership role again. "Given the imminent barbecue, our first order of business is to liberate the hostages, and I shall do that." He held up the jingling iron ring of keys. "The rest of you know what to do."

"I love it when a scam comes together," Affonyl said.

"Rust, I love it when a scam *works*," Reeger said.

Sir Dalbry was glad to have his sword as well. Not only would he liberate the imprisoned nobles and art aficionados, he needed them to take part in the grand finale. But he had to whisk them to safety before the orcs decided to eat them.

After the others went their separate ways, Dalbry headed off to the main dungeon level. Holding his sword, he emerged from the hidden doorway, glanced from side to side to make sure that no orc sous chefs had arrived early to prep the meal.

Seeing the knight approach, the nobles rose to their feet, haggard and shaking. They were a miserable lot, thin from near starvation, with hollow eyes and gnawed fingernails. Empty blue tins of Sue-Pam littered the cell floor.

"Have you defeated the orcs yet?" asked Darylking.

"How long does a haunting take?" asked Pattilane.

Dalbry approached the cell door, sorting through the keys on the ring. "The orcs have indeed decided to leave." The prisoners managed to smile, shuffling toward the barred wall. "But the bad news is that they have decided to throw a farewell feast before they go —and you're all on the menu. Thus, it's time for me to liberate you from the dungeon and take you into hiding."

The captives looked uneasy, but Dalbry couldn't let their intransigence grow. It was all a matter of timing now, with his companions each doing their parts. "You'll be happy to know that we have snacks in the secret hideout."

That was enough to convince them.

He swung open the rusty cell door, and the captives stumbled into the dungeon corridor, shaking and chattering. The knight directed them toward the hidden doorway, waving his sword for good measure. "You will all help with the final phase of our haunting. Rest assured that this desperate plan was developed by professionals."

The nobles were duly reassured.

He closed and locked the cell door after the last captive had left, then followed them into the hidden passages. "We're going to the guest bedrooms and the spare linen closet. This castle needs more ghosts."

After sneaking out of the castle, Reeger hurried to the stables. The mounts were waiting, munching contentedly on hay, though the mule gave him a look that suggested it was time to change the water in the trough.

Reeger chided the mule. "No drinking until after work. We've got an important job to do."

He patted Drizzle on the side of the neck, and the gray-and-brown gelding snorted, ready to become a powerful steed again. Pony wanted to take part, too, but Reeger doubted he would need a third animal. "I'll come back for you, if there's a job opportunity."

He saddled the horse and mule using the tack stored in the stables, then searched among the barrels, gardening tools, spare roofing shingles, and hardware supplies, until he found two coils of rope. He ran out into the courtyard fog, secured each end properly, and tugged to make sure that the knots were tight. He returned to the stables, unrolling the ropes along the way. Leading the gelding and the mule to the side of the stables, he secured the ropes to their harnesses, checking the knots.

Drizzle seemed disappointed to be treated as a plow horse instead of a knight's steed, but Reeger patted him again. "Just remember, every member of the team has to play a particular role in the dragon business."

The mule let out a soft, annoyed bray that demonstrated his disinterest in being a cooperative team member. Instead, he munched on the fresh dewy grass in the courtyard.

"Now we just wait," Reeger said. Giving incentive to his team members, he produced wrinkly old crabapples he had found in a storage barrel. He tossed one each to Drizzle and the mule, then trotted off to give Pony a treat as well.

Reeger ate the last crabapple and waited for the mayhem to erupt.

In the castle kitchens the ovens were stoked and spits mounted in the big fireplaces. Some brutes ransacked the pantries for herbs, vinegar, and honey so they could mix special basting sauces from orc family recipes. Despite their general fear of the ghosts, they were glad for a large barbecue cookoff. One giant cauldron hung over low coals to simmer because King Borc wanted some cuts of meat to be slow-cooked.

Goil, Jerx, and Olugg marched down to the dungeon level with nets, barbed spears, and filleting knives. They had instructions to take a few nobles right now, so the orc chefs could start the first course of the feast, but other guests would be brought up hourly so the banquet could continue until dawn. The orcs were frustrated and disappointed that they had never found any treasure, but the prospect of an all-you-can-eat buffet made everything better.

When the three orcs reached the dungeon levels, however, they were astonished to find the dungeon cell meat locker empty.

Olugg trudged up and down the corridors to double-check the cell address, but there was no sign of the captives. Goil pressed his face against the bars, peering into the dim cell. A lone rat scurried around the edge of the chamber, snuffling in empty blue cans on the floor. It stood up on its hind legs and raised its forepaws in a shrug.

Olugg spoke through chattering teeth. "Maybe the ghosts ate them."

FORTY-FOUR

Affonyl had never been fond of the spoiled, tedious members of the nobility. From growing up in the court of King Norrimund the Corpulent, she remembered the pompous nobles she'd endured at jousting contests, court banquets, and seemingly endless recitations of heraldry and lineage. Thanks to her training, she knew how to fake a mildly interested expression, while occupying her real thoughts with Wizard Edgar's natural science lessons.

Still, the former princess did have compassion. The noble prisoners—not to mention the king—needed to be rescued from their horrible fates. So, while Borc and his band were distracted throughout the castle, running about with barbecue preparations, she knew it was her true princessy duty to un-display King Longjohn.

When the throne room was empty, she darted into the hall, where chairs were overturned and dishes strewn about. If she'd had a chance, she might have taken Ugnarok's charred metal helmet from Borc's closet and stuck it in a flower alcove here, for additional scariness.

More important, though, was for her to do a solo rescue. Dangling in manacles on the wall, the lanky king blinked at her in surprise and actually brightened. He shifted his shoulders in the oversized frame. "It's Affonyl NoLastName!" His beard had grown shaggier in the days he had been on artistic display. "Sorry about your grand unveiling, but I'm glad you got away. You must continue to create great art."

She stood on her tiptoes beneath him and fumbled with the shackles around his ankles. "We'll reschedule the unveiling once the orcs are gone." She heaved a sigh of relief. "Good, these are just screw-bolt fastenings." She worked the first thumbscrew to loosen the iron band. "Orcs have trouble keeping track of keys, I suppose."

"As do I," said King Longjohn.

When she got the first ankle band free, the king heaved a sigh of relief and flexed his leg, though his other three limbs were still fastened to the wall. Keeping her ear cocked for any oncoming orcs, she worked swiftly on. Her fingers were sore by the time she undid the two wrist bands and the last ankle, but she had built up callouses since she'd stopped being a princess.

At last, she helped lower the gangly king to the floor. He collapsed weakly. "That's quite a relief."

"It's not over yet," she said, taking his elbow. "The orcs are still in the castle, but we're trying to scare them off. One more ambitious haunting."

Longjohn rose to his full height and shook his head. After dangling for days, he had been stretched another inch or two taller. "I honestly didn't know my castle was cursed. Those ghosts never bothered me before."

Affonyl hurried him to the nearest secret passage. "Ghosts are what you make of them—and now you have to be a ghost with the rest of us."

When she yanked his arm, he winced. "Do you think we could stop by the apothecary in the lower level, get some willow-bark tea—"

"Later." She pulled him into the hidden passageway. "To the linen closet, where you can join Dalbry and the other ghosts."

In all of the castle's secret places, the only real gold Cullin and his companions had found was Longjohn's petty-cash fund. For the plan, they would have to make the best of the limited treasure.

Leaving Dalbry with the nobles in the linen closet to prepare for their final assault, Cullin and Spam carried the small chest of gold coins out to the side courtyard. Reeger was already in position by the stables, but there was one more thing to prepare before they could call the orcs.

In the dead of night, Cullin could see only a blur of the full moon behind the ever-present fog. Even the screeching seagulls overhead seemed confused as to the time of day.

They lugged the heavy chest to Affonyl's tarpaulin-covered landscape art. After setting the burden down, he and the scullery girl worked at the anchor ropes to remove the canvas. While Cullin fumbled to undo the tight knots, Spam found a faster solution by slashing the cords with her knife. Then they pulled the sheet off of the enormous slab of rock.

He stood with his hands on his hips and felt disappointed for the former princess. "That's not quite the unveiling Affonyl wanted."

Spam just made a rude huff.

With the artwork on full display, the two carried the chest underneath the overhang, where Affonyl had sat in her folding chair during Longjohn's preparatory banquet. They scattered handfuls of gold over the ground in a redistribution of wealth, though they were each wise enough to pocket some of the coins for their own future expenditures.

When the chest was empty, they moved it to the shadows underneath the rock slab, lid tantalizingly closed, so the orcs could imagine it might still be full. With all the gold scattered to attract the orcs, the two dashed away to find Reeger.

When the freed noble prisoners and art aficionados had finished preparing in the spare-linen closets, Dalbry drilled them on their duties, had them practice their ghostly chants. The knight did not have his shining armor, but there were plenty of bedsheets to go around—and that would do.

Just in time, Affonyl joined them with a shaky King Longjohn, rescued from his manacles on the wall. He walked with a wobbly gait, but Dalbry was glad to see him. "Right this way, Sire. We have a bedsheet for you. High thread count—I believe it was originally from your own bed."

The sheets had been distributed to the noble prisoners, clean white linens for all, except a few stragglers who had to use spring floral prints. Dalbry put those people in the back of the group, where they wouldn't be immediately seen.

Affonyl donned a designated sheet for herself, while the knight inspected his linen-covered crew. They seemed a hopeless lot, but he was counting on the fog as well as the confusion and gullibility of the orcs.

The former princess and Dalbry pushed the nobles along the corridor to the outer doors.

Longjohn staggered forward, swinging his long arms and legs, which made the bedsheet ripple ominously. "I can't see a thing," he said. The sheet was too long and tangled around his feet.

Dalbry straightened the hem to give him more room. "You must be at the forefront, Sire. You are the king, after all. Their true leader." He lowered his voice to a mutter. "Even if it is the blind leading the blind."

As they hurried to get into position, the king raised a gangly arm. "Onward! We must drive out those monsters and avenge the damage they've done to my art collection."

Dalbry adjusted the bedsheet on his head.

CHAPTER

FORTY-FIVE

When he learned that the noble captives had disappeared, Borc felt his stomach growl. He had been looking forward to the feast as a way to salvage this invasion debacle. His orcs were difficult to control on a good day, and the presence of ghosts, curses, and burning orc skeletons did not make his job as king any easier.

He stalked restlessly through empty dungeons, the empty kitchens, the smelly empty bunkroom. The tiny crown weighed heavily on his head.

If only they had found some token amount of treasure, the orcs could have departed in imagined victory. Now, Borc was fed up—and yet entirely unfed. Without the noble prisoners, they couldn't even have a farewell feast! He would go down as a failure in the great orc histories, even if orcs didn't write any histories.

Then a miracle happened.

From the side courtyard, someone shouted. "The treasure! We found the treasure!"

Borc didn't recognize the voice, but he had trouble keeping track of his band anyway. He still didn't really know how many of his band were dead, or which ones.

"Treasure!" was the operative word in the shouts, and he grabbed his battle axe and strode out of the bunkroom. "As your king, I will investigate."

Also hearing the word "treasure," the remaining orcs decided to accompany their king as bodyguards, as well as participants in the wealth. They all charged out into the courtyard, where the thick fog obscured details.

"It's over here!" the voice called out again.

Borc increased speed, stomping on the wet grass. He saw the immense propped slab on display, no longer covered by the tarp, but what caught his eye was the gleam of gold coins scattered on the ground. They were definitely shiny.

"The treasure!" He glanced at the discarded gray tarpaulin that lay crumpled off to the side. "Didn't anybody think to look there?"

"We did! Honest!" More orcs rushed forward.

Borc ran ahead and bent down to snatch up the coins. He held them in his palm. Definitely gold pieces. Lots of them.

Three other orcs dropped to the ground and grabbed at the shiny coins. Others discovered the treasure chest tucked in the back. "There's more!"

Borc experienced a warm satisfaction at last. "Yup, it's here. The treasure's all here!"

Cullin and Spam ran up to Reeger by the stables. "The orcs found it! King Borc is with the gold!"

The joyous orc shouts had already told Reeger all he needed to hear. He remembered the challenge of erecting Affonyl's great masterwork. Now it would become a piece of proper performance art.

"Step back, lad." He pushed Cullin behind him.

Drizzle and the mule stood with the ropes tied to their harnesses, ready to go, and Reeger yelled into the gelding's ear. "Hyaah!" With a greenwood switch from an ornamental shrub, he smacked the mule's buttocks.

Both animals lunged forward, pulling hard. The taut rope strained and creaked, its other end tied to the wooden support pole.

The orcs reveled in the treasure they had found, scrambling to gather the gold pieces. A dozen of them crowded together, grabbing the coins. The rest of the orcs tried to shove their way forward, but there was no room under the rock.

With a great scrape and groan, the rejected ship's mast popped out of place and tumbled forward. Rock in Its Natural State collapsed into place with a heavy squish.

A sudden, horrified silence fell over the foggy courtyard as the rest of the orcs gaped at what had happened.

Cullin shook his head. "King Borc simply didn't understand art."

Reeger grunted, "Worse, he didn't understand gravity."

After the resounding thud, more than two dozen orc warriors staggered back with a simultaneous gasp of horror. On the edge of the courtyard, even more brutes struggled to see through the murky fog. The nearer orcs stumbled away, confused by the now-horizontal rock slab.

Milling about, they all remembered the curse. As the orcs looked back at the castle silhouetted in the mist, an outcry arose. "King Borc is dead! King Borc is dead!"

Then in a second chorus, "Ugnarok is dead, too! Ugnarok is dead, too!"

Those two details slowly worked through the minds of the orcs until they concluded that this was a dangerous place. They raised weapons as their paranoia increased and they prepared to evacuate the premises.

Then all the ghosts arrived.

After rushing through the empty castle, the sheeted nobles suddenly hesitated at the side courtyard, reluctant to run unarmed into an orc army.

"I can't see a thing," Longjohn repeated, plucking at the covering over his face.

"The important part is that they all see you," Affonyl urged them forward. She was disheartened by the collapse of her ambitious work of landscape art. But the poignancy of a true masterpiece was to know its transience and fragility.

At the front of the group, Dalbry yelled, "You're doing great. You're all terrifying." He gave Longjohn an encouraging shove. "Now, charge!"

As instructed, the gangly king raised his long arms and lifted the bedsheet. Behind him, the other cloth-covered nobles lurched out and waved their arms, moaning in a united chorus. "Booo!"

Shocked by the rock slab and their squashed king, the orcs whirled in panic to see a crowd of terrifying ghosts in pale, flapping sheets. The orcs screamed like whinnying horses.

"Orcs must leave!" Dalbry yelled in a deep voice.

"This castle is cursed!" Affonyl added.

The nobles hadn't had enough time to rehearse their lines, but they managed to say "Booo!" again and again. They flowed across the courtyard.

The orcs crashed into one another, slugging and punching to get away from the castle.

Just then Longjohn's shoe caught on the sheet in front of him, and he tripped. As he sprawled on the ground, the ghostly disguise came off. Behind him, two other nobles ran forward unable to see, and fell on top of their king.

Confused, the orcs stuttered to a halt in their headlong flight.

The sheet-faced nobles continued to run about making ghostly sounds, but the ones at the rear flailed their flower-print sheets, looking springlike instead of terrifying.

King Longjohn picked himself up, shook his head to clear his thoughts. Affonyl pulled him to his feet. They both yelled "Booo!" again.

A few of the orcs realized that something was wrong.

"Those aren't real ghosts," one said.

"Hey, that's King Longjohn. From the frame on the wall!"

"Those are floral prints!"

Affonyl groaned in dismay as the plan fell apart before her eyes. Trying to convince the invaders, she shouted, "No, they're real ghosts!"

"They killed King Borc."

"They killed Skeez and Urml."

"They killed Otto and Ditto."

Raising their ugly weapons, the orcs shifted from a frightened gaggle to a menacing horde. They greatly outnumbered the haunting crowd.

Dalbry flung off his sheet and raised his sword, seeing this was going to be a fight. He stood next to the former princess. "This is unfortunate."

Cullin, Spam, and Reeger joined the front line of ghosts. This was not the way any of them had wanted the evening to end. Subbaron Darylking waved his white sheet as if it were a surrender flag.

With a bloodcurdling battle cry, the brutes stormed forward, eager to prove that they could bash ghosts after all.

Longjohn looked as if he might have preferred to be back up on the wall.

Suddenly, the air split with a boom of magical thunder. A flare of lightning skittered from turret to turret in the castle, then lanced into the side courtyard right where folding chairs would have been set for a summer concert. Green and yellow smoke boiled up, thicker even than the fog.

Accompanied by more lightning, a terrible figure appeared wearing a fearsome iron helmet much like Ugnarok's but black with bold yellow lightning bolts painted on the sides. The helmet's eye holes flared a dazzling orange.

The orcs gasped and shrank away. The sheeted nobles had a similar reaction, but in the opposite direction.

In a terrifying voice as loud as the thunder, the ominous figure demanded, "Where is Ugnarok?"

The invaders reeled away, and some fell on their butts. Blue lightning ricocheted around the courtyard and struck two orcs, turning them into smoking piles. The helmeted wizard-mage demanded again, "Are you hard of hearing? Where is Ugnarok?"

Needing no further encouragement, the remaining orcs picked themselves up as fast as they could. Like a stampeding herd, they raced away from the castle grounds, intending to run all the way across Longjohn's kingdom and into safer lands.

Sadly for them, the disorienting fog remained so thick that they lost all sense of direction. Instead, they ran directly over the headlands cliff and plunged down to the rocks and the crashing surf far below.

Seeing the cowled figure looming in a haze of ozone and electrical power, Affonyl swallowed hard and considered running in panic herself.

For the third time, the specter demanded, "Where is Ugnarok? Help a guy out?"

The former princess gathered her courage and stepped forward. "Ugnarok's not here right now. We would take a message, but ... he's dead."

"Dead?" the voice boomed, then the figure's shoulders slumped. The lightning dwindled away in the air, and the helmet's blazing eyes turned toward her. "Well, that was a waste of time."

With gauntleted hands, he reached up to twist the helmet and lift it off his head. "Wait—Affonyl, is that you?"

Amazed to hear her name, the former princess cautiously approached. She recognized the gray hair, the unruly beard, the kindly eyes that had all been covered by the mask. "Wizard Edgar!"

CHAPTER
FORTY-SIX

M y dear Affonyl, it's good to see you!" She ran forward and gave her former mentor a hug. He patted her on the back. "Your hair is different, isn't it? And that bedsheet—"

"A lot of things are different," she said. "I'm a *former* princess now, living a life of adventure."

"And keeping up your natural science studies, I hope?" His expression grew troubled, and he spoke at a rapid clip. "Whatever are you doing in an orc-infested castle? You're not hanging around with that Ugnarok? He's a bad apple—and a disgrace."

"No, we're here for artistic reasons," she said.

Cullin ventured closer, as if hoping to protect her. "Did you say ... Wizard Edgar?"

She grabbed the young man's arm and pulled him forward. "Cullin—this is the man who taught me all about natural science and alchemy!"

Dalbry, Reeger, and Spam also joined the conversation. After introducing them, Affonyl asked Edgar, "Are you still with the consortium of evil wizards?"

Edgar nodded. "Yes, it's a decent job, and I've learned a lot since leaving your father's service. The consortium only accepts the very best."

"Of course! They accepted you, didn't they?" Affonyl said, feeling the warmth grow in her voice.

"Huh, they also accepted Ugnarok." Edgar tucked the black helmet under his arm and looked away. "That man clearly didn't fit in, never took the job seriously, always joking, trying to be the class clown—but none of it was funny, just mean spirited. The bosses reprimanded him several times, and finally gave him his pink slip. But before he left, Ugnarok stole one of our most valuable HTPs and fled."

"What's an HTP?" Cullin asked.

"Helmet of Terrible Power." Edgar held up his own black model with the painted lightning bolts. "The consortium dispatched me to retrieve it. Ugnarok constantly groused that he wanted to get even with King Grog for ruining his comedic aspirations, so this was the first place I came to look." He glanced around the side courtyard, noted the collapsed rock. "Might you know where the HTP is?"

"The helmet was last seen in King Longjohn's closet," Dalbry said with a satisfied smirk.

Reeger chuckled. "Ugnarok wasn't using it anymore."

Edgar seemed perplexed, then caught his breath. "Ah, yes, you said he's dead."

Affonyl crossed her arms over her chest. "The Helmet of Terrible Power apparently didn't have enough power to protect him against a peanut allergy."

Edgar nodded. "Ah, yes—peanut ex machina. It's what he deserved. No joke." He scratched his matted hair, which looked unruly because of the helmet. "Perhaps you'd better explain from the beginning, Princess Affonyl."

"It's just Affonyl now—and that'll be part of the explanation. I have quite a story."

"Too bad we don't have a minstrel present," Cullin said.

With interruptions and additions from her companions, Affonyl rapidly told the highlights of their tale.

When they had finished, Spam was eager to contribute. "We can go fetch Ugnarok's helmet from the closet. Do you want the orc skeleton, too?"

The wizard shook his head. "No, that won't be necessary, dear girl, but I would appreciate the HTP as soon as possible. I'm on a deadline."

She grabbed Cullin's arm, and Affonyl felt a twinge of jealousy at the pesty affection the scullery maid showed him.

As the two ran off, the wizard let out a heavy sigh. "I apologize for the hassle my delinquent colleague caused. Now, however, I can complete my important mission for the conglomerate. I might be promoted to the head of their collections department."

Affonyl took advantage of the few spare minutes to catch up with her mentor. "I'm impressed that you rose to such a high level! You're their enforcer and bounty hunter."

"Enforcer and bounty hunter?" He chuckled. "Ah, yes, you always held me in such high esteem, dear girl. That sounds much better than lost-and-found retrieval. I think I may use that."

Panting hard from running, Cullin and Spam came back, handing Ugnarok's polished but singed helmet to Edgar. After inspecting it, he was obviously relieved. "Now, they're sure to put a gold star in my employee folder. I might even get a raise. Enforcer and bounty hunter!"

He seated his own black helmet on his head, but he looked less fearsome now that Affonyl knew it was Wizard Edgar inside. He propped Ugnarok's helmet under his arm, and summoned thunder and lightning again. Green and yellow smoke curled out, engulfing him.

"I hope we see you again, Edgar!" Affonyl called.

The rest of the friends waved, and the towering wizard vanished.

They gathered by the stables for a celebration. Cullin was thrilled with the successful grand finale of their scheme, but he saw Affonyl looking at the collapsed stone with a resigned expression. He wanted to be supportive. "Sorry about your art. I wish others had been able to see the great unveiling."

She blushed and looked away. "It doesn't matter, Squirrel."

He dredged up hope and optimism. "But the name of Affonyl NoLastName should be known throughout the land!"

Reeger looked at the enormous fallen rock and the fallen ship mast. "Rust! You're not going to want us to prop it all back up again, are you, Princess?"

Dalbry joined them, waxing philosophical. "Everyone experiences art differently, and Borc experienced it as a crushing blow."

"You might say he felt the full weight of it." Spam gave a satisfied huff. "Ha! I bet he's smeared all along the bottom of the rock like peanut butter."

Cullin chuckled. "Smeared like *jam* might be a better metaphor."

Affonyl drew a breath. "Leave it as it is. We've proved that Rock in Its Natural State is ... flat on the ground."

CHAPTER
FORTY-SEVEN

As the captive nobles recovered from their ordeal, King Longjohn assessed the damage to his art collection, his castle, and his pride. Well fed again, and with Affonyl's great unveiling canceled, the visiting guests soon began bickering over esoteric art opinions. One discussion about the most effective uses of burnt umber nearly drove Darylking and McCowan to a duel, but when no armed champions offered to fight in their stead, the two agreed to disagree.

The few remaining members of the castle staff began scouring away the remnants of the orc invasion. Carpenters fixed the smashed garderobe seat that had allowed Reeger's escape. The dreamcatchers, macrame, and decoupage were repaired and put back on display.

Spam returned to her dream job with a bucket of soapy water and bristle brush, cleaning seagull droppings from statues. The fog lifted at last, leaving a bright blue sky, which improved the seagulls' aim, thereby giving the scullery maid more to do.

The story of the orc invasion, the fatally allergic wizard-mage, and the brave haunting of Longjohn's castle was told, retold, and exaggerated. Cullin, Reeger, Dalbry, and Affonyl milked the tale for many free rounds at the harbor town taverns. When Affonyl wanted a reminder of princessy finery, they dined at a classy, high-end bistro, and they all agreed that the thin consommé and tiny petit fours were less satisfying than a bowl of hot chowder. Reeger ate tray after tray of the local oysters, though he preferred the mountain ones.

After drink-buying audiences grew weary of the orc story, the friends told the tale of Amnethia's lake monster. In retrospect, Cullin was glad that scaring off the orc army had not required large explosives.

King Longjohn tried to give them an allowance from his petty-cash chest, but he found that the orcs had taken it. Instead, he let them charge their food and drink on his kingly tab, since he still believed the companions were avant-garde artists and well-respected critics. Some of the tavern owners were hesitant, because Longjohn's tab was as long as his legs, but he was the king, and they considered it their taxpayer dollars at work.

On a bright afternoon, Cullin and the former princess walked along the docks, browsing exotic items from the New Lands. Reeger tagged along, even though the young man would rather have been alone with Affonyl. She liked to peruse the scientific curiosities from the research ship and talk with the naturalist about the specimens preserved in alcohol.

Reeger snorted, considering it a waste of the fine moonshyne for which the kingdom was renowned. The naturalist turned to him with a sniff. "Where do you think most of the kingdom's profit came from, sir? A substantial portion of King Grog's distilled moonshyne was reserved for scientific endeavors. There's a scientist duke up north who has an entire dragon preserved in a giant tank filled with alcohol. Just imagine how many barrels of moonshyne that took!"

Reeger turned his attention to a different item just arrived on a merchant ship: dried leaves from the tobacco plant, which smelled thick, rich, and foul at the same time. A merchant hawking the product lured Reeger in, while Cullin and Affonyl kept their distance. "You smoke these leaves just like pipe-weed." The merchant waved a roll of the brown, stinky leaves. "But it's better than pipe-weed, far more addictive."

"Rust, are you serious?" Reeger took a rolled wad of leaves that looked like a thick stick.

Grinning, the other man nodded. "Light one end until it smolders, then inhale the smoke through the other."

Cullin felt sure it was a scam, but Reeger had a penchant for trying unpleasant things. The merchant ignited one end of the rolled tobacco leaves and coached him in how to puff and inhale, to roll the smoke around inside his mouth and lungs. "They're called cigars. I sell only the finest quality—straight from the New Lands. It's certain to take off as a smelly but pervasive habit among the upper classes."

Much coughing ensued, and Reeger applied significant peer pressure to convince Cullin and Affonyl to puff on the cigar, too. The young man's eyes watered, his mouth and throat burned, and he choked out, "It's very nice."

With a few of the gold coins he had pocketed, Cullin bought a fine box of cigars as a keepsake.

Later in the day, Dalbry brought them to see Ugnarok's dragon ships that had crashed up against the rocky shore—swift and sturdy vessels that had carried the orc army into the harbor. "I wonder what the harbormaster will do with them, now that the wizard-mage owner is dead." The knight seemed to be deep in thought.

"Send them to the lost and found?" Cullin said.

Dalbry studied the carved dragon figureheads. "Impressive vessels, don't you think? We do claim to be kraken hunters. Perhaps the four of us could cruise down the coast in one of these boats, telling our tales, finding new adventures."

Cullin admired the snarling reptilian head, which reminded him of the rare times he had faced a real dragon, as well as the many times he and his friends had faked such an encounter. "We do know a lot about dragons. It would fit with our image."

"Does anyone know how to sail?" Affonyl asked. "Or row?" She glanced at the long oars.

"Rust, I'm not pulling one of those!" Reeger said. He still reeked of cigar smoke.

Dalbry was not dissuaded. "How hard can it be? King Longjohn owes us a substantial reward for liberating his castle, and I certainly don't think he'll pay us in cash."

"I did deliver the landscape art as commissioned." Affonyl pursed her lips. "He owes us for that as well."

They knew the state of King Longjohn's treasury and the scarcity of liquid cash. The prospect of actual payment seemed dim, and after a brief discussion they decided they should take what they could get. Reeger suggested they might be able to sell it on a used dragon-ship lot.

With their minds made up, they headed up from the harbor town toward the castle. Once more, they would appear as Dalbry the art critic, Cullin the executive assistant, and renowned unknown artist Affonyl NoLastName. Reeger didn't need to put on any airs as a landscape artistic engineer.

King Longjohn had sent out a recruiting call for more men-at-arms, but received few good candidates. The castle remained mostly unguarded, and the companions didn't even need to get guest passes.

The lanky king sat on his restored throne with one long leg crossed over the other. He no longer had a crown, since Borc was wearing it when Rock had shifted Its Natural State. To serve the temporary need, Longjohn had fashioned a paper crown that rested on his head. An empty, tilted frame still hung on the wall above the throne.

With Cullin beside him, Dalbry sauntered up to the dais and presented himself. Affonyl stood just behind them, the eccentric artist, while Reeger hovered at a safe distance near the entrance. The supposed critic reminded the king that his client had provided the artistic services for which she'd been hired. Cullin looked down at Ye Olde Journal as if it were an executive ledger, also pointing out their "extensive and invaluable services" in driving the orc invaders out of the castle.

King Longjohn made the distinctive awkward fidgeting of a man with insufficient funds, until Dalbry suggested the royal gift of a dragon ship as payment in full.

The king's long face showed immediate relief. "I was planning to repurpose those vessels into merchant ships for the New Lands ... but I could spare one of them as compensation for your collective bravery and ingenuity." He nodded again. "May you find it, ah, inspirational in your endeavors."

He looked at Affonyl, even more embarrassed. "Your new masterpiece was remarkable, breathtaking, but the unveiling was not acceptable for an artist of your caliber. It pains me to the bottom of my creative heart." He squared his shoulders, determined. "As an added reward, you may each choose one rare and precious item from my prized art gallery. Thus, you will think of me on all your travels."

Dalbry bowed with utmost gravity. "We accept with immense gratitude, Sire."

Longjohn folded his long fingers together. "It is the least I can do!"

"It is," Reeger muttered.

Cullin couldn't imagine what he would do with the strange art objects, but they couldn't turn down a royal gift. Even if the piece wasn't monetarily rewarding, it was the classy thing to do. He mulled over which item he might like to take for himself.

Now it was Affonyl's turn. She approached the throne, looking both shy and pleased. "I have one last thing for you as well, King Longjohn. You commissioned an original work from me, and so you shall have one."

Delighted, Longjohn lurched up from his throne, unfolding his long limbs. "An original work by Affonyl NoLastName! I cannot express my joy!"

The former princess withdrew a rolled sheet of paper from her long peasant skirts. "I did this down in the harbor town while we were waiting for service at the bistro."

"Service?" Cullin muttered. "It took an hour just to get coffee."

The king's eyes were bright as Affonyl presented one of her cartoony caricatures: a striking, exaggerated resemblance of King Longjohn with his slack jaw, scraggly beard, and wide eyes. Behind him were silly drawings of Borc the orc and Wizard-Mage Ugnarok. They were all grinning.

Longjohn began to weep. "This art is profound and moving—and it looks just like me! I shall frame it and keep it on the wall of my bedchamber."

FORTY-EIGHT

Departing from the castle for the last time, they passed through the statue garden. Reeger thought about taking one of the statues as his reward, perhaps the elephant with the purring kitten in its trunk, but decided it would be too difficult to carry. The mule brayed, putting an end to the discussion.

Cullin was glad to see Spam scrubbing away at the seagull droppings. He picked up her spare brush and dunked it in the bucket of water to help the ragamuffin girl with her chores. "Maybe you want to come with us? See the world? Have a life of adventure? You can be pretty useful."

Spam flushed. "You think I'm pretty?"

"Not quite the way I meant the sentence to be taken ..."

Spam scrubbed a gray glob from the statue of the thinking troll. "And leave all this? It's everything I could possibly want."

"Maybe you could want ... more?" Cullin asked.

Spam gave another one of her endearing huffs. "Ha, I'll leave the dragon slaying to the experts. I've got a castle and a job. It doesn't get better than that. And I have my side business selling tins of Sue-Pam."

She went back to scrubbing, obviously avoiding saying goodbye. Cullin had really enjoyed getting to know the scrappy scullery maid. Just as he left, though, she cocked her eyebrows. "But if I ever change my mind, I'll find you."

"How?" Cullin asked.

She huffed. "You'll be sailing a dragon ship and telling stories about conquering orcs and wizard-mages. You don't exactly keep a low profile."

Dwarfed in his overstuffed leather chair, Prince Maurice dares to take one last sip of the expensive brandy. This time he manages to cover most of his grimace. "So that's how you defeated a wizard-mage—by sheer coincidence?"

"And a deadly allergy."

"And the orc army ran off in terror because a bunch of nobles pretended to be ghosts by wearing bedsheets? And another wizard-mage appeared just in the nick of time?"

I look down at the stubbed-out cigar. "It was much more intricate than that, son. The simplest solutions are rarely that simple. That's the mark of being a good king."

"And a good confidence man," Maurice says.

"There are many similarities between the two. Haven't your tutors been teaching you about politics?"

The boy stands up and stretches. The hour is late, and by now the thunderstorm has diminished. Still, we'll have to put up with seeping dribbles throughout the night.

"King Longjohn let you choose among his art masterpieces. Which one did you take? After all this time, it must be really valuable—where is it?"

Even after my wonderful tale, the prince remains skeptical. I suppose that's to be expected for someone his age. As an independent emo teenager, he tends to doubt his father.

"I thought you'd never ask. I still cherish the painting—the mastery, the brushstrokes, the innate humor, the composition."

"Now you sound like an art critic," Maurice says.

"Dalbry taught me much. I know the proper words to say."

I step to the back of the man cave. Preparing for this evening, I covered up the frame on the wall behind us. "Look, son—isn't it just the way I described it?"

With a flourish, I yank away the cloth to reveal the colorful painting of cute puppies in medieval costumes playing cards in the tavern.

Maurice gasps and comes forward. "You mean it's real? The whole story was real?" He seems impressed.

"And here's the proof, lad."

"It's a little kitschy, don't you think?"

"You see kitschy, I see a clever satire on the human condition using canine metaphors." We stand together, father and son, king and prince, admiring the masterpiece.

A voice comes down to us through the vent hole in the wall. "Are you two almost done down there? It's Maurice's bedtime!"

"Yes, dear!" I shout back. "We've had a great time—even had a father-son moment."

"A moment?" I can hear the frown in her tone. "You're smoking those New Land cigars again. I can smell it through the ventilation shafts."

"Putting it out now, dear," I call up. With a spare cup of water, I douse the still-smoldering cigar in the ashtray.

As I lead him out of the private man cave, I clap my hand on the boy's shoulder. "Come, Maurice. A dozen more sessions like these, and I'll teach you everything you need to know to be a man and a king."

ACKNOWLEDGMENTS

A complex dragon business operation involves lots of helpers and c0-conspirators. For *Skeleton in the Closet* I had great input and support from my wife Rebecca Moesta, Tracy Griffiths, CJ Anaya, and Marie Whittaker. My sharp-eyed test readers included Hannah Sheldon, Kate MacEachern, Scott Padgham, Heather Jones, and a special shout-out to Tracy Eire, Sean Smith, Tina Allen, Andrew Bulthaupt, Daryl King, and Patricia Lane for their extra support in making this book happen.

ABOUT THE AUTHOR

Kevin J. Anderson has published more than 170 books, 58 of which have been national or inter-national bestsellers. He has written numerous novels in the Star Wars, X-Files, and Dune universes, as well as unique steampunk fantasy novels *Clockwork Angels* and *Clockwork Lives*, written with legendary rock drummer Neil Peart. His original works include the Saga of Seven Suns series, the Wake the Dragon and Terra Incognita fantasy trilogies, the Saga of Shadows trilogy, and his humorous horror series featuring Dan Shamble, Zombie P.I. He has edited numerous anthologies, written comics and games, and the lyrics to two rock CDs. Anderson is the director of the graduate program in Publishing at Western Colorado University. Anderson and his wife Rebecca Moesta are the publishers of WordFire Press. His most recent novels are *Gods and Dragons*, *Dune: The Heir of Caladan* (with Brian Herbert), *Stake*, *Kill Zone* (with Doug Beason), and *Spine of the Dragon*.

facebook.com/KJAauthor
twitter.com/TheKJA
instagram.com/TheRealKJA

Printed in the USA
CPSIA information can be obtained
at www.ICGtesting.com
JSHW021908190424
61528JS00001B/2